A WILL
TO KILL

'I love RV Raman's Harith Athreya with his cool, curious resourceful-
ness. *A Will to Kill* is a good traditional mystery with twists and turns
set in a colonial-era mansion in the Nilgiri Hills'

OVIDIA YU,
author of CWA-shortlisted *The Mimosa Tree Mystery*

'Like stepping back to the Golden Age of the classic mystery'

RHYS BOWEN,
international bestselling author of *The Tuscan Child*

'A modern-day take on the classic locked-room murder mystery…
Athreya is a fine detective with a curious mind'

New York Times

'The influence of Agatha Christie and John Dickson Carr on the narrative is compelling… influences of author Ngaio Marsh… subtle,
clear, ironic, but always elegant and peppered with wit; characters
sharply, sometimes hilariously, drawn'

The Telegraph India

'Intriguing contemporary whodunit and series launch… fans of
golden age mysteries will look forward to the sequel'

Publishers Weekly

'We may not have our own Sherlock or Poirot, but the narrative
tradition of Christie and Doyle has found a worthy successor in RV
Raman. I cannot wait to read more of Harith Athreya's adventures'

' *Herald India*

Following a corporate career spanning three decades and four continents, RV RAMAN now lectures on management, mentors young entrepreneurs, serves as an independent director on company boards, and writes.

A Will to Kill is the first novel in the Harith Athreya series. *A Dire Isle*, the next Harith Athreya mystery, is forthcoming from Pushkin Vertigo in 2022.

www.rvraman.com

RV RAMAN

A WILL TO KILL

PUSHKIN VERTIGO

Pushkin Press
71–75 Shelton Street
London WC2H 9JQ

A Will to Kill was first published by HarperCollins India,
2019 and then Polis Books in North America, 2020

First published by Pushkin Press in 2021

1 3 5 7 9 8 6 4 2

ISBN 13: 978-1-78227-732-3

Designed and typeset by Tetragon, London
Printed and bound by CPI Group (UK) Ltd, Croydon, CRO 4YY

www.pushkinpress.com

A WILL
TO KILL

1

The visitor was ill at ease, fidgeting with his watch's metal strap, locking and releasing the clasp repeatedly. He had already made two attempts to convey the message he was carrying, and had pulled up short both times. He glanced around the near-empty, wood-panelled restaurant at Chennai's New Woodlands Hotel where the late-afternoon crowd was yet to arrive. Across the table, under a large painting of young Lord Krishna stealing butter, Harith Athreya waited, studying the willowy young man who had given his name as Manu Fernandez. The sealed envelope Manu had brought remained unopened on the polished wood table, beside a steaming tumbler of filter coffee.

Manu had just invited Athreya to his family mansion in the Nilgiris on his father's behalf, and was ineffectively trying to pass along the rest of the message. When he made little headway the third time, Athreya stepped in to encourage him.

'You are only the messenger, not the author of the message,' he said quietly. 'Don't feel awkward about it.'

He paused as a waiter brought them hot, steaming idlis. Manu leaned back in his green-covered chair to let the waiter serve the snack with sambar and chutney. A determined look crept on to his lean, clean-shaven face as he watched the waiter do his job. Once he was out of earshot, Manu squared his shoulders and took the mental plunge.

'You see, Mr Athreya, Dad has written two wills,' he blurted.

'Surely, that isn't a problem. The later will would prevail.'

'Normally, yes. But in this case, both wills are dated the same, and Dad has gone to the extent of writing the exact same time on both. He has also got witnesses to sign the wills simultaneously, in the presence of a lawyer. Neither of the two can be said to supersede the other.'

'That's interesting!' Athreya's curiosity was piqued. He had not encountered such a situation before. Manu's father seemed to be an unusual man. Athreya found himself looking forward to meeting him, for he already knew that he would be accepting this intriguing invitation. He leaned forward. 'Why did your father do that?' he asked.

Manu shrugged, avoiding both the question and Athreya's eyes. Instead, he spooned a piece of idli into his mouth.

'From what you say,' Athreya went on, 'both wills would be considered equally valid.'

'Yes.'

'Then which one will take effect when your father... er... passes away?'

Manu dropped his spoon and touched his lips with a napkin.

'That would depend on the manner in which he dies,' he replied.

Athreya's eyebrows rose in surprise.

'I'm afraid you lost me there,' he said.

'It... it's like this...' Manu stuttered. 'If Dad dies of natural causes, one will takes effect. But if he dies... unnaturally, the other one comes into force.'

'By "natural causes", you mean—'

'Old age or a naturally contracted illness,' the younger man explained.

'But if he dies as a result of anything else, the other will takes effect?'

'Yes. That includes death by accident as well.'

'I see,' Athreya murmured, frowning as his right index finger traced invisible figures and words on the tabletop. Clearly, the developing puzzle had captured his imagination. As a retired investigator, his interest in commonplace crimes had waned. Although no crime had yet been committed, the situation at the Fernandez family mansion intrigued him.

'Does your father expect to die... er... unnaturally?' he asked Manu.

'That is a question you should ask *him*.'

'I can't, as he is not here. But you are, so tell me what you know.'

After an uncertain pause, Manu's face suddenly broke into an apologetic smile.

'Some say that a curse hovers over Greybrooke Manor, our family mansion. According to legend, every past owner of the house has died a violent death, and every future owner will die violently too. I don't know if it is true, but I remember my grandfather laughing it off when I was a kid. My grandmother was furious that he had talked about this dark legend with us kids.'

'How did your grandfather die?' Athreya asked softly.

'In an accident. He was standing by the open door of a moving train, smoking his pipe, when he slipped and fell out. His head was crushed when he hit a rock. Death must have been instantaneous.'

Athreya sat back and gazed at the younger man for a long moment, stroking his fine-haired beard, which had a patch of silver at the chin.

'An accident, no doubt?' he asked.

'Of course. No reason to believe otherwise. He had been drinking heavily on the train.'

'And who had owned the mansion before your grandfather?'

'A string of Britishers. I don't know much about them, except the last one, whose heir sold the estate to my grandfather. This was after the heir's father had died.'

'And how did that Englishman die? Do you know?'

'Had his throat slit when he was asleep in bed. He was said to have molested a local girl the day before. The girl's father slipped into the mansion at night and killed him.'

'I see… am I to assume that your father wrote two wills on account of this legend?'

'It could be the legend, or it could be his fascination with crime fiction. He absolutely devours those books. Sometimes I feel that he lives in a world of his own—part fictional, part real. I really can't think of any other reason. As I said, this is a question that is best put to him directly.'

'Tell me,' Athreya asked as he stirred his coffee, 'who benefits from your father's death?'

Manu squirmed in his chair. It was apparent that he had hoped Athreya wouldn't ask this question. But he answered it nevertheless, presumably due to his father's instructions.

'That depends on which of the two wills comes into force. The contents of one will—let's call it the first will—are common knowledge. This is the one that takes effect if he dies of natural causes. But the contents of the second will are a secret known only to Dad.'

'OK. Who are the beneficiaries in the first will?'

'Several people, but I benefit the most. As his only child, I inherit the lion's share of the estate, including Greybrooke Manor.'

'And who are the other beneficiaries?'

'My cousins and some neighbours. What they will receive isn't trivial by any yardstick. The pieces of the estate due to them are pretty valuable at today's prices.'

'Not trivial, eh? Your father seems to believe that the chances of his dying unnaturally aren't trivial either.'

Athreya took a sip of his coffee and studied Manu over the rim of his tumbler. He was beginning to understand why Manu's father, Bhaskar Fernandez, had invited him to Greybrooke Manor.

'One practical way of looking at it,' Athreya went on when Manu didn't respond, 'is that some people have a reason to kill your father. But if they do, they will not inherit their share. It's a stalemate of sorts. Is your father trying to protect himself by writing two wills?'

Manu shrugged and dropped his gaze.

'Why does he want me to come to Greybrooke Manor?' Athreya asked.

'Honestly, Mr Athreya, I don't know.' Manu's gaze was riveted to the tabletop. 'But I suspect he wants to consult you. Besides, being crazy about crime fiction, he would love to chat with you. He has his own stories to tell, too. He's wanted to meet you since he heard about you from a mutual friend. We are having a house party with family and neighbours. He probably wants to take advantage of that and have you, too.'

Fifteen minutes later, Athreya was dialling the number of the mutual friend on his mobile phone, a retired judge by the name of Suraj Deshpande. On the table was the invitation. It was a single sheet of off-white handmade paper. In the top left corner was an inscription in bold dark-grey lettering: 'GREYBROOKE MANOR, NILGIRIS'. The top right corner read: 'BHASKAR FERNANDEZ'.

The rest of the sheet was covered with an old-school slanting cursive. The letter was written in purple ink, with a broad-nibbed fountain pen:

> Dear Mr Athreya,
>
> I heard of you from our mutual friend, Suraj Deshpande. From the first time Suraj spoke of you, I have wanted to meet you. I would be greatly obliged

if you would consent to spend a few days with me at my estate in the Nilgiri Hills.

I have been an aficionado of crime writing (both fiction and non-fiction) for much of my later years, and would truly welcome an opportunity to talk to someone who has so much knowledge and understanding of such matters.

Unfortunately, my health does not permit me to travel as much as I used to. I have therefore asked my son (the bearer of this letter) to extend a personal invitation on my behalf. I can promise you excellent food, a comfortable stay and company that you will find both varied and interesting.

As an additional inducement, may I point out that Greybrooke Manor is a colonial-era mansion? It has been renovated to offer every modern amenity one could reasonably expect. It is a salubrious retreat away from the crowds and bustle of Ooty and Coonoor, and is as close to nature as one can get without sacrificing comfort and convenience.

I do hope that you will not disappoint me. I look forward to receiving your acceptance.

I am also wondering if you could help me professionally on a personal matter. We could perhaps discuss it when we meet.

Yours faithfully,

Bhaskar Fernandez
8 November 2019

As Athreya waited for Suraj Deshpande to answer the call, he tried to recall the last time he had received a formal handwritten letter, particularly one inscribed with a fountain pen. These days, letters that were not electronic were invariably typed. Except for the signature at the bottom, such letters showed little in the way of character.

But Bhaskar Fernandez's letter was pleasingly different. The firm writing hinted at a man of strong will, while the choice of words suggested grace. The distinctive letter paper, which was clearly expensive, was indicative of wealth and refinement. And the colour of the ink spoke of the individuality of the writer.

Even without considering the riddle of the two wills that Manu had spoken about, Athreya found himself inclined to accept Bhaskar's invitation. The opportunity to spend a few days at a colonial-era mansion in the lap of nature was a temptation that was difficult to resist. All that remained was to have a word with Suraj.

'What can you tell me about Bhaskar Fernandez?' he asked the retired judge, once the niceties were behind them.

'A cultured man with excellent taste,' Suraj replied. 'You will agree once you see his collection of antiques and paintings. It must have taken a lot of time and effort to build a collection such as his. Not to mention money, of which he has plenty.

'At the same time, he is a tough nut to crack. He can be more stubborn than a mule. When he digs his heels in, there is no power on earth that can move him... except perhaps his niece Dora. He is a fascinating man, even if some of the stories he tells are a little over the top.'

'What did he do before he retired to the Nilgiris?'

'He was an antique dealer. I think he used to deal in paintings, too. He has travelled widely, especially in Europe and Asia, but also a bit in the Americas. He lived in Vienna for a number of years. Made a pile of money and returned to India twenty-five years ago.'

'Do you know he has two wills?' Athreya asked.

13

'*Two* wills?' Suraj repeated. 'I know of one.'

Athreya summarized what he had learnt from Manu.

'There is a bit of history there,' Suraj said, his voice dropping a notch or two. 'The Greybrooke estate has been the subject of a long and bitter legal battle. Bhaskar's father bequeathed it solely to him, his eldest son. But Bhaskar's sister and brother challenged the bequest. After years of delay, the challenge was finally thrown out of court early this year, and the estate came completely into Bhaskar's hands. In the meantime, both his brother and sister had passed away.

'Bhaskar, being the man he is, made a voluntary pledge—in public—that he would not leave his nephew and two nieces unprovided for. However, the will stipulates that their bequests will go to them only after his death. Similarly, Bhaskar has bequeathed things of considerable value to neighbours and servants.'

'In other words, there are people waiting for him to die?' Athreya asked.

Suraj paused. Athreya imagined his friend's mind working in high gear. He was relieved that he had called Suraj. During the twenty-odd years they had known each other, Athreya had always found Suraj to be reliable—both as a source of information as well as in his assessment of people. Suraj too had often relied upon Athreya's uncanny knack of imagining potential possibilities and opening up new avenues to explore. Consequently, a strong bond had formed between the judge and the investigator, and had lasted beyond retirement.

'If that is so,' Suraj responded slowly, 'Bhaskar is in no hurry to oblige. There are many more years in him. He may be wheelchair-bound, but he is only sixty-five.'

'And what is this party he is organizing next week?' Athreya continued. 'Do you know anything about it?'

'He wants to put an end to the acrimony the legal battle has created. He wants the family to come together again, as originally intended by Bhaskar's father—wipe the slate clean and let the family start over afresh. I believe they are all gathering at Greybrooke Manor: Bhaskar's nephew and two nieces, along with a few neighbours.'

'When did Bhaskar's siblings die?' Athreya asked.

'Bhaskar is the eldest. Mathew, his brother, died three years ago, and Sarah, his sister, passed away last year. Their children are all that's left of the extended family. Bhaskar's wife passed away almost ten years ago—a wonderful lady who died too young.'

'Yes,' Athreya agreed. 'That's what I was thinking... too young. Bhaskar is the oldest of them all and he is only sixty-five. All the others—his siblings and his wife—seem to have died too young.'

2

Nilgiri Mountain Railways' toy train crawled up the incline like a fat blue caterpillar. It was perhaps the slowest way to get from Mettupalayam to Ooty; from the foothills to the plateau at the top. At an average speed of less than ten kilometres per hour, the train—a part of the Mountain Railways of India, collectively deemed a UNESCO World Heritage Site—took almost five hours to cover the forty-six kilometres that separated the two towns. In the first half of its journey, it ran even slower, inching along at a little over eight kilometres per hour.

With time at his disposal, Athreya had decided to make a vacation of the travel by taking the much-acclaimed train, which was the only one of its kind in the country: a rack railway that used a rack-and-pinion arrangement to climb the steep hills. How he had managed to get a ticket at such short notice was a mystery. He had already sent ahead his suitcase to Greybrooke Manor the previous day from Coimbatore, so he could travel light on the toy train.

Sitting across from Athreya in his first-class compartment was an elderly man with a stiff, pointed moustache that would have done Hercule Poirot proud had it not been for its unmitigated whiteness. Swathed in a muffler and a hat, the jacketed man had a bearing that hinted at a background in the armed forces. Next to him sat a snow-haired lady, who had her arm around a little girl.

The train, with its steam engine, had left Mettupalayam behind and begun its wheezing ascent, when the man, who had been watching Athreya with twinkling eyes, broke the ice.

'On vacation, sir?' he asked in a good-natured baritone, with a friendly smile that stretched the ends of his moustache further apart.

'Sort of,' Athreya responded with a smile and a nod. 'I have an invitation to spend a few days in the Blue Mountains.'

'This is a good time of the year to visit, Mr—?'

'Athreya. Harith Athreya.'

'How do you do?' The man stretched out his hand for Athreya to shake. 'I'm Wing Commander Sridhar.' He gestured to the woman and girl sitting next to him. 'My wife, Sarala. And my granddaughter.'

'My name is Mariebelle,' the little girl chirped, her big brown eyes taking in Athreya's smiling, avuncular visage, topped by a fine-haired mane that had a patch of silver in the front that matched the patch on his chin. 'I am a fairy *queen*.'

'Hello, Queen Mariebelle.' Athreya humoured her with a mock bow. 'Have you hidden your wings? I can't see them.'

'That's because ordinary humans can't see them unless they are princes.'

'Oh, I'm no prince! But, Your Highness, where is your wand?'

'Wand?' the little girl asked, perplexed.

'Fairies have magic wands, don't they?'

The girl cocked her head to one side, looking uncertain.

'Would you like a wand, Queen Mariebelle?' Athreya asked.

The girl nodded, her eyes sparkling in anticipation. Athreya reached into his duffel bag. Slowly and theatrically, he pulled out a pencil a foot-and-a-half long. The girl's eyes lit up and her little hand reached for the enthralling object.

'Say "thank you" to the nice gentleman, darling,' her grandmother urged, but the little one's attention was fully taken up by the unexpected gift.

'As I was saying,' Wing Commander Sridhar said, taking up the conversation again, 'this is a nice time of the year to come here, if you don't mind the mist and the rain. The summer rush is long gone, and the winter chill is not yet upon us.'

'A lot of mist, eh?' Athreya asked dreamily, watching the fog shrouding the faraway hilltops and distant valleys.

'It can get pretty tricky, especially if you are not watching where you are going. What with it being slippery underfoot and hazy all around, a misstep is never very far.'

'I can imagine,' Athreya replied, glancing at the steep, rugged ground outside the window and the patches of loose, slushy soil left behind by cascading rainwater.

'First time to these hills, Mr Athreya?' Sarala asked.

'Oh, no,' said Athreya with a laugh. 'I've been to Ooty a few times, but usually for work. Even on the few occasions when it was not, I found the town a tad commercialized.'

'That it is! That it is!' the wing commander agreed enthusiastically. 'You need to stay away from the hustle and bustle of it all, Mr Athreya. Somewhere a few miles out where you can enjoy nature. Then it can be divine. You are going to Ooty, I presume?'

'I'm getting off at Coonoor. The last leg of my journey will be by road. My destination is somewhere north, I believe—towards the border with Karnataka.'

'Ah! That's welcoming wilderness, all right. As close to nature as you can get. Where are you staying?'

'A place called Greybrooke Manor.'

Abruptly, the wing commander's face seemed to freeze. His wife's eyes widened a trifle, and the polite smile on her face faltered. But only for a moment. She recovered her poise and averted her eyes, busying herself with her granddaughter.

'Ahem!' The wing commander cleared his throat more loudly than necessary. The twinkle in his eye had faded.

'Greybrooke indeed! Interesting place, interesting place! So, Bhaskar has invited you to his place?'

'You know Bhaskar Fernandez?' Athreya asked, wondering why the mention of Greybrooke Manor had ruffled the couple.

'Oh, yes. Oh, yes. I knew his father too, Thomas Fernandez. Tom, we called him. Bit of a shock when he died. He fell off a train, you know.' His voice dropped. 'Poor old Tom. Going to stay at Greybrooke, eh?'

'Yes. I'm quite looking forward to it.'

'Are you?' the wing commander asked doubtfully. Sarala's eyes had returned to Athreya's face. They were guarded now. As she held his gaze, Athreya thought he sensed a trace of apprehension.

'Bit of a chequered history, Greybrooke has,' he heard the wing commander say. 'Rather dark, unfortunately. I'm sure you've heard of it.'

'I'm afraid I don't know much about Greybrooke,' he said. 'Perhaps you can enlighten me?'

'It's an old mansion. Quite old, quite old. Was built by the Brits at the cost of how many native Indian lives, I don't know. An imposing structure, strong as a fortress. I wonder how they hauled all that stone to such a remote place. Why the English buggers chose such a location in the first instance beats me. Must have been the back of beyond when it was built.

'Anyway, an English bugger built it, but he didn't enjoy it for more than a year. Lost his footing one misty night and fell into a ravine. Broke his neck. The mansion passed on to another Brit. Every English blighter who owned it thereafter—there were three or four of them, I think—fell prey to something or the other, and the mansion began acquiring a reputation. Greybrooke Manor is no stranger to violent death, Mr Athreya.'

'Many locals don't go near the mansion, you know,' Sarala interposed. 'They say that the man who built it was a devil worshipper. That's why he built Greybrooke Manor in such an out-of-the-way place, far away from prying eyes. They believe that he even practised human sacrifice.'

'Nonsense, Sarala!' the wing commander boomed.

'Look at the way the chapel at Greybrooke Manor was built,' Sarala persisted. 'The sun never enters it. It's always dark, even in the daytime. Exactly how the devil—'

'Devil worship, my foot!' the wing commander thundered. 'Human sacrifice, my left eye! Nonsense and old wives' tales, Sarala. Don't you go about putting silly ideas into Mr Athreya's head.'

Athreya suppressed a smile, thinking that was precisely what the wing commander had been trying to do.

'I was only—' Sarala began to protest, but her husband cut her off.

'I know, I know, my dear. But there's no need for that.' He returned his attention to Athreya. 'Don't you believe the baloney people tell you, Mr Athreya. Don't let anyone spook you. Remember, there is no terror on God's earth that a reliable six-shooter can't handle.'

'Don't worry, madam,' said Athreya, turning to Sarala with a chuckle. 'I've seen my share of spooks. I've spooked a few spooks, too!'

'Now, that's the kind of man I like. Drop in if you have the time, Mr Athreya. I can offer you some fine Scotch. We live not far from Wellington. Here is my card. Call me, and I'll have my driver come pick you up.'

The wing commander pulled out a visiting card and gave it to Athreya.

'Thank you,' Athreya nodded, taking the card. 'Back to Greybrooke Manor… you were telling me about the Englishmen who once owned it.'

'Ah, yes! So I was, so I was. As the English buggers copped it, one after another, someone floated a myth about the mansion, saying that it was cursed. My own view is that the locals started it to get even with the Englishwalas. But, you know how it is… you repeat a thing often enough and you start believing it yourself. That's what happened, and this silly legend took root.'

'The one about the owners of the mansion dying violently?'

'So, this is not the first time you're hearing about it, right? Who told you?'

'Manu Fernandez.'

'Ah! Interesting, interesting. I didn't think Manu believed it. Anyway, the Englishwalas also fell for the legend and grew scared. The last heir sold the mansion to old Tom Fernandez and fled. Sold it for a song, he did. With all that acreage around it.'

'How are you planning to get from Coonoor to Greybrooke Manor, Mr Athreya?' Sarala asked. She had regained her poise. 'I hope you are not planning to find your way there? You seem to be travelling alone.'

'He can't find his way there, my dear,' the wing commander boomed. 'Not after all the road signs were washed away in the downpour we had last week. Most local taxiwalas and autowalas won't take him there either. Too scared.'

'Oh, I'm fine, madam. Manu has promised to pick me up late afternoon and drive me there. I'd like to spend a few hours in Coonoor first. I have an acquaintance there I'm meeting.'

'Best to get to Greybrooke Manor before sunset, Mr Athreya,' Sarala said.

'Nonsense, Sarala!' the wing commander barked. 'Manu knows his way around. He is no kid.'

Pleasantly satiated after a traditional four-course lunch at a popular restaurant, Athreya and Rajan strolled leisurely along the streets of Coonoor, making their way back to the latter's house. An ex-Indian Police Service officer, and a widower, Rajan had settled in Coonoor after his retirement two years ago. Athreya had helped Rajan solve a couple of difficult cases, for which the latter voiced his gratitude each time they met.

'I think I've heard of Greybrooke Manor, but I don't remember in what context,' Rajan said in response to Athreya's question. 'The name Bhaskar Fernandez is vaguely familiar. What do you want to know about him and his mansion?'

'Oh, nothing in particular,' Athreya responded. 'Just curious, as I will be staying there. A retired air force officer I met on the train had some interesting things to say about the place.'

'Unfortunately, I can't help you there. I've been here only for a couple years, during which I have been away at my daughter's place in Chennai more often than not. But I do know someone who would know about Greybrooke Manor. We can visit him if you like.'

'A long-timer of these parts, is he?'

'That's right. A retired postmaster who has lived here for as long as anyone can remember. His wife was, at one time, one of the very few doctors in this part of the world. If anyone would know about Greybrooke, it's them.'

'That's wonderful, thanks. Does he live far from here?'

'Not at all,' Rajan smiled. 'He is my neighbour.' He glanced at his watch. 'He should just be getting up from his siesta.'

'Siesta?' Athreya asked. 'So early?'

'He is a traditional man. Has brunch, not lunch. After a nice snooze, he wakes up to have his habitual afternoon coffee. In fact, we might just be able to get an excellent cup or two if we land up at the right time.'

'Good idea!' Athreya grinned. 'Let's gatecrash.'

To refresh his memory, he pulled out a piece of paper on which he had scribbled the Fernandez family tree and studied it. He had sketched it from a text message Suraj had sent him after their telephone conversation.

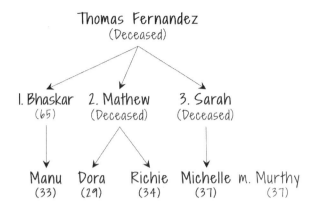

Thomas Fernandez
(Deceased)

1. Bhaskar (65) — 2. Mathew (Deceased) — 3. Sarah (Deceased)

Manu (33) | Dora (29) | Richie (34) | Michelle (37) m. Murthy (37)

Fifteen minutes later, they were settled in the front veranda of a quaint little cottage, with a strong aroma of coffee wafting towards them through the open door. Ramanathan, the retired postmaster, was swaying gently in his rocking chair, while Rajan and Athreya had occupied two cane chairs across from him, a small cane table between them. Beside Ramanathan was Susheela, his wife—a frail old lady with a kindly smile.

'So, staying with Bhaskar, eh?' Ramanathan asked in a sand-papery voice. 'He is a colourful man, and generous too. Never a dull moment when he is around.'

'Very energetic too,' Susheela added. 'Despite being in a wheelchair, he does so many things. I remember him being a live wire when he was younger. Full of beans and always trying out something new.'

'Yes,' her husband agreed with a nod. 'Full of energy, but he has little respect for rules.' He chuckled. 'Just like his father, old Tom Fernandez. Very adventurous, old Tom was, and didn't know the meaning of fear. Bhaskar has taken after him.'

'Thank goodness, Manu hasn't taken after them,' the old lady said with a trace of approval. 'Nice, decent boy, Manu is. I wish he would get married and settle down soon. Heaven knows he is old enough. What Greybrooke needs is a woman's hand.'

Athreya listened happily as the old couple continued to talk unprompted. Rajan had warned him about the couple's penchant for talking. They had little else to do in their old age, and all they needed was a willing listener. For a newcomer wanting to know about their region and its people, it was an opportunity that could not be allowed to pass.

'Why, madam?' Athreya asked.

'It's been a while since Greybrooke Manor had a woman running it. Since old Tom's wife passed away, it has been run by servants. First, by Tom's servants; then, after he died, by Sebastian and Bhaskar's servants.'

'Sebastian?' Athreya asked. It was not a name he had heard before now.

'Bhaskar's loyal caregiver and major-domo of sorts. Also his secretary, when the occasion demands it. With Bhaskar largely confined to his wheelchair, Sebastian looks after everyday matters at the mansion. He does a good job, mind you; I'm not complaining. Very diligent and keeps the place clean and tidy. But it's not the same as having a woman run the household.'

'Bhaskar may be confined to his wheelchair, Susheela, but he does get around pretty well,' the retired postmaster butted in as soon as he got the chance. 'He has one of those newfangled electric wheelchairs and he zips around the mansion and its grounds. Even at his age, he manages to dash around as recklessly in the wheelchair as he had done in cars. Drives it too fast for his own good, if you ask me. What he doesn't want is another accident.'

'You know that Bhaskar almost lost his legs in a car crash, don't you?' Susheela asked when her husband paused for breath. 'Was pushing a car way beyond the speed limit, I'm told. Lucky to have come out alive. But the poor man's legs were mangled forever. He required half a dozen surgeries after the crash.'

'Never afraid to take risks, good old Bhaskar,' the retired postmaster pronounced. 'Just like his father. One must be careful as one gets older, you know. He doesn't want another accident in the family.' He squinted at Athreya through his thick glasses. 'You know how old Tom died?'

Athreya nodded. 'I believe he fell off a train.'

For a brief moment, Ramanathan seemed annoyed at having been denied the opportunity to narrate the incident. But he recovered quickly and continued nevertheless.

'It was the middle of the night,' he said, getting into the details unasked. 'Old Tom must have had half a bottle of whisky inside him. He went to the compartment door to smoke his pipe. He probably liked to stick his head out and feel the air on his face. Think about it, Mr Athreya—a swaying train and a tipsy old man leaning out of the door. One hand must have been holding his pipe.

'That meant that Tom must have been holding on to... whatever he was holding on to with just one hand. What would happen if that hand slipped? Eh? That was Tom for you, a devil-may-care outlook, and reckless.'

'That's when Greybrooke Manor passed on to Bhaskar Fernandez, isn't it?' Athreya prompted.

'Yes,' said Susheela, nodding. 'That was a little hard on poor Sarah, Bhaskar's sister. It was she who looked after Tom as often as she could, whenever she could get away from the scoundrel of a husband she had. Bhaskar visited her only rarely, what with him being wheelchair-bound. Tom should have left a part of the estate to Sarah. She was really upset about it. Cried her heart out when Tom's will was read out. She never came back to Greybrooke Manor... except to be buried in the family cemetery.'

'What good would it have done if Tom had left a part of the estate to Sarah?' Ramanathan demanded. 'Sarah's husband would have gambled it away within a year. Tom did the right thing in leaving her an annuity. In any case, Sarah's health was failing. It was only a matter of time before she followed her father.'

'It is astonishing how people don't learn,' his wife said, changing the topic. 'I'm talking about Michelle, Sarah's daughter. One would have thought that living with that scoundrel of a father, and growing up under the shadows of his misdemeanours, would have been enough to make a young woman avoid thugs like her father. But, no. As soon as she comes of age, Michelle goes and marries Murthy—a crook of the first water, just like her father was. Maybe worse. He has his eyes on the Greybrooke estate, I can tell you. And he wouldn't think twice about gambling away her inheritance. Poor Michelle.'

'History repeats itself.' Ramanathan nodded sagely. 'Michelle took after Sarah and is stuck with a scallywag of a husband.'

'What about Bhaskar's other niece and his nephew? Athreya asked. 'His brother Mathew's children.'

'Ah, Mathew's kids. Well, Richie, the son, has turned out to be a rascal as well. There isn't one attractive young woman within miles of Greybrooke he has not propositioned or coveted.'

'Does he live there?' Athreya asked.

'No, but he visits often enough. He holds no regular job, you see. He gets free food, drink and lodging at Greybrooke Manor. Even when the estate was under dispute, Bhaskar kept it running, and allowed the extended family unrestricted access. That had been Tom's wish.

'Murthy, Michelle's husband, also used to drop in often. But one night, a few years ago, he got badly drunk and abused Bhaskar in the most profane terms. After that incident, he stopped coming to Greybrooke. Bhaskar and he are not on speaking terms now.

Murthy still comes to Coonoor, but he stays elsewhere. He's always trying to get Michelle to chisel Bhaskar out of some money.

'Richie may be good for nothing, but Dora is an angel. Nice, sweet girl, with a good head on her shoulders. She will do well, I'm sure. Bhaskar loves her as he would his own daughter.'

'Dora and Manu are sensible young people,' Susheela agreed. 'I'm happy that the estate will pass on to Manu. He will look after Dora, too—despite all the bad blood the disputed will created. They are like brother and sister.'

'The bad blood was only between Bhaskar and his siblings,' the retired postmaster protested. 'Not between the cousins of the next generation.'

'No?' his wife asked sharply. 'Haven't you heard what Richie and Michelle have been saying? Not to speak of the venom Murthy spews when he is drunk?'

3

Crown Bakery, in the heart of Coonoor, reputed to have been established in 1880, was among its oldest institutions and a veritable landmark. Manu had somehow managed to find a place to park his jeep on the crowded road that served as one of the main thoroughfares.

Lounging beside Manu was a pleasant-looking young woman, who appeared cheerful and at ease in her light-blue jeans and dark pullover. Willowy like Manu, she was of a build that spoke of wiry strength and easy movement. Their faces were remarkably similar. Had Athreya not known that Manu was an only child, he would have taken her to be his sister.

'This is Dora, my cousin,' Manu said, as Athreya walked up to them.

'Hello, sir.' Dora's agreeable face split into a grin as she shook hands warmly and with a surprisingly firm grip. 'Welcome to Coonoor. I hope you had no difficulty finding Crown Bakery? I was telling Manu that we should have picked you up from where you were.'

'No difficulty at all,' Athreya responded, returning the smile. 'Everyone seems to know it. I hope I've not kept you waiting?'

'No, no, sir. We arrived not more than five minutes ago. Shall we go? Your suitcase is already at Greybrooke Manor.'

Dora swung herself into the driver's seat of the jeep they had been leaning against, and Manu insisted that Athreya sit in the front. It was, he said, far more comfortable than perching at the back. Dora wriggled into her jacket and zipped it up to her chin.

A slight thrill ran down Athreya's spine when he realized that the canvas hood of the jeep was down and the windscreen had been laid flat on the bonnet. He would be experiencing the full rush of crisp mountain air as they drove to Greybrooke Manor.

The jeep pounced forward and darted between bikes, buses and pedestrians as it made its way north, past the bazaar. From the effortless way Dora drove the jeep while keeping up a steady chatter, it was apparent that she was adept at handling the vehicle. With a suppressed smile, Athreya realized that if there was one thing she didn't share with her cousin, it was his reserve.

Soon, they had left the town behind as they headed north. Dora pointed out various sights and places, reeling off names in the dwindling light. Wispy mist—sometimes white, sometimes grey—glided along the hillsides and dales, clinging to groves and lingering over ponds. Here and there, thicker fog cloaked the valleys and the hilltops at a distance, veiling tea plantations and woods alike.

Wherever the dying fingers of sunlight touched the scenery, the foliage erupted in different shades of green, from a bright pea hue to a dark olive. But where the grey mist enwrapped the slopes and shut out the sun, colour seemed to drain from the picturesque landscape.

What was amply clear was that the area they were driving through had recently seen copious rainfall. The ground was drenched, and puddles of water dotted the roads. Here and there, patches of earth had come loose and had slid down the hillside. Landslides, Manu had earlier said, were common at this time of the year.

All the while, Dora continued her chatter, drawing smiles and chuckles from Athreya. From time to time, Manu butted in with his wry one-liners. Athreya found himself enjoying the company and the drive, even if he had to narrow his eyes to slits to face the cold onrush of air.

By now, they were well away from Coonoor, and were driving along winding roads cut into the hillside, climbing and descending alternately. Traffic on the roads had reduced to the occasional car or bike. Every now and then, they passed clusters of shops and houses, which invariably sent the resident dogs barking and chasing the jeep, much to Dora's amusement.

As the sun began to settle down behind the hills in the west, and signs of habitation grew scarce, a thought struck Dora.

'Manu,' she gushed, 'why don't we take Mr Athreya to the hilltop? He can see the valley at sunset. What say you? We have lots of time.'

'Yup,' Manu agreed. 'Good idea. You'll have to do it quickly if you want to get there before sunset.'

Dora swung the steering wheel to the right and turned on to a mud road, pausing only to engage the four-wheel drive. Athreya found the jeep was ascending steep inclines as she manoeuvred it through twisting mud paths. She raced against the setting sun, making for the top of the hill.

They reached the vantage point just as the huge red sphere of the sun began to touch the distant horizon. But there was more than enough ruddy light for Athreya to marvel at the vista before him. Far below was a shallow valley that was close to a kilometre wide. Meandering leisurely across the plain of the vale was a narrow stream, more like a brook. From the distance, it resembled a long grey vein. Along its near side was a scattering of four buildings, one large and the others significantly smaller.

'That's the brook from which Greybrooke takes its name,' Dora said in a whisper, pointing to the grey water. 'The large building is the mansion, Greybrooke Manor. The long, boomerang-shaped one closer to the brook is the annexe. Uncle Bhaskar had it built a few months ago.'

As Athreya gazed at the estate from afar, the thought upper-most in his mind was how far away it seemed from everything else. There appeared to be no other habitation close by. Except for the mud road that snaked down into the vale and ran along-side the estate, there seemed to be no other access, unless one trekked cross-country to get there. Among a cluster of trees, around a kilometre and a half to the right, he saw a few green-shingled rooftops that seemed to blend in with the treetops around them.

The vale itself was breathtakingly beautiful. It was as close to nature as Athreya had imagined it to be after reading Bhaskar's letter. The three of them stood silently, taking in the stunning panorama as the sun gradually settled in the west.

He didn't know if he was imagining it, but, in the distance, the Greybrooke estate seemed to convey a sense of loneliness to him. There was also something secretive about the silent vale, something enigmatic.

'Come,' Manu said gently, disrupting Athreya's thoughts. He sounded almost as if he was afraid of disturbing the tranquil air. 'Let's go. We should get off this hill before the light vanishes.'

Athreya nodded silently and climbed into the jeep. Dora stole one last look at the scene and got into the driver's seat.

'Thank you,' Athreya said quietly, as they began descending the hill. Hearing himself speak, he thought he sounded awestruck. 'Thank you for bringing me here. It is indeed a marvellous view.'

'My pleasure,' Dora murmured. 'It's always gratifying to come here with someone who appreciates it. There is something poetic about the view, something lonely.' She smiled as Athreya shot her a surprised glance. 'You sensed it, didn't you? I thought you did. I always sense a suppressed loneliness in the vale when I view it from here. As if it has a secret that it cannot tell.'

Unwittingly, Athreya found himself agreeing with her.

'Yes,' he whispered. 'I was trying to find words for what I felt. You express it perfectly.'

Dora flushed with pleasure at the compliment and fell silent. Athreya welcomed the quietness as he revisited the vista in his mind's eye. Soon, they returned to the point at which Dora had taken the detour to climb the hill. The mist was thicker now and all around them. The light was considerably dimmer. Greyness pervaded the landscape. A moistness enveloped them, making Athreya wish that he had worn his jacket as Dora had worn hers.

'Careful, Dora,' Manu said softly, as Dora picked up speed. 'The soil for the next kilometre or two seems to be loose. Small rocks and loose earth have been sliding down. Turn on the headlights.'

Two shafts of brilliance pierced the gathering gloom, and a milky aura sprang up around the jeep. The beams only partly illuminated the mist as they cut through a thickening haze. He could see no other points of light, near or far. The croaking of frogs and chirping of crickets were gradually becoming louder.

With her entire attention focused on the road in front of them, Dora had stopped talking. Looking round, Athreya saw Manu's keen face was tight as he too peered forward, scanning the road ahead. For some reason, Athreya felt a chill touch him. But only for a moment. Immediately, his pragmatic nature reasserted itself.

They had been going along for about ten minutes when a sudden noise from behind shattered their concentration. Instinctively, Dora slowed the jeep down to a crawl.

'What was that?' she demanded without taking her eyes off the road. There was a distinct edge of anxiety in her voice.

Athreya turned and saw Manu had swung around to face the rear from where the noise had come. In his hand was a powerful torch, the kind forest rangers carry, which he had switched on. The next moment the beam illuminated a huge mound of earth and foliage under a cloud of dust, around thirty yards behind them.

It was a landslide. A mass of loose soil had come crashing down, into the space they had vacated just a few seconds earlier. Even as Athreya watched, another rumble shook the ground. More soil and rocks slammed down on top of the existing heap. The new mass engulfed the road and poured down the hillside beyond. Two tall trees tumbled down into the gloom and crashed on to the road a dozen yards behind them.

'Move!' Manu urged. 'Move, Dora.'

Even in his urgency, Manu had possessed the presence of mind to not shout. Raised voices and loud sounds, Athreya recalled reading somewhere, were best avoided around avalanches and landslides.

'It is dangerous to hang around a fresh landslide,' Manu explained as the jeep leapt forward. 'There is no telling when it will widen and take you with it. Every landslide unsettles the soil around it, making the area vulnerable. Until it settles down, it's best not to go near the site.'

'How bad is it, Manu?' Dora asked without turning her head. They were pulling away from the devastation. 'The noise was deafening.'

'It's a big one, Dora. The largest I've seen in a while. It's going to take a couple of days at least to clear it up and reopen the road. Thank God, it missed us.'

'Yes, thank God, it came down *after* we passed the spot. Greybrooke Manor is going to be cut off for a few days. But at least all of us will be there.'

Ten minutes later, they turned off of the tar-topped road on to a mud road that led into the valley they had seen from the hilltop. Darkness had all but descended upon the hills, and the valley looked all the greyer for it. Everywhere around them was mist, which seemed to have thickened still more with the onset of dusk. The nip in the air reminded Athreya of his jacket again.

Presently, a huge iron gate loomed ahead of them, its black-painted bars gleaming with dew. With surprise, Athreya noted the total absence of light at the gate and the gatehouse beyond, and wondered why that was so. On either side were tall eucalyptus trees, standing like silent sentinels in the night. Beyond the gate was a gravel driveway, which vanished into the misty gloom, past the reach of the jeep's headlights.

A Gurkha guard materialized in the spill of light from the jeep and opened one of the gates. He cracked a crooked grin and threw them a salute as the vehicle rolled up to him, shouting, '*Namaskar, saab*! *Namaskar*, madam!'

Dora stopped the jeep as Manu told the guard about the landslide and enquired if everyone else was home. Satisfied that everyone was, Dora let in the clutch. The guard, who had answered to the name of Bahadur, shut the gate behind them with a heavy clang.

The gravel driveway, now hemmed in by trees on both sides, curved to the left ahead. Lamp posts bordering it stood dark, making Athreya wonder again at the absence of lighting.

'Power cut,' Manu explained, as if reading his mind. 'A couple of power lines snapped in the deluge we had last week. They have yet to restore them. We have been having long power cuts and low voltage for a week.'

'Don't worry, we have a generator,' Dora interposed, as if to mitigate the shortcoming. 'But it can't take the load of the entire estate. We just have to be selective about what lights we turn on. Outdoor lights are the first to get the axe.'

As the jeep took the bend, a massive grey edifice loomed ahead. Greybrooke Manor turned out to be a two-storey mansion of stone, topped by a sloping shingled roof. The nearest outer wall, which was one of the shorter sides of the rectangular mansion, was covered with dark-green ivy that looked almost black in the diffused light from the jeep. Neat rectangular openings in the ivy marked the windows and doors.

Light spilled out from a pair of wide French windows on the ground floor and a smaller window. A solitary figure stood behind the long windows, peering out at the jeep. On the floor above, three curtained windows remained dark. To the left on the ground floor was a wide porch with the front door to the mansion.

The porch lights came on as the jeep approached the mansion, and the front door swung open to let out a patch of light into the night. A man appeared in the doorway and stood silhouetted against the glow.

'Welcome to Greybrooke Manor, Mr Athreya,' Dora said lightly as she brought the jeep to a halt. 'It may not look like much in the dark, but it is a comfortable place. It's actually quite lovely in the day.'

She jumped out of her seat as Manu unwound himself at the rear of the vehicle. Athreya took a moment to stir, then stepped out cautiously on to the gravel. As the man came down the front steps to greet them, a boy darted out from behind him to take Athreya's bag and some packages from the jeep.

The silhouette turned out to be a straight-spined, sharp-featured, middle-aged man of quiet bearing. He was dressed simply in a pair of dark trousers and a light-coloured shirt.

'Welcome to Greybrooke Manor, sir,' he said genially, with a welcoming smile and a slight, old-fashioned bow. 'I hope you had a comfortable journey?'

'Yes, thank you,' Athreya replied, noting that the man hadn't offered a handshake. He reasoned that this was perhaps Sebastian, Bhaskar Fernandez's caregiver, secretary and major-domo.

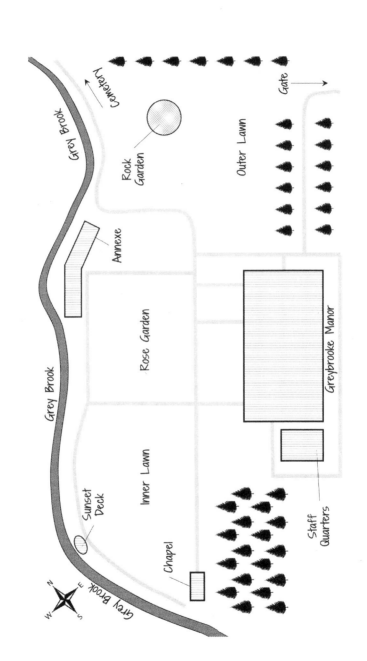

'My name is Sebastian,' the man confirmed, as he ushered Athreya through the porch and up the front steps. 'Your room is two doors away, and is ready. Would you like a drink now, or would you rather freshen up first?'

'I'm sufficiently refreshed after riding in an open jeep late in the evening.'

'Very good. Shall I take you to Mr Fernandez?'

'Have a heart, Sebastian,' Dora cut in before Athreya could answer. She put her arm through Athreya's, leading him through a wide double-door to their right and into the drawing room, which was dimly lit. 'Let Mr Athreya grab a drink first. I'll take him to see Uncle after that,' she called over her shoulder. Manu busied himself with some letters lying on a table in the hall.

'Mr Fernandez is in the study, Dora,' Sebastian called out after her. 'I'll tell him that Mr Athreya is here.'

As Dora poured out his preferred drink at the bar counter, Athreya suddenly realized that there was another person in the dimly lit room. A lady of the same willowy and athletic build as Dora and Manu, but a shade heavier and a few years older than Dora, was watching him intently from near the French windows.

Just as Athreya was about to greet her, Dora let out a hiss of frustration.

'No ice!' she griped. 'Half a second, Mr Athreya, I'll get some.' She caught sight of the other lady and waved as she strode to the door. 'Oh, hi, Michelle. I didn't see you there. Mr Athreya, this is Michelle, my cousin. Just have a chat with her while I find us some ice.'

As soon as Dora left the room, Michelle strode forward purposefully.

'Good evening,' said Athreya pleasantly.

'Good evening,' Michelle replied, acknowledging his greeting with only a flicker of a smile. She came up very close and asked in a low voice, 'Are you a lawyer, Mr Athreya?'

'Oh, no.' Athreya shook his head. 'Not at all.'

'Are you…' She hesitated for a moment. 'Are you a policeman?'

'Not any longer.'

A perplexed frown darkened Michelle's face. 'Then why are you here?' she asked in a whisper.

Before a surprised Athreya could respond, Michelle's hand flew up to her face in embarrassment, and she flushed red.

'Oh, I'm so sorry. I didn't mean it that way. It came out all wrong. I am so rude! Please forgive me, Mr Athreya.'

But Athreya was all smiles in return.

'There is nothing to forgive,' he said comfortingly, but she shook her head anxiously. 'Don't give it another thought. Please.'

In the low light, he studied the overwrought lady's face, now partly hidden by her hand. Along with the embarrassment was a palpable tension. He was now sure that she was the person who had watched his arrival through the French windows. Some unknown anxiety was gnawing at her, and her disquiet seemed to have something to do with his arrival. At an unguarded moment, when Dora stepping out had providentially presented her with a brief opportunity to find out who he was, she had unthinkingly blurted out the question foremost in her mind.

'I'm sorry, Mr Athreya,' Michelle repeated earnestly. 'I am not usually like this.'

'I can well imagine,' he said. 'No harm done anyway, and I take no offence. But allow me to respond to your question. As you probably know, your uncle invited me here.'

'You know Uncle Bhaskar, then?' Her wide brown eyes were searching his.

Athreya shook his head. 'Never met him in my life. A common friend connected us. I'm looking forward to meeting him today.'

'Oh.' Michelle was at a loss for words. Her mouth remained open for a couple of seconds. 'Then how… why…' She trailed off, a look of utter confusion clouding her face.

Just then, Dora returned with an ice bucket, and Michelle took the opportunity to retreat.

'I need to run,' she said aloud. 'I'll see you in a little while, Mr Athreya.'

Just as she turned away, she added in an undertone, 'Thank you.'

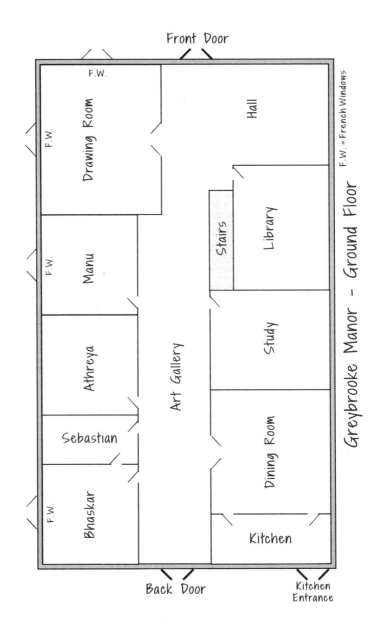

Front Door

Greybrooke Manor – Ground Floor

F.W. = French Windows

Drawing Room

F.W.

F.W.

Hall

Manu

F.W.

Athreya

Sebastian

Art Gallery

Bhaskar

F.W.

Stairs

Library

Study

Dining Room

Kitchen

Back Door

Kitchen Entrance

4

Athreya ambled over to the bar, where Dora was struggling with the lid of the ice bucket. After a brief tussle and a muttered curse, the young lady prevailed and the lid came loose in her left hand. She dropped it and picked up a pair of tongs to add two ice cubes to Athreya's drink.

'Some more?' she asked, glancing at Athreya.

'No, thanks. Two is fine,' Athreya replied, watching her wield the tongs expertly with her left hand. 'Left-handed? I didn't notice it in the jeep. But then there is little to distinguish a left-hander from a right-hander as far as driving is concerned. You have to operate the controls, whichever side they are.'

'They say lefties are creative,' Dora said, mixing herself a mild drink with lots of ice. 'Do you buy into that?'

'I'm not sure, but my personal experience—entirely anecdotal, of course—suggests so. The left-handers I've known have been more creative on the average than the rest of us. Especially in the arts.'

'Really? Mr Phillip is right-handed. He is the best artist I've ever seen—by a mile.'

'Mr Phillip?' The name was new to Athreya.

'A neighbour. He lives a kilometre or two down the vale. You'll meet him. Uncle has invited him for the do that starts tomorrow. Do you know many artists—'

She broke off and turned towards the door of the drawing room, through which a whirring sound was now coming.

'Here we go. Brace yourself!'

Athreya followed her gaze in time to witness a wheelchair barrel into the room at high speed. The pitch dropped a notch as it slowed down slightly, and veered towards Dora and him. The driver was a bearded man with powerful shoulders and a grizzled mane. He wore a bright chequered shirt of red and white. His left hand gripped a joystick, while the right rested lightly on a touchscreen console mounted on to the chair. A red-and-green woollen blanket was draped over his legs. Despite being seated with his legs covered, the willowy build of the Fernandez clan could not be missed.

Bhaskar Fernandez had entered the drawing room considerably faster than a walking man might have. He had hurtled in at the speed of a sprinting boy. The wheelchair was still moving swiftly as it approached Athreya. Athreya did what he would have done had overexcited children burst into the room and begun scampering around recklessly with little regard to their safety or that of the others around them—he stayed rooted to the spot. Dora too had frozen where she stood.

'Mr Athreya!' Bhaskar boomed in a gravelly baritone, as he yanked the joystick to stop the missile he was riding. 'Welcome! Welcome to Greybrooke Manor.' He thrust out a long arm and shook Athreya's hand heartily, and held on to it, 'I hope you had a good journey?'

'Thank you,' Athreya replied, with a wide smile. 'Yes, the journey was fine, and I'm delighted to be here. Thank you for inviting me. A quaint place you have here.'

'Wonderful, wonderful,' Bhaskar exclaimed, still shaking Athreya's hand. 'Dora look after you well, eh?'

'Very well. She and Manu have been entertaining me from the moment they picked me up. I think I know every spot worth knowing between here and Crown Bakery. And she insisted on giving me a drink as soon as we got here.'

'Wonderful, wonderful,' Bhaskar repeated and finally let go of Athreya's hand. He wrinkled his nose theatrically. 'From *this* bar?' he queried.

'We went to the hilltop, too,' Dora piped in quickly, avoiding the last question. 'Mr Athreya loved it.'

'He did, eh?' Bhaskar's brilliant eyes were studying Athreya, assessing him. 'Did it touch him?'

'It did. See, I'm not the only one who senses things there. He did too.'

'I know, girl. Your aunt used to feel it too… every time. She and I used to go up there every so often. There were times it touched me, too.' He turned to his niece and continued in a more serious tone. 'Sebastian tells me that you escaped a landslide by a whisker. Thank goodness! How bad is it?'

'I didn't see it, Uncle. I was driving, and the landslide happened behind us. Manu was sitting at the back and saw the whole thing. He should be able to tell you.'

'Can't seem to find him,' Bhaskar grumbled. 'Anyway, he'll soon be here.'

'I saw a bit of it,' Athreya chimed in. 'Manu shone a torch at the landslide. It actually happened in two parts, less than a minute apart. The first slide was smaller, the mass of earth that was dislodged being twice the length of this room and twenty to thirty yards wide.

'Then came the second, which was far larger. This one covered the entire road and spilt over downhill. Two big trees came crashing down a dozen yards behind us, accompanied by a lot more rocks and soil. The noise was deafening. That's when Dora rushed us away from there. I'm not sure how much more came down, but I looked back as we took the curve in the road. The mass seemed much wider than it first was—perhaps a hundred yards wide. It was difficult to make out much in the dark, but the dust cloud was massive.'

'A hundred yards, eh?' Bhaskar's eyes glazed over in contemplation. 'That's going to take a few days to clear—'

He broke off as Manu and Sebastian walked into the room. At a touch of the console and with a reflexive twist of the joystick, Bhaskar turned the wheelchair to face the newcomers.

'There you are, Manu,' he said. 'Mr Athreya tells me that the landslide might have been as much as a hundred yards wide.'

'That's right,' Manu nodded. 'It was a big one.' He went on to narrate what he had seen.

'Hmm,' Bhaskar went on. 'I hope the road isn't too damaged. Are we stocked adequately, Sebastian? Nobody can come or leave, except the others down the vale.' He threw a quick glance at Athreya, and said, as if to clarify, 'The valley is cut off.'

'We are well stocked, Mr Fernandez,' Sebastian confirmed. 'We can easily last for a couple of weeks. But we may have to be more careful with the diesel for the generator.'

'Do what it takes, Sebastian. Don't get bullied into switching on more lights than necessary. And make sure that the generator doesn't run more than twelve hours a day.' He turned to Athreya with an apology. 'I'm sorry about this, Mr Athreya. I hope it won't inconvenience you too much, but I don't think it will affect your comfort. We can light an old-fashioned fire in your fireplace if your room gets too cold. There is no shortage of wood.'

Before Athreya could respond, Bhaskar turned back to Sebastian and went on, 'Go there in the morning and make a first-hand assessment. See what the Roads Department has to say about how long it'll take to fix it. In any case, from what Manu and Mr Athreya say, it's going to take a few days…'

Bhaskar lapsed into silence, frowning like a grumpy bear, sinking his chin into his chest. Such was the presence and personality of the man that none of the others, including Athreya, spoke. Bhaskar was thinking; he would soon have something more to add, so instinctively, they all waited. Athreya took the opportunity to study the man.

White and black shared his mane in equal measure, while white had gained ascendancy in his beard. However, it had not yet touched his arched eyebrows. He had a large head, bigger than that of his son and Dora. In the few minutes Athreya had shared with him, it had become apparent that Bhaskar was an intelligent man who knew his mind and got his way. His swarthy skin was tough and lined beyond his sixty-five years. Athreya guessed that he had seen a lot of the outdoors in his earlier years.

Strong shoulders extended into long, powerful arms that must have developed their taut muscles over years of manipulating and propelling wheelchairs. Perhaps he had not had the benefit of an electric wheelchair for long.

At length, Bhaskar looked up and spoke to Sebastian.

'We must ask Enrico to delay his visit,' he said. 'He was contemplating coming the day after tomorrow. Now, with the landslide, that is not going to be possible. See if you can reach him now. Tell him I'll call him tomorrow, after we get a clearer picture from the Roads Department.'

'Enrico?' Manu asked as Sebastian went away to make the call.

'An art valuer,' Bhaskar replied. 'Art critic, too. Didn't I tell you that I'm having my painting collection appraised? Enrico happens to be in India now, and I thought I'd use the opportunity.'

'Oh, the valuer,' Manu nodded, his face clearing. 'I didn't know his name.'

Just then, Michelle returned, in time to hear the last bit of the conversation. She was totally composed now, and smiled pleasantly at Athreya. She had changed into fawn-coloured trousers and a dark woollen top. Her black-brown hair was brushed back and hung just below her shoulders.

'The valuer is coming?' she asked. 'When?'

45

'It'll take a few days,' Manu replied. 'There's been a landslide. The road is blocked. No casualties, thank heavens. We escaped it by a whisker.'

'Landslide?' she asked in alarm. 'Where?'

'On the main road, before you turn into the valley; it came down not more than a dozen yards behind our jeep.'

'Oh!'

For a brief moment, Michelle's features froze. Just when Athreya thought that she was going to commiserate with her cousins on their close shave, she excused herself and went to the French windows, where she pulled out her phone and began texting.

'Dora,' Bhaskar growled. 'Are you going to leave me thirsty, girl?'

'Thought it might do you good to be sober for a little while,' she rejoined cheekily, winking at Athreya. 'Your usual poison?'

Bhaskar grunted something unintelligible that Dora seemed to understand. She picked up a glass from the bar counter and walked over to a cupboard near the French windows at the far end of the room, which was in shadow. She opened it to reveal a row of bottles, a collection of finer liquor.

'And give Mr Athreya something decent from my cupboard,' Bhaskar called after Dora. 'Not your varnish that passes for whisky.'

Just as she was about to bring down a bottle from the upper shelf, a male figure came in through the French windows. In his hand was a polished cane about three feet long, which he was trying to twirl between his fingers. In the low light, he didn't see Dora and almost cannoned into her. He managed to avoid her, but his cane, out of control from his clumsy twirling, did not.

The swishing end struck the glass in Dora's right hand and shattered it. With a muted cry of pain, she dropped the remaining shards. The next moment, maroon blood oozed across her palm and began to drip on to the wooden floor.

'Richie!' Manu called with suppressed anger, as he sprang forward and switched on a light. 'Watch where you are going, man.'

'Who, me?' the newcomer retorted petulantly. 'She was in the way! What is she doing in front of the French windows?'

'Fixing me a drink, you blundering oaf!' Bhaskar bellowed. 'Now make yourself useful and fetch the first-aid kit. You have cut your sister's hand!'

For a brief moment, Richie Fernandez seemed to contemplate a tart response. He quickly thought better of it, and ran the length of the room and out of the door. It didn't escape Athreya's notice that he had neither expressed regret at having hurt his sister nor shown any form of remorse. The sole emotion on his strikingly handsome face was anger.

'It's nothing, Uncle,' Dora said in a small voice, coming to her brother's aid. 'It's just a cut, that's all.'

'When will you stop defending your brother, girl?' Bhaskar asked in a voice that reminded Athreya of muted thunder. 'Now let the doctor look at your hand.'

Michelle was already striding towards Dora, saying, 'Let me see, Dora.'

On studying the injury for a second, she called to Manu over her shoulder, 'Can you fetch my medical bag from my room, Manu? This is going to need some dressing. Bring it to the hall; I'll need more light.'

'Is it bad, Michelle?' Bhaskar demanded darkly.

'A little deep at one end, but nothing that won't heal in a couple of days. Dora has seen worse. Come, Dora, let's go.'

Michelle had wound a napkin from the bar around the injured hand to stem the bleeding. She was calm and assured as her doctor persona took over. Her earlier edginess was nowhere in sight.

As Michelle and Dora went out, an elderly man with a serious face walked in. He was roughly Bhaskar's age, but was balding and clean-shaven. His rimless glasses glinted in the dim light of the drawing room as they caught and reflected the brighter light from the hall.

'What happened?' he asked in a quiet, cultured voice. 'Dora seems to have hurt herself.'

'A small accident,' Bhaskar rumbled. 'Cut her hand. Michelle says it's not serious. Let me introduce you to Mr Athreya. Mr Athreya, this is Varadan, an old friend of mine and my lawyer for many years.'

Athreya shook hands with Varadan, looking with interest at the man who had helped Bhaskar write the two curious wills.

'Did you drive up from Coimbatore?' Varadan asked, after pleasantries had been exchanged.

'No,' Athreya replied. 'I took the toy train from Mettupalayam.'

'How on earth did you manage to get a ticket for it at such short notice?' Bhaskar asked. 'Some government connection?'

Athreya smiled enigmatically and changed the topic. He didn't want to talk about his network. 'By the way,' he said, 'I met someone on the train who knows you.'

'Who?'

'One Wing Commander Sridhar and his wife.'

'Ah! Sridhar!' Bhaskar exclaimed. 'Entertaining man. Did he say anything about Greybrooke Manor?'

'Yes, he did.'

'Must have talked about "English buggers" and "Englishwalas", I guess?'

'Yes!' Athreya grinned. 'Does he always do that?'

'He is a pukka sahib, that man. Would fit in perfectly if you were to send him back a hundred years into the past and insert him into the British-Indian army.'

'He is Air Force, Bhaskar,' Varadan teased, flashing a quick, mischievous smile at Athreya. 'Not Army.'

'There was no Air Force a hundred years ago, genius,' Bhaskar shot back. 'Sridhar would have had to settle for the Army.'

'I also met Ramanathan and his wife. They too spoke about you.'

'Ramanathan?' Bhaskar asked. 'The retired postmaster?' He let out a guffaw. 'Been making enquiries about me, have you?' he asked with a grin. 'Quick work! I'm impressed.'

Bhaskar lowered his voice and thrust his head forward at Athreya.

'Before the youngsters return,' he said, 'I wanted to tell you this. I'd like to spend some time with you and Varadan tomorrow, before the guests start arriving. Manu told you about the two wills, I take it?'

Athreya nodded.

'I would like to tell you why I did that,' Bhaskar went on. 'Varadan, of course, knows all about it. And once you have heard me out, and I've answered your questions, I would like to offer you a commission. In the event of any... unpleasant developments.'

Dinner turned out to be an informal affair in the form of a buffet. Athreya had expected Bhaskar to have ordered a formal five-course meal, which would have been in keeping with the colonial, old-world atmosphere that Greybrooke Manor asserted. At about nine p.m., Murugan, the chief of staff, came to the drawing room and discreetly announced that dinner had been served. All the residents of the mansion, with the exception of Richie, who had not been seen for over an hour, drifted to the dining room, chattering as they went.

Treating him as the guest of honour, Dora ushered Athreya to the tables where the buffet was laid out, and recommended dishes to him. Already informed that Athreya was a vegetarian, Bhuvana—Murugan's wife and the mansion's cook—had prepared a number of meatless dishes.

Soon, all of them were sitting around the long dining table with full plates.

'Mr Athreya,' Michelle asked with a twinkle in her eyes, 'do you believe in ghosts?'

'Ah!' Bhaskar exclaimed from the head of the table. 'One of my favourite dinner-time topics. Of course, I like it even better over cognac after dinner. Come on, Mr Athreya, tell us. Have you encountered the world of phantasms and apparitions?'

'Not the kind of ghosts you probably have in mind, Michelle,' Athreya replied unhurriedly and entirely in earnest. 'Not in spirits, ghouls, ectoplasm and that sort of thing. Not in the ones you read about in horror stories. But I do believe in ghosts of a different sort—ones that are far more dangerous.'

'What sort?' Michelle asked in a hushed voice.

'The kind that exist only in the minds of men and women. The ones that make them do things they would not otherwise attempt... from thievery and debauchery to murder and massacre. Such phantoms can ravage the minds of the weak-willed and the insecure. That's the kind of ghost I do believe in.'

'Poo,' Bhaskar exclaimed. 'For a moment, I thought you were going to tell us a thrilling ghost story. I fear you have disappointed Michelle.'

'Have I?' Athreya asked her with a smile. 'I'm sorry. But I have faced my share of spooks and phantoms.'

'Well, I guess you are too sane, Mr Athreya, too pragmatic to believe in such otherworldly things. But there are many here who do believe in them.'

'I'm sure there are.' Athreya smiled. 'That's so everywhere, all around the world. But do *you* believe in ghosts, Michelle?'

'I don't want to… but sometimes…' She stopped.

'Sometimes what?' Athreya prompted.

'Sometimes, you see or hear things you can't explain away.'

'Are you talking about the Parker thing, girl?' Bhaskar asked.

Michelle nodded and looked up at Athreya.

'There was an Englishman called Parker,' she said. 'He was one of the early owners of Greybrooke Manor. He was reputed to have been a devil worshipper, and there was a rumour that he had sacrificed a young girl at the chapel. Her nude body was found a mile away.

'Parker was killed horribly, apparently in retaliation, and was denied a Christian burial. His chopped-up body was scattered along the length of the valley, and not all of it was found. Because of that, they say, his spirit is unable to be at peace. It keeps wandering in the valley, searching for the missing pieces of its long-lost body. Sometimes it comes to Greybrooke Manor too.

'Many people claim to have seem him at night, walking about in the vale. The tale has been around for ages, well before Grandfather bought the Greybrooke estate.'

'A practical man would say that the tale served its purpose,' Athreya said cautiously, bringing his eyes back to the food on his plate. 'It allowed an Indian to purchase this vast property for a song. Wasn't this story one of the reasons behind the last English heir offering the estate at a throwaway price?'

'Sounds like Wing Commander Sridhar,' Bhaskar said. 'But he is not wrong. This tale and the larger legend contributed to my father getting the estate cheap. But the legend and its related tales still live on, you know. It will not be easy for me to find a willing buyer for this estate, should I wish to sell it. Myths and legends are powerful stuff.'

'That they are,' Athreya agreed wholeheartedly. 'Myths, legends and well-spun fiction send sane men and nations to war.

History is full of such incidents. If you've read Yuval Harari, you'll know what I mean. Fiction drives men to the ends of the earth. And beyond.' He turned to Michelle and continued, 'Do you have reason to believe in these tales?'

Michelle seemed to struggle with putting together a response. She tried a couple of times and pulled back. Athreya waited patiently.

'You see, Mr Athreya,' she finally managed, 'I have seen Parker's ghost.'

'You?' Bhaskar demanded. 'When?'

'Three times, Uncle. The latest occasion was last night.'

'Where, girl?'

'In the vale,' Michelle said in a low voice. 'A little beyond the cemetery.'

'What were you doing in the cemetery at night?' Bhaskar's voice was a soft growl, not unlike a mother wolf's.

When Michelle did not answer, Bhaskar let out a soft groan and rubbed his face vigorously.

'Murthy is around, isn't he?' he asked kindly. 'You went to see him.'

It was more a statement than a question. Michelle didn't answer. Her eyes were riveted to the tabletop.

'My dear girl, ask him to come here.' Bhaskar's tone had softened. 'He doesn't have to see me if he doesn't want to. He can stay in the annexe instead of that rundown Misty Valley Resort. Michelle, girl, whatever words he may have uttered, he is still family. He is *your* husband. Ask him to come over. Tell him I said so. At least you will not have to wander about the vale in the night. It's dangerous, Michelle. Not that I believe in Parker's ghost. There could be more deadly things aprowl.'

'I tried, Uncle. But he…' Her words petered out, and she shook her head mutely.

'Is he OK, Michelle?' Dora asked suddenly. 'Not affected by the landslide, I hope?'

Michelle threw her cousin a grateful glance and smile.

'He's OK, Dora. Thanks.'

In a flash, Athreya understood why Michelle had rushed to the French windows as soon as she had heard about the landslide. She had immediately begun texting. She must have been trying to reach her husband to check if he was safe.

The conversation was abruptly broken off when Richie sauntered in, looking a little dishevelled. From the droplets of dew on his jacket, and from his sodden shoes, Athreya guessed that he had been walking in the open. Without a word, Richie went to the buffet and began loading a plate with food. Silence fell.

He then went to the far end of the dining table, opposite Bhaskar, and sat down to eat, keeping his gaze down. He didn't even look at his sister to see how her hand was faring. Nor did he bother to exchange pleasantries with their guest.

After a few long moments of embarrassed silence during which Dora bit her lip and turned away from the table, forced talk began. Dora's eyes were swimming with tears. A strange expression suffused Bhaskar's face, one that was a mixture of sadness and outrage. For a brief moment, disgust flickered across Michelle's face.

Clearly, the family knew something Athreya didn't. Glancing at Varadan, Athreya saw that the lawyer was studiously focusing his entire attention on his dinner.

5

It took Athreya a couple of seconds to remember where he was when he awoke the next morning in a large, square room about ten yards across. A five-seater sofa set, two upholstered chairs, a gleaming writing table and three low tables dotted the room, around the huge four-poster bed he was lying on. The only time he recalled waking up in bigger rooms was when he had visited some of the palaces in Rajasthan.

Diffused light filtered in through the large barred windows he had left open overnight. Outside, a thick blanket of fog shrouded the lawns and the garden. Sunlight was struggling to infiltrate the murkiness, giving the vista a pearly quality.

Athreya rose and walked to the window, where he deeply inhaled the crisp mountain air. At once, he felt invigorated, as a pleasant tingling spread across his body and the lingering lethargy from a restful slumber fell away. The eucalyptus-scented air felt moist and fresh. He decided to take a walk outside.

Ten minutes later, he stepped out of the front door, which he had found unlocked. Before him was dense fog, through which he could barely make out the tree-lined driveway by which he had arrived yesterday. The fog reminded him of the comparison many an English writer has used—a thick pea soup. There was no sound to be heard, not even that of the breeze or the brook.

He went down the broad steps and across the porch on to the paved walkway, patterned with interlocking blocks of three colours. But now, he could only see them as three shades of grey. The aspect that struck him was that the hazy world around him was almost entirely devoid of colour. The fog was so thick that he would not have detected a man ten yards away, and, even at a shorter distance, he wouldn't have recognized anyone unless he knew the person well.

He walked a few paces and turned left along the walkway, treading along in a leisurely manner. At a junction where the walkway met another walkway at a right angle, he stopped and turned to look at the rectangular mansion.

The ivy-covered shorter side of the rectangle, along which he had come, appeared black. The openings in the ivy that marked the doors and windows were a shade darker. The longer side, along which he now wanted to walk, looked grey, as it blended into the fog at a distance. The mansion stood silent and still. A slight shiver ran down his spine as his imagination seemed to perceive something baleful and ominous in the scene.

Shrugging it off with a hiss of irritation, Athreya began walking down the pathway that ran parallel to the longer side of the mansion. The first room to his left was the large drawing room where he had spent several hours yesterday. One of the two pairs of French windows, he knew, must open on to the track he was on. Sure enough, he came upon a set of steps that led down to a path that met the walkway.

The room next to the drawing room also had a set of French windows, and a set of steps leading down to a path, which then met the walkway. At the top of the steps, framed against a soft glow from the room, was an indistinct shape. Man or woman, he could not tell, but it seemed to be peering out at him.

Abruptly, the figure ran down the steps and hastened towards him. Athreya could make out the contours of a hand a clutching heavy stick or cane of some sort. When it was a couple of yards away, he recognized who it was, just as the person too seemed to identify him.

'Mr Athreya,' Manu called in surprise. 'Good morning! You are up early.'

'Morning, Manu,' Athreya acknowledged. 'Force of habit, I suppose. I'm usually an early riser. It's a wonderful morning. Even if I can't see beyond my nose.'

'That's the valley for you. Fog can get really thick here. But it should lift within an hour. Not every day is like this, you know. Sometimes, it is bright and sunny.'

'Oh, I'm not complaining, Manu. I am quite enjoying this. A novelty for a city dweller.'

'It is, indeed.' Manu paused for moment and looked around as if seeking something. 'Say, were you walking along here ten to fifteen minutes ago?' he asked.

'No. I just came out of the front door.'

'Did you see or hear anyone when you stepped out?'

'No. Why?'

'I saw someone on this walkway. I saw him from my window.' He jerked his thumb back at the French windows through which he had come. 'That's my room. He seemed to be prowling around.'

'Prowling?'

'That's the impression I got. There seemed to be something stealthy about the way he was moving. But that could be due to the fog as well. You, too, were walking slowly. But, come to think of it, he was shorter than you, smaller build. He was walking faster.'

'I wanted to see the garden and the grounds. But not knowing my way around, I thought it best that I go about cautiously.'

'Of course. Say, why don't you come in and have a cup of tea? In a short while, the fog will thin out sufficiently for you to see the estate. I'll take you on a short tour.'

'Sure.'

Half an hour later, they were back on the walkway. The world was much clearer now, although wispy mist still hugged the dew-drenched ground and lingered among the trees. The mansion was more visible, with its stone walls, severe and grey, stretching for fifty yards along the longer side.

A third set of French windows led from a room at the furthest end of the mansion. A part of the steps had been converted into a ramp. This, Athreya guessed, must be Bhaskar's room. The ramp must have been added to facilitate the passage of the latest owner's wheelchair.

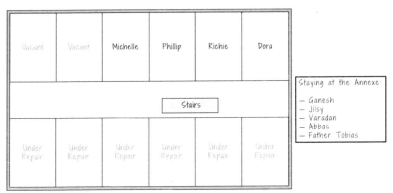

Greybrooke Manor - First Floor

The upper floor of the mansion was punctuated by six large windows, all barred. All of them were dark. Three of these rooms were occupied by Dora, Richie and Michelle. The other side of the upper floor also had six rooms, Manu said. But they were currently not in a state to be occupied, as the plumbing and electrical wiring were awaiting repairs.

On their right, enclosed by hedges, was the rose garden with an impressive array of bushes sporting roses of different hues, from white to dark red. Beyond that was a low single-storeyed building, which Manu said was the annexe. It comprised six guest rooms, only one of which was now lit. It was occupied by Varadan. Bhaskar had invited four neighbours to the party, who were to

57

arrive later in the day, and some of them would be housed there. Athreya mused, not for the first time, on the true nature of party.

They continued on the walkway, past the mansion to a stretch that had a grove of tall trees to the left and the manicured inner lawn to the right. At the end of the walkway stood a building with a steepled roof covered with grey shingles. Like the front of the main house, this building too sported ivy. But the creepers had not crept up the walls completely, as they had the mansion's facade. Questing fingers of dark green had reached halfway up, and had closed over the structure's entire height here and there.

This was the chapel. Manu pushed the door, which swung open with a creak of protest. It turned out to be a long room with an altar on a dais raised three steps at the far end. The gilded altar looked new and heavy, and was made of a combination of wood, metal and stone. Its top comprised a long stone slab, with its middle section supported by five metal pillars and the bottom section at both ends supported by wooden cabinets. Five tall candlesticks, finely engraved and polished, stood on the altar.

An aisle ran down the middle of the room with pews on either side. Between the front row of pews and the dais was an open space, about five yards in length, that was covered with a number of rectangular mats. At either end of this space was a door, which were shut and bolted.

The far wall behind the altar bore a cross and a mural depicting Jesus. On the dais, between the altar and the mural was enough space for three or four people to stand or sit. Two long wooden benches ran along the wall on either side of the mural. Two large cupboards were embedded in the wall at both ends of the dais. All the windows on the side walls of the chapel were closed and latched.

'Do you have a priest here?' Athreya asked.

'No,' Manu replied. 'But Father Tobias lives up near the main road from which we turned into the valley yesterday. He runs a small church not far from where the landslide took place.'

'I remember Dora pointing out a church just before we turned into the mud road that took us to the hilltop.'

'That's the one. We send word to Father Tobias if we need him at the chapel, and he willingly obliges.'

They left the chapel and went behind it to the Grey Brook. Crystal-clear water gurgled as it flowed over rocks and stones worn smooth over time. The brook was a good fifteen feet below them, where dark rock dropped sheer to meet it. The blackish colour of the rock bed and the pebbles made the brook look grey—hence the name 'Grey Brook', Athreya surmised.

Along the brook was another pathway that went upstream and around the other side of the inner lawn. A little distance up this path, on the very bank of the brook, was a raised structure with no walls and a shingled roof. Sunset Deck, Manu called it. From there, the pathway curved and went back towards the rose garden and the annexe.

'Further upstream, another walkway leads to the rock garden and the family cemetery,' Manu said as they reached the annexe and turned right to head back towards the mansion. 'You can probably take a stroll that way after breakfast. Past the cemetery is the open vale. Ten to fifteen minutes away is the Misty Valley Resort and a couple of dwellings.'

'These walkways have been laid out very well,' Athreya said appreciatively. 'Most places where I have seen such interlocking blocks have a few ups and downs, and you can sometimes stub your toes on them.'

'Yes. The people who built them took special effort to ensure that the blocks were laid evenly, without edges or bumps. The idea is to afford smooth passage to Dad's wheelchair. It needs an even surface, especially at the speed Dad drives it.'

They had reached the mansion, and had turned to enter Manu's room through the French windows when a raised voice came from their right.

'I will not let you spoil the family name!' Bhaskar thundered, anger crackling in his voice.

'Manu has briefed you on the matters relating to the inheritance of the estate,' Bhaskar began evenly as Athreya and Varadan sat in his study after breakfast. His voice was the usual dignified baritone. None of the anger that Athreya had heard through the window earlier that morning was in evidence. 'To put that into perspective, it would be useful for you, Mr Athreya, to understand a bit of history.

'My father, Thomas Fernandez, was a wealthy man by most standards. By all accounts, he ran a tight business, but he was also a fair-minded man. He is said to have helped freedom fighters and anti-British rebels extensively before Independence. But in those days, anyone who wanted to succeed had no option but to do business with the British, and that's how he learnt about the Greybrooke estate and eventually ended up buying it.

'My parents had three children. I am the eldest, followed by my brother, Mathew, who was two years younger. My sister, Sarah, followed Mathew into this world a year and a half later. There is this peculiar thing about the Fernandez clan... all the Fernandez boys have little respect for convention and are often overly venturesome. They are often given to eccentricity, and do crazy things. I myself am no exception. Thankfully, Manu seems to have broken the mould.

'But let me start with Sarah, my sister. As luck would have it, she married a leech named Gonzalves. That is what set off a chain of events that continue to this day. When my mother—a divine soul by the name of Anjali—died, my father decided to begin transferring his wealth to his children. Mind you, the Greybrooke estate, which he bought dirt cheap, was only a part of his assets. He had more in the form of investments, property and his business.

'The first thing he did when he began planning his bequests was to take care of his daughter. He settled a minor fortune on Sarah, and gave her a large property in Madras, now Chennai. Together, the money and the property accounted for roughly a third of his wealth. That, he said until his dying day, was the biggest mistake of his life. That's because Gonzalves, Sarah's rascal of a husband, liquidated the inheritance and ran through it in a few years.

'As if that were not enough, Gonzalves then made Sarah pester Dad for more money. He even resorted to emotional blackmail, but Dad didn't budge. Sarah used to come here to Greybrooke and spend long periods of time with Dad. Partly to get away from her badgering husband, partly in the hope of getting some money. She succeeded to some extent, but Dad would never give her large sums.

'He made sure, however, that the needs of Sarah's daughter, Michelle, were fully met. He directly funded her education and sent her money every month for her expenses.

'Coming to my brother, Mathew, it was a different story. Mathew was an inveterate rebel, who liked to wear his defiance on his sleeve. His pet target was Dad. He and Dad were perpetually at war with each other. On anything and everything, from the smallest thing to the biggest, they would clash. Eventually, there came a time when Dad thought it best that they didn't live under the same roof.

'Unlike me, Mathew had always shown interest in Dad's business, which was doing very well. By this time, Dad was getting old, and was finding it difficult to run the business. Besides, my mother's health was failing, and he wanted to spend as much time with her as possible.

'It was therefore a very agreeable solution to all parties concerned when Dad gave his business to Mathew, who gladly accepted it and moved away. The unequivocal understanding was that Mathew would not get a significant amount of Dad's remaining wealth, which would largely come to me. Mathew's share had, for all practical purposes, been settled.

'But, by the time Dad died, things had changed. Mathew had been reckless and had run the business into the ground. Dad had finalized his will in which the Greybrooke estate—now of substantial value—would come to me. I also inherited a chunk of his financial investments, while Sarah and Mathew got smaller portions.

'Dad had been clear in his mind that he had divided his assets into three roughly equal parts, which he had given to his three children. Two of these three, he had largely given away before he wrote the will. This distribution he documented meticulously, lest his will be contested by people who did not know the history of the family.

'But when Dad died and the will was about to take effect, Mathew disputed it in court. Abetted by Gonzalves, who was still hoping to gain from Dad's death, Sarah joined Mathew in the challenge. In their plea, they made no mention of the inheritance they had already received—and squandered—from Dad. Given the clear documentation Dad had attached to the will as his reasoning, there was little merit to their case.

'But our courts are what they are. The challenge dragged on, stoking bitterness and resentment along the way. By the time it came to a proper hearing, both Sarah and Mathew were gone. Sarah had been diagnosed with cancer, and her last two years were painful for the family. I did what I could financially, but there was no changing the inevitable.

'Mathew always had a weak heart. Unable to handle the stress of running a failing business and unable to stomach the bitterness arising from his imagined grievances against Dad, he too succumbed.

'At the final hearing, it turned out to be a no-contest case. Within minutes, the court struck down Mathew's challenge. But it had cost us years, and had engendered needless acrimony in the family. At the end of it, Michelle, Richie and Dora had been left penniless.

'That's when I did something I hope I will not regret. After the court had passed the order, I publicly pledged that I would provide for my nephew and nieces. I vowed to give them some of what I had inherited from my father. Manu would get the lion's share as was rightfully due to him, but his cousins too would get something.

'I wrote a will bequeathing parts of the Greybrooke estate to Michelle and Richie, and a Bangalore property to Dora. Some other locals here also received smaller bequests. I left my paintings collection to Phillip, whom you will meet shortly. He is an artist I've known for seven years, and he happens to be a major contributor to my collection. You will see a number of his paintings in the gallery. My antiques, of course, go to Manu. Similarly, I left some money and a small piece of land to a local church run by Father Tobias. A Coonoor hospital gets some money, and a number of charities receive grants.

'I wrote this initial will about a year ago. But soon, I found reason to change it. After lengthy discussions with Varadan, I cancelled the earlier will and wrote the two wills that are now in force—one that will come into effect if I die naturally, and the other if I die of unnatural causes.

'I sent copies of my revised will to Michelle, Richie and Dora. This is the one that takes effect if I die of natural causes. In this will, Michelle gets a part of the Greybrooke estate as before, and Dora gets the same Bangalore property. But Richie no longer gets a part of the estate. Instead, he gets a twenty-year cash annuity. At the end of twenty years, he gains control of the corpus.

'The reason I made this change was this: I'd come to realize that Richie is wayward and a spendthrift. His judgement is terrible, and he has habits that he cannot support. If he gained control of a property, he would sell it immediately and squander the money. Similarly, he would fritter away any large chunk of money I might leave him. The best way to protect him against himself is to give him a cash annuity, the corpus of which he cannot touch until he is older, and hopefully, wiser.

'When I sent them copies of this will, I also made it clear that there was another will that would supersede this one should I die of unnatural causes. I explained what "unnatural causes" meant, but I did not reveal the contents of the second will. Even Manu is unaware of it.

'This, Mr Athreya, is a summary of the woes that have plagued my family. Any questions?'

'Several,' Athreya replied, 'but the one that is foremost on my mind is why you chose to write two conflicting wills. Does it have anything to do with the legend of Greybrooke Manor?'

'The one about all future owners of the mansion dying violent deaths?'

Athreya nodded.

'It's probably true that some of the British owners of the mansion died violently. My own view is that their deaths were the result of how they had conducted themselves. Dad's death, on the other hand, was an accident. The idea that future owners will die violently is just bunkum. Hogwash.'

'Yet,' Athreya said, 'you seem to expect that you may die unnaturally. Why?'

Bhaskar inhaled deeply and let out a long sigh.

'That's because something started happening immediately after I wrote my initial will a year ago.'

'The one in which you unconditionally bequeathed portions of your assets to your nephew, nieces and neighbours?'

Bhaskar nodded. His arms were lying limply on the cushioned armrests of his wheelchair.

'Yes… yes. It occurred to me that someone was not idly waiting for me to die. He or she was trying to hasten it.'

'Hasten it?' Athreya asked. 'In what way?'

'Within a month of writing that initial will, death began to stalk me. Of course, it may just be coincidences or tricks of my imagination, but peculiar things began to happen.

'My car's brakes failed in a surprising manner—a rubber hose had been cut with a sharp blade. A venomous snake appeared in my bed out of nowhere. I was almost run over in Coonoor by an apparently out-of-control van. And to top it all, there was a break-in at this mansion. Disregarding valuable items that he could potentially have stolen, the intruder made straight for my room. That's when I began thinking about writing two conflicting wills.'

'What happened to the intruder?'

'I shot him. Varadan will tell you that I am a pretty good shot. I could have killed him if I wished to, but I thought it better to wound him so that I could find out whom he was working for. I shot him in the leg. Unfortunately, he broke the glass of the French windows in my room and escaped. I had been lying in bed when he came, and couldn't follow him. Had I been in my wheelchair, I would have pursued him. By the time Sebastian and Murugan heard the gunshot and came to me, the man was gone. It was after that that I had bars put on my French windows too.'

'It should not have been difficult to find a wounded man,' Athreya protested. 'Especially in a place like this. Did you check with the local doctors?'

'All of them in Ooty, Coonoor and nearby towns. The police made a thorough search. They came up with nothing.'

'That can mean one of two things,' Athreya mused. 'Either the police were hand in glove with the intruder—which I have no reason to suspect—or the person who had engaged the man was close by. They must have transported him away to Coimbatore or elsewhere, to a doctor who kept his mouth shut for a price.'

'I think so, too,' said Bhaskar, nodding. 'Let me answer your next question before you ask it. Did the attempts on my life stop after I rewrote the will? Yes, but it's only been a few weeks since I wrote the new ones. Only time will tell.'

'OK,' said Athreya. 'So where do I fit in? Why did you bring me to Greybrooke and tell me all this?'

'You see, Mr Athreya, I am not entirely convinced that my two-will trick can work. There is a chance that I may have miscalculated. In the event that I do die unnaturally, I want you to investigate my death.'

'Is that the commission you wanted to offer me?'

Bhaskar nodded and allowed himself a wry grin. 'A posthumous commission, if you will. I wonder if you have ever been offered such a thing. But seriously, Manu and Varadan have instructions to appoint you if something nasty happens to me or anyone else here.'

6

The previous night after dinner, Michelle had offered to show Athreya around the vale. They now set off together, going up the path that led to the cemetery and the vale beyond. They stopped briefly to admire the rock garden in the outer lawn. It was a circular arrangement of tastefully laid rings of rocks and plants, rising higher with each ring. Around the outermost ring were three stone benches for people to sit on.

About 500 yards from the inner lawn, the walkway ended in a quiet little cemetery demarcated by stone pillars. The grass in the square piece of land had been mowed, and small flower beds had been laid out around the five gravestones that occupied one corner of the cemetery.

Michelle walked up to the graves and solemnly placed the flowers she had brought with her. Athreya stood back a few paces, his arms folded in respect for the departed. Michelle bowed her head and said a silent prayer before she turned to Athreya with a little smile.

'I always feel at peace when I come here,' she said softly. 'Somehow, I feel my mother's presence here, as if she is standing beside me. Poor Mom, she went too young.' She gestured to the gravestone closest to her. 'This is her grave. The large one near the corner is my grandfather's. The ones next to it are my uncle and aunt. And this is my father's.'

Athreya had detected a hint of suppressed emotion when she had talked about her mother, and, to a lesser extent, about her grandfather. But when she mentioned her father, her voice was flat and expressionless.

'There are two people from the family who are missing from this cemetery,' she continued. 'Do you know who and why?'

'Well, I heard that your grandmother's name was Anjali and Bhaskar's wife's name was Sujata. I presume they were cremated, not buried.'

'That's right.' Michelle flashed him a quick glance. 'That was fast. You hadn't met any of us till yesterday evening.' A sheepish look came over her. 'I hope you have forgiven me for yesterday's foolishness?'

'There is nothing to forgive, Michelle,' Athreya said.

'As you would have gathered over dinner last night, we are going through a difficult patch. You know that Uncle and my husband are not on talking terms, and quite frankly, my husband and I could do with some help from Uncle. With the two of them staying at the ends of the vale, I have to be the go-between. I don't mean to bore you with my troubles, but I thought I owed you an explanation for yesterday's rudeness.'

'Come, Michelle, you need to explain nothing.'

By now, they were walking out of the cemetery and away from Greybrooke Manor. The walkway had ended, and they were now on a mud path with wild grass and shrubs on both sides. A dozen yards to their left ran Grey Brook, whispering to itself, flowing placidly. A short distance to their right was an irregular stand of trees, beyond which the hill began its climb gently.

They continued walking slowly, with Michelle providing a running commentary, just as Dora had done in the jeep. With a smile, Athreya appreciated the fact that everyone at Greybrooke Manor, with the exception of Richie, was being hospitable, and was going the extra mile to make him feel welcome.

Further down the valley, they came to a clutch of low buildings to their left, one of which was larger than the rest.

'Is that a resort?' Athreya asked.

'The Misty Valley Resort. This path leads straight past it.' She gestured towards two cottages to their right that were standing alone. 'These have nothing to do with the resort, and stand on Uncle's land. A very good painter lives in one of them.'

'Ah, Mr Phillip, I presume? I believe he is coming to the party tonight?'

'That's right. A quiet man who says little, but smiles a lot. The other cottage is occupied by an ex-army major and his wife. They too will be coming to the party.'

Michelle broke off as a youngish-looking man appeared further down the path. He had just come from the resort, and hailed Michelle as he strode towards them. He was immaculately dressed, and must have been in his mid-thirties. His dark hair was carefully brushed back, and he seemed to have freshly shaved. His clothes were obviously expensive. Athreya's first impression was that he gave considerable attention to his looks.

'This is Ali Abbas, the owner of the Misty Valley Resort,' Michelle said. 'And this is Mr Athreya, who is visiting Uncle.'

'Technically,' Abbas said as he shook hands with Athreya, 'I am not the owner. My father is. But he is too old to run the place, so I do what I can. A pleasure meeting you, Mr Athreya.' He looked down at Athreya's long fingers and continued, 'Of course! A valuer would be an artist too.'

For a second, Athreya was confused. But light dawned the next moment. Abbas had mistaken him for the art valuer Bhaskar had invited to Greybrooke Manor.

'I'm afraid I'm neither, Mr Abbas,' he said good-humouredly. 'I do sketch a bit and fool around with pencils and pens, but I am not an artist by any stretch of the imagination. I'm visiting Mr Fernandez casually.'

As he spoke, he caught a flash of puzzlement on Michelle's face, and recalled the question she had blurted out unintentionally: *'Why are you here?'* She had mistaken him for a lawyer or a policeman, and Abbas had now assumed that he was the art valuer.

Michelle intervened to change the topic.

'You sketch?' she asked enthusiastically. 'I would love to see some of your work. The vale abounds with excellent subjects. The eastern side of the mansion, which faces the hills, presents a lovely scene.'

'Perhaps I'll try my hand at it,' said Athreya, smiling. 'The afternoon may be a good time, with the sunlight falling on the hills from behind the mansion.'

'If we have sunlight,' she said with a nod. 'Even otherwise, it's a fine sight. Oh, Abbas will be joining the party too. It's going to be great fun with a dozen people. Bhuvana, our cook, is outdoing herself for the party. I'm really looking forward to it.'

Athreya wondered how true that was. With her husband staying fifteen minutes away at the Misty Valley Resort, she must be torn between the two places. On the other hand, being alone at Greybrooke Manor might be a welcome sojourn away from her badgering spouse.

After some more pleasantries, they said goodbye to Abbas and went further down the valley. Half an hour later, they turned back and headed towards Greybrooke Manor. The walk in the vale, preceded by the discussion with Bhaskar, had stimulated Athreya's appetite. He now looked forward to lunch.

When they reached the mansion, a little later than expected, lunch had been laid out and the others were waiting for them. Dora and Manu were arguing about some trivial matter as cousins and siblings often do. Sebastian and Varadan were discussing a pair of colonial-era swords mounted on one of the walls of the dining room. Bhaskar was in his wheelchair, talking to a bearded, bespectacled man with unruly, grizzled hair. Bhaskar broke off as they entered and hailed Athreya.

'There you are,' he said. 'Enjoyed the walk?'

'Yes, thank you,' Athreya responded. 'The valley is beautiful.

Almost as if it is frozen in time. I can't believe that we are just an hour away from crowded Coonoor. We may as well be on a different planet.'

'That's true,' Bhaskar agreed. 'That's precisely why some of us have decided to settle here. Let me introduce you to my friend and neighbour, Phillip. You would have walked past his cottage on your walk. Phillip, this is Mr Athreya, who has very kindly consented to visit me. He is a retired investigator whose work you would have heard of, but not his name.'

'Why not?' Phillip asked.

'Because he keeps his name out of the papers. He is the one who cracked the triple murder at Qutub Minar last year, retrieved the stolen Nizam jewels the year before and proved that the British diplomat's recent suicide was actually murder. My police friends say that his success rate is unmatched.'

Phillip ambled across and took Athreya's hand in a firm grip. His long artist's fingers curled around Athreya's palm and gave it a brief squeeze; and though they looked fragile, they exerted more pressure than Athreya had expected.

'Pleasure to meet you, sir,' Phillip said shyly in a gentle voice, with a wide smile.

'Same here,' Athreya replied. 'Michelle showed me your cottage. A very pretty place, I must say. Did you come by the same path we took?'

'No other way unless you take to the woods,' the artist said laconically, the wide smile still in place. As Michelle had said, here was a man who smiled more than he spoke.

'Phillip goes around on his mountain bike,' Bhaskar chimed in, expertly piloting his wheelchair into their midst, avoiding Dora by a whisker. 'It doesn't take him very long to get here. You must have been further down the vale when he left home.'

Athreya recalled seeing a high-end mountain bike outside the mansion's front door. That explained why he had not seen Phillip entering Greybrooke Manor. The conversation moved to mountain bikes, and how they were so useful in the vale. Most well-to-do people in the valley had one, including Manu, Sebastian, Abbas and the retired army major. Phillip, it turned out, was an avid cyclist, testimony of which was borne by his muscular shoulders and arms.

As they partook of the informal buffet lunch, conversation meandered and finally came to the topic of art and paintings. Phillip lost his reticence and spoke at length about the various forms and styles of paintings, and how watercolours were very different from oil paints. He and Bhaskar argued like schoolboys over matters of detail.

'The trouble with Phillip,' Bhaskar grumbled to Athreya as they finished lunch, 'is that he has very little imagination for an artist. But to his credit, he is the first one to admit it. His fingers, however, weave magic on the canvas. There are over a dozen of his paintings in my art gallery. All of them are of scenery or people; none are abstract or from his own imagination. Come, let me take you around my gallery.'

Flanked by Phillip and Athreya, Bhaskar careened his way to the hall. The wide corridor that ran the entire length of the mansion, from the front door to the rear one, had been converted into the art gallery. Mounted along the entire length of the long corridor, except where doors pierced the walls, were paintings of different shapes and sizes. Along the walls were glass display cases that flaunted antiques and smaller works of art: figurines, sculptures, tablets, fine china, jewelled daggers and miniature paintings.

They stopped at a large painting of a mountain scene that dominated the wall near the front door. The familiar-looking scene was done in strikingly vivid colours that seemed to bring it alive. At the bottom right corner was a scrawl in maroon that said 'Philipose'.

'Recognize it?' Bhaskar asked. 'It's one of Phillip's early works.'

'Aren't these the hills at the far side of the vale?' Athreya asked. 'The western side beyond the brook?'

'That's entirely right.'

'Is this how pretty it is during the summer?' Athreya enquired with a hint of wonder.

'When the sun is shining and the fog absent, this valley is heaven on earth. But at this time of the year, we are hostage to the mist.'

'Mr Phillip,' Athreya said, turning to the artist, 'I congratulate you. This is absolutely terrific. I am no connoisseur of art, but this is as beautiful a painting as any I have seen.'

To Athreya's surprise, Phillip blushed.

'Thanks,' he said bashfully. 'As Bhaskar said, I can faithfully reproduce what my eyes see. When it comes to painting the unseen, my mind is sightless.'

'This one,' Bhaskar said, propelling his wheelchair to a mid-sized painting, 'is the Danube valley. An excellent reproduction by Phillip. And that there is the Buda Castle in Budapest.'

They spent an enjoyable hour going up along one wall of the gallery and down the other. More than half of the works were by European painters, a couple of which seemed vaguely familiar to Athreya. Phillip spoke at length about his paintings and a few others, while Bhaskar expounded on the rest. When it came to antiques and other pieces of art, Phillip fell silent.

But Bhaskar was unstoppable as he gave a continuous commentary on the antiques. The erstwhile antique dealer in him came to the fore. Metal works of art from Europe competed with wood carvings and masks from Africa and with delicate porcelain pieces from South-east Asia—and even a totem pole and a suit of armour at one end.

At the end of the hour, Athreya was left enlightened and inspired. He decided to accept Michelle's suggestion to sketch the hills on the mansion's eastern side. He went to his room and took out a sketching pad, pencils and erasers from his suitcase. As he stepped out and went towards the front door, a shadow fell over him.

It was Richie.

'I saw you with Phillip and my uncle,' he said without preamble.

His voice was sophisticated and well-modulated. Intelligent brown eyes gazed out from a handsome, well-proportioned face, under hair that was set in a calculatedly casual manner. There was an air of elegance and virility about him that was sure to make him attractive to some women.

'Good afternoon,' Athreya greeted him non-committally in response.

'You've had a look at all the paintings?' Richie asked briskly.

'Not the ones on the upper floor. I believe there is a similar gallery upstairs?'

'Not of consequence.' Richie dismissed the question with a wave of his hand. 'It's half-empty, and what is there is not of much value.'

'Do you share your uncle's interest in art?' Athreya asked mildly.

Richie's face split into a roguish grin.

'To the extent that they represent a valuable investment, yes,' he responded unabashedly. He cast a quick glance around the hall and lowered his voice. 'I know that you haven't had the time to make a detailed assessment, but do you have a ballpark estimate of how valuable the collection is?'

So, Richie was making the same mistake that Abbas had committed earlier. For a moment, Athreya wondered if the two were good friends. They seemed to be of a similar mould at first glance.

'I am not the valuer your uncle has invited,' he said aloud.

Immediately, as if a switch had been turned off, Richie lost interest. His expression suggested that he had mentally dismissed

Athreya the moment he learnt that he was not the valuer. With neither apology nor acknowledgement, he turned on his heel and strode out of the front door.

Michelle had been right. The view of the hills to the south-east of the mansion was indeed impressive. The hills began their gradual ascent at an intermediate distance, after which they grew steadily steeper. The undulating skyline, from the rolling hills on the left, to the hilltop from where Dora had shown him the valley, to the gentler slopes on the extreme right, made a fine sight. The velvety green fuzz on the slopes of the rightmost hill looked like tea gardens. Closer in the foreground, the mud road by which he had come to the estate snaked up the hill.

But the sunlight that Athreya had hoped for was playing truant. It was patchy and far too intermittent. Propelled by a steady breeze, low clouds had darkened much of the western horizon. The hills and the slopes under them had already grown misty and taken on the familiar grey mien. Rain seemed to be falling in some places too. Within half an hour, Athreya guessed, gloom would reclaim Greybrooke Manor and mist would shroud the hills. That was all the time he had for sketching.

He took a seat on a stone bench beside the long south-eastern wall of the mansion and balanced his sketchbook on his knee. Two minutes later, he was engrossed in reproducing the vista before him. His pencil sped across the paper, laying down confident strokes—some short, some long; now faint, now dark.

Soon, a grey picture in the likeness of what he was looking at took shape. It was not nearly of the class of Phillip's creations, but the likeness to the landscape was unmistakable. A short while later, he sat back and studied the sketch critically. Not bad, but he could think of at least a dozen improvements he could make.

He looked up at the sky and found that the first traces of grey were reaching over the mansion. Perhaps there was time for one more sketch. But what should he draw? Another scene that was before him, or something that existed only in his mind's eye? Perhaps the latter.

As he was about to begin, a familiar voice sounded from behind him. He turned and realized that the bench he was sitting on was close to a window, which he guessed was the study's. Through it came Bhaskar's voice.

'What did Murthy say?' he asked. 'Did he agree to stay here?'

'No, Uncle,' said Michelle's voice. 'He'd rather stay at the resort, he said.'

'Heaven knows you can't afford it,' Bhaskar barked. 'Why does he waste your money so?'

'Well... he is not paying.'

'Not paying?' Bhaskar demanded, 'Is Abbas letting him stay for free?'

'Yes. He and Abbas are discussing a business proposal.'

'Business proposal!' Bhaskar sounded alarmed. 'Don't touch his proposals with a bargepole, girl. You will lose every rupee you have.'

'We are not investing any money, Uncle. Abbas is.'

'Out of love and affection? Don't tell me that Abbas has turned altruistic all of a sudden.'

'Well... not really.'

'Then what? Out with it, girl.'

'That's what I wanted to see you about, Uncle.' Bhaskar made an unintelligible sound that reminded Athreya of a bear's growl.

'The land that you are bequeathing to me...' Michelle said slowly.

'What of it?'

'We want to use it to start a resort.'

'A resort? Here? You want to create another Misty Valley? Are you out of your mind, Michelle?'

'Well… Abbas and Murthy say that Misty Valley is not doing well because it doesn't have access to the main road. People can only reach it by the narrow side road, and that makes the resort difficult to find.'

'So?'

'The piece of land you are giving me is on the main road. It connects the main road with Misty Valley.'

'Oh, Lord!' Bhaskar exclaimed. 'I think I am beginning to see.'

'If we merge my land with Abbas's, we'll have a larger resort that has access from the main road. It should do well.'

'Let me guess the rest of the proposal… Abbas wants you to put in your piece of land as your investment and he will bring in the money to develop it. Is that right?'

'Exactly! And for investing the land, Abbas will give us a stake in Misty Valley too. Isn't that wonderful?'

'Did he ask you to give the land on a rent-free lease for ten or twenty years?'

'Ye—yes.'

A long, inarticulate rumble sounded from Bhaskar. At the end of it, he spoke slowly, as if addressing a child.

'I'll say this as gently as my ornery disposition allows me,' he said. 'You are a good doctor, Michelle. But you are a bad judge of character, just as Sarah was. And you make a terrible, terrible businesswoman.'

'Uncle!'

'Do you think this is the first time this proposal has been made? Abbas's father approached me years ago with something similar. Get this into your head, girl—Abbas is a cheat and a swindler. Don't do any kind of business with him. He will take

77

away your money, and leave you high and dry. What will you have once the property I give you is also gone?'

'If you have such a low opinion of him,' Michelle asked hotly, 'why are you inviting him to the party?'

'We have to be neighbourly,' Bhaskar said evenly. 'In this out-of-the-way place, we have no other option. In times of crisis, we have only neighbours to turn to. And they have only us to lean on. Inviting him to a party and doing business with him are entirely different things.'

'Coming back to the proposal,' Michelle went on after a pause, her voice calmer, 'we don't have to put in any money and we'll still get a share in the business. We can be settled for life.'

'Indeed? You may as well kiss the land goodbye. Does Abbas have the money to develop a whole new resort?'

'Apparently.'

'Do you know where he gets his money from, Michelle?'

'How does that matter? Let him beg, borrow or steal.'

'Misty Valley is sucking more money than it generates.'

'OK. So?'

'And Abbas's father was never a wealthy man.'

'I don't get the point.'

'Then where does he get his money from? Developing a resort will take crores.'

'I don't know.'

'I'll tell you. He gets it from selling drugs.'

'Uncle! That's just a rumour.'

'No, it isn't. He supplies drugs along the Western Ghats, from Kodai to here to Coorg.' Bhaskar's voice had risen. 'That makes all the bloody difference. What kind of a character do you think a drug pusher has?'

'So you won't help me, Uncle?' Michelle asked after another pause.

'I have always helped you, and will continue to help you. But I will not become party to your financial suicide. My notion of doing you good is not falling into Abbas's traps. You are a fool, Michelle, and I have to protect you from yourself.

'Your grandfather gave one-third of his wealth to Sarah, and your father squandered it. Murthy will do exactly the same thing with your land. History repeats itself, Michelle, history repeats itself. One would have thought that, after growing up with a father like Gonzalves, you would have known better than to hook up with a similar man. But no, you go and choose Murthy, another loafer.'

'Uncle!' Michelle wailed. She let out a wretched sob. 'Won't you let the past be the past? I will not have you speak ill of my mother.'

'You are right. I'm sorry. I shouldn't have brought Sarah into this. Poor thing, her only fault was that she trusted the wrong man. Unfortunately, you are making the same mistake.'

'If that's how you feel, I'll leave this place tomorrow.'

'No, Michelle. We will have visitors for three days. The family must stick together and present a common face. Let's not wash our dirty linen in public.'

'Some family!' Michelle retorted. 'A family where people don't help each other.'

A long pause dragged in silence. Athreya imagined Bhaskar being angry and Michelle crying. When Bhaskar broke it, his voice was soft and injured.

'Michelle,' he said gently, 'look up, girl.' Another long pause. 'Look up… that's the spirit. Now, look me in the eye and repeat what you said. Say that I don't help you.'

Michelle sobbed uncontrollably, and when she finally calmed down, she apologized profusely.

'I shouldn't have said that, Uncle,' she concluded. 'I'm sorry. You pay the rent for my clinic and my flat. It was uncharitable of me to have said what I said. I'm terribly sorry. Will you forgive me, Uncle?'

'Of course, girl. Don't be silly.'

'But what am I to do, Uncle? I'm stuck.'

'Do what you should have done a couple of years ago. Do what your mother should have done after you were born. Had she cut your father loose, you wouldn't have been in this plight. Sarah was a wealthy lady once, wealthier than I am now. You do what I say, and I'll reconsider every decision I made about you.'

'You mean…' Michelle trailed off.

'Reclaim your life, Michelle. Cut Murthy adrift. Divorce him.'

7

The party was nicely underway in the spacious drawing room, which could have easily accommodated double—or even triple, in a pinch—the number of people there in it. Bhaskar had planned to have twelve people in all, exactly a dozen. Eleven was an unlucky number for the Fernandez clan, he had insisted, and thirteen even more so: it was the unluckiest number of them all, especially for dinner. That, in part, explained why he had invited Abbas.

'I don't want this to be my last supper,' he had said earlier. 'And today is Friday. The number thirteen and the day do not mix well either.'

Coming from a brutally pragmatic man, this had surprised Athreya. The other members of the family had nodded in agreement, especially Michelle. Athreya had wondered who the thirteenth person could potentially have been. Murthy? He could think of no one else.

The room was lit dimly by several low-wattage lamps that together cast a soft radiance. Cocktail snacks—samosas, vadas, paneer tikka and other delicacies—were placed at different spots within easy reach of where people had gathered, and Murugan was continually replenishing the plates. Bhaskar, with a bright red-and-green woollen blanket covering his legs, was in his wheelchair at the centre of the room, along with Sebastian, playing the sociable host to Abbas, Phillip and Varadan.

Abbas was immaculately dressed in expensive clothes, while Varadan was neatly turned out in understated professional attire. Phillip's shirt was similar to Bhaskar's, but the overall look was that of a shabby painter.

The four cousins were having a ball of a time near one of the French windows, all of them sounding pleasantly inebriated. Michelle looked charming in her grey divided skirt and white frilly shirt. Dora's light-blue jeans looked freshly ironed under her purple kurti. Manu and Richie were in jeans too, but with very different T-shirts. Manu's was light grey and minimalist, while Richie's was bright maroon.

Athreya found himself with Major Ganesh Raj and his pretty wife, Jilsy, the latest residents of the vale he had met. Ganesh was talking enthusiastically about his favourite topic, of which Athreya knew little: superheroes. It appeared that comics and graphic novels were the primary reading material the retired major consumed, despite his pushing fifty. While he drank only strong dark rum, Jilsy, who looked to be in her early thirties, was clearly enjoying her red wine.

Dressed in a canary-yellow wrap-around that ended at her knees, she was the inevitable centre of attraction. Along with matching heels, an orange scarf and maroon lips, she did make for a pleasant sight, and male eyes in the room frequently drifted towards her. Even without the get-up, she was an undeniably attractive lady. As she tried to conceal her ennui at her husband's incessant monologue about superheroes and their powers, her eyes darted over to people of her own age, lingering especially on Manu.

Both pairs of French windows in the drawing room had been flung wide open so the smokers could step outside for their nicotine shots if they wished to. The mist outside was thicker than it had been the previous evening, and the low-hanging clouds flashed intermittently, lighting the murky night with an aura of diffused luminescence.

The clouds had dumped their burden earlier in the evening, drenching the vale and thickening the all-pervading mist. Even the walkways, which were but a few yards away from the French windows, couldn't be seen. The world outside was an unmitigated sea of grey. Barely a leaf stirred. It was just the kind of milieu to arouse the crime-fiction aficionado in Bhaskar. He rescued Athreya from Ganesh's tiresome discourse.

'Athreya, is it true that women murderers prefer poison, while men favour more physical means to kill?' he asked loudly. 'Is it because most women wouldn't have the strength to wield, say, an axe?'

'Or a heavy, blunt instrument,' said Athreya, sauntering away from the major in relief, towards the centre of the room. 'While it is very much a matter of strength, the choice of murder weapon depends more on three other factors: the victim, the nature of the motive and the opportunities the victim offers.

'Pushing someone off a moving train or off a railway platform as a train approaches may not require the same strength as throwing the victim off the top of a tall building. Women have been known to do it even in our crowded railway stations and trains. All you need to do is to tip a person over or trip him. A woman pushed another out from a running Mumbai local train just last month.

'Crimes of passion—love, hate, revenge, infatuation—tend to be less planned, and are often opportunistic. Poisoners, on the other hand, are more likely to plan their crimes meticulously. Coming to the victim, it is obviously easier to poison a strong man than to physically assault him, especially if the killer is a woman or a smaller man.'

'Access to firearms changes that, I suppose?' Varadan asked.

'Certainly, especially a silenced one. But here, access to guns is far more limited than it is in the western world, especially among the common public.'

'And access to poison?' Jilsy asked. She and her husband too had walked over to the group.

83

Athreya turned and met her flattering gaze.

'If you consider the entire spectrum from the crude rat poison that kirana shops sell, to naturally occurring toxins, to more refined substances like cyanide, you have plenty of access. Even potatoes can be poisonous, especially those that are green below the skin or ones that are sprouting.'

'Wow!' Ganesh exclaimed loudly. 'I didn't know that. So easy, eh? Supervillains always carry belts with pouches of poison.'

'What weapon would you use, Mr Athreya?' Dora asked mischievously. 'If you were to commit murder, that is.'

She and her cousins had gravitated to the centre of the room where everyone else sat or stood.

'I would choose one that would result in death, but would leave no indication that it was murder,' Athreya said. 'The best way to go scot-free would be to not let even the faintest suspicion of murder arise.'

'Ah.' Ganesh cut in with a fatuous grin. It was clear that he hadn't understood Athreya. 'Me, I would go for a gun. Nothing as dependable and sure-shot as that. *Boom*! And *khalas*! The matter is over. The bugger is dead.'

'Oh, let's go around the room choosing our preferred weapons,' Jilsy said excitedly. 'Each of us will say how we would commit a murder. Come on, it's just a game.'

'A silenced gun for me,' Richie declared, surprising Athreya by going first. He had shed his sullen reticence and turned on his charm. He was gazing covetously at Jilsy. 'If I can't get one, I'll settle for a long dagger. Wouldn't want blood spilling on to my hands.'

'Ooh,' Jilsy tittered in morbid delight, her eyes wide. 'I'll choose poison, like Mr Fernandez said. I can't use any of Ganesh's guns. The kick is so powerful that I would topple over backwards. I don't think I can use a dagger either. I am not as strong as

Michelle or Dora.' She turned her flashing eyes to Bhaskar. 'You go next, Mr Fernandez. Choose your weapon.'

'I carry an automatic, my dear lady, and I am a pretty good shot,' he rumbled drily. 'You probably know that I shot an intruder recently, but chose not to kill him. It was obvious that he had come to stab me. I would have been well within my rights if I had killed him. Self-defence.'

This was greeted with stunned silence, and Athreya quickly scanned the faces in the room. Stumped, Jilsy was staring at Bhaskar, wide-eyed and with her mouth open. Ganesh had a stupid expression on his face. Sebastian's jaw was set and he looked grim. Manu and Varadan remained impassive, while Dora's and Michelle's eyes had widened. There was a contemplative look on Phillip's face, in addition to the perpetual half-smile he always wore. Athreya couldn't see Abbas's and Richie's faces.

Most of them would know about the break-in and its apparent connection with the two wills. As the awkward silence dragged on, Varadan took it upon himself to break it.

'There are so many other ways to kill,' he said. 'Just read some of Bhaskar's crime-fiction collection in the library. People drown in rivers, fall down stairs, have heavy objects fall on them, die of suffocation in airless rooms or dungeons, and even get scared to death. In books, people even drink acid, thinking it is water. And in one old story, a scientist, most improbably, drinks liquid nitrogen.'

'Don't forget "The Speckled Band",' Sebastian added, joining in the effort to move the focus away from the recent incident. 'It took all of Holmes's courage and ingenuity to crack the case. Some writers like Poe have even more bizarre ways of killing their victims. Edgar Wallace too.'

'Indeed,' Athreya concurred. 'Murky London fogs in these stories invariably result in someone falling off a bridge or an embankment into the Thames.'

'Why go as far as fictional London?' Abbas joined in. 'We've had instances of people breaking their necks in this valley during foggy nights. The man who built this mansion is said to have died that way.'

'Did he fall or was he pushed?' Richie quipped. 'That's the question. What say, Ganesh?'

'A gun for me any day,' the retired major responded, apparently not having followed the conversation very well. '*Boom*! And *khalas*!' he repeated before sauntering away to the bar to pour himself a large portion of dark rum.

'And what about that Parker bloke?' Richie went on, his eyes riveted on Jilsy. 'Nobody knows how he died, or where. Least of all himself. He still roams about the vale searching for pieces of his body. Michelle saw him as recently as the day before yesterday.'

A frisson of fear seemed to run down Jilsy's body, making her shudder. She cast a nervous glance through the French windows, but the grey mist outside was impenetrable, especially when seen from inside the lighted room. A low rumble of thunder shook the drawing room.

'That's why I don't walk around the valley after dinner, Richie,' she said in a small voice. 'They say that the time between midnight and four a.m. is when ghosts are most likely to roam about. Isn't that true, Mr Athreya?'

Déjà vu. First Michelle, now Jilsy. Athreya chose to respond differently to Jilsy than he had to Michelle.

'This Parker's ghost,' he asked her, 'how do you know it is him?'

'Who?'

'Parker, of course.'

'Everyone says it is.' Jilsy seemed confused. 'He is deathly white in colour and wears the old British uniform.'

'How do you know?' Athreya countered. 'It must be pitch-dark in the valley at night.'

'It is not misty on some nights, Mr Athreya, and sometimes the moon is out,' Abbas broke in, coming to Jilsy's rescue.

'Have you seen him, Abbas?'

'You bet.'

A flash of lightning lit up the mist outside the French windows. A peal of thunder sounded a few seconds later, this time louder and nearer. The lights in the drawing room flickered for a few moments in response.

'Can you describe him?' Athreya asked, when the reverberations died away.

'Certainly. Medium height, reasonably thin, a fleshy face like that of a tippler, blond hair, similarly coloured beard... what else, Richie? Dora?'

The siblings shook their heads.

'I've never seen him,' Dora said.

'Michelle?' Abbas asked.

'Don't ask me!' Michelle squeaked. 'I run when I see anything remotely resembling the Parker ghost.'

'Thus spake the woman of science,' Manu teased. 'A doctor to boot—'

'I have seen him,' Sebastian broke in unexpectedly. 'Several times. So has Phillip. Abbas's description is quite accurate.'

'Ever accosted him, Sebastian?' Dora asked impishly. 'You are the most fearless of us all, except perhaps Uncle.'

'No, Dora,' said Sebastian, smiling indulgently. 'Perhaps I should waylay the ghost one of these days.'

'Don't mess with things that don't concern you, Sebastian,' Bhaskar cut in. 'Let sleeping dogs lie. Of course, if he comes into Greybrooke Manor, kill him.'

'Kill a ghost, Uncle?' Dora laughed. 'How?'

'With a silver cross and a stake through the heart,' Manu retorted, with a wide grin. 'Don't you know? That's what they do in horror novels. Sure-shot way to slay ghouls, vampires and werewolves.'

'Stop it, you two!' Michelle barked, and pointed with her eyes to Jilsy. 'Can't you see she's scared?' Michelle herself seemed a shade paler.

'Ha, ha!' Ganesh guffawed and threw his bear-like arm around his wife's slim shoulders. 'Don't worry, my dear. Nothing can touch you when I am around.' He pulled her close and gave her a squeeze that emptied her lungs. 'Neither Parker nor anything else.'

'Don't take this lightly, Ganesh,' Abbas warned with a seriousness that surprised Athreya. 'And you too, Manu and Dora. You don't know what you are talking about—'

A bright rod of lightning fell outside the French windows. A moment later, a terrific crash of thunder sounded overhead, vibrating around the room. It seared the valley with a momentary brilliance that hurt the eye, making everyone in the room wince.

When they recovered from the intense flash, they found themselves plunged in impenetrable darkness. All the lights in the drawing room and the hall outside had gone off. The few lights that had illuminated the walkway between the mansion and the annexe were also off. Night invaded the drawing room through the open French windows.

Someone whimpered in the darkness. A sharp intake of breath followed the sound. Silence fell.

Athreya felt his senses suddenly sharpen as if he was expecting something to happen. His imagination took flight. He thought he heard a soft moan and a rustling sound coming from his right. He tried to recall which direction he had been facing when the lights had gone out, but couldn't remember.

He turned his face in the direction the rustling sound had come from. Another flash of lightning lit up the mist outside, and he found himself looking directly at the French windows at the far end of the room.

Framed against the lightning's blaze was a figure clad in a shapeless, hooded robe that covered it from head to toe. Two billowing arms were outstretched on either side to touch the frame of the French windows.

In its left hand was something long and slender.

Jilsy screamed. Someone dropped a glass. Several gasps sounded. The person behind Athreya drew his breath sharply. A faint glow sprang up from the wheelchair's touchscreen console, showing Bhaskar's keen face in sharp relief, hunched forward and peering through the darkness at the French windows. The glow also fell on his right hand.

In it was a handgun.

Another flash from the heavens lit up the room, showing that the robed silhouette had come in a pace or two. Its arms were still outstretched. A new voice, hoarse and quivering, said a name.

'Bhaskar!'

Jilsy screamed again, and, in the glow from the wheel-chair's console, Athreya saw Sebastian move swiftly and pick up something.

The next moment, the lights came on. Murugan had restarted the generator. Two steps away from the French windows stood the robed figure, clad in black from head to toe and clutching a cane walking stick. The hood fell away to reveal a bald pate and a smooth face wearing glasses. The eyes behind the glasses blinked rapidly in response to the sudden light.

'Father Tobias!' Manu exclaimed and strode forward towards the newcomer. 'What are you doing outside on such a night?'

Behind him, Jilsy collapsed into the nearest chair with a soft moan of relief. Michelle, her face as white as a sheet, had both her hands covering her mouth in terror. Her glass lay in pieces at her feet.

Sebastian, who had been standing behind Bhaskar when the lights went out, was now beside him. In his hand was a heavy brass candlestick from the nearby mantelpiece. He now moved swiftly to return it to its place. The others hadn't moved, save Bhaskar, whose right hand was disappearing under the blanket covering his knees. He was putting away his automatic.

'Oh, I'm so sorry to barge in, Manu,' the priest said, smiling ruefully. 'I got lost in this blessed fog and didn't know where I was until I saw your lights from a distance and came here. I hope you don't mind.' His timid gaze flickered across the room. 'Oh dear, I seem to have startled you. I'm so sorry.'

'No harm done, Reverend.' Bhaskar immediately took charge. 'The ladies got a bit of a shock, but nothing a stiff drink can't remedy. Pity you don't take an occasional drink yourself. This is the perfect night for one. Anyway, come in and warm yourself.'

'Would you like some hot tea, Father?' Dora asked, stepping forward. She had collected the shards of Michelle's broken glass from the floor and handed them over to Murugan, who had come in with a mop to clean the mess.

'Bless you, Dora. Yes, I could do with some tea. If you don't mind, that is. I don't want to trouble you.'

'No trouble at all, Father. I'll be back in a jiffy.'

The priest shook out his cassock and picked up the two leaves that fell from it. He looked around apologetically and nodded his head in silent greeting at each person.

'I seem to have gatecrashed this party. My profound apologies. Please, please, don't let me interrupt you.'

'Join the party, Reverend,' Bhaskar boomed. 'You are always welcome at Greybrooke Manor, party or not. Come and rest your feet. You must have been on them for a while.'

'For a couple of hours.' The cleric lowered himself into a chair that Sebastian brought for him. 'Good evening, Sebastian, Phillip, Major.'

'This is Varadan and this is Mr Athreya. My friends.' Bhaskar waved towards the two men. 'Father Tobias is our local priest, who also presides over our little chapel on occasion.'

Tobias beamed at them with an air of muddled benevolence, blinking every so often. Soon, Dora brought him tea in a large mug, which Tobias sipped in appreciation. Everyone had moved on from the disrupting lightning and thunder, and from the sudden appearance of Tobias.

'Bless you, my child,' he said. 'What happened to your hand?'

'A small accident, Father. Nothing serious.'

Michelle came up and chatted with the priest, as did Jilsy. Everyone other than Richie and Abbas seemed to be on good terms with him. As soon as Tobias finished his tea, he sought out the two younger men and greeted them.

Soon, the party had regained its momentum, the disconcerting interruption forgotten. Ganesh got progressively more drunk as he downed peg after peg of dark rum. He buttonholed Varadan, and held forth on superheroes and supervillains. Jilsy drifted away from them and began chatting with the four cousins and Abbas.

Athreya found himself with Sebastian, who turned out to be a pleasant man to talk to. Both of them were partaking of the same whisky from Bhaskar's liquor cupboard. It turned out that Sebastian had spent a good part of the day at the site of the landslide.

'It's going to take at least two days to clear the road,' he said. 'And perhaps a day or two more to make it motorable. But we have nothing to worry about. We have enough supplies for this three-day party, and for at least another week after that. You must enjoy yourself to the hilt, Mr Athreya. That's what Mr Fernandez would want.'

'A generous man, Mr Fernandez,' Athreya said, thinking about the conversation he had overheard outside the study window.

'Oh, yes.' Sebastian agreed emphatically. 'Very large-hearted. I've been with him since I was an uneducated teenager, you know. From before the accident that smashed his legs. He educated me, and taught me so many things. I owe everything to him.'

'Did he take the family quarrel badly? From the way he spoke about it, the challenge his brother mounted in court seems to have cut deeply.'

'Yes, it did. A very sad affair. It achieved nothing but delay and bad blood. Mr Fernandez was very fond of his sister, Sarah. It broke his heart when she joined Mathew in the challenge.'

'But Mr Fernandez is a strong man, isn't he? He came out of all of this unscathed. Despite the bad blood, he is doing everything he can for his nieces and nephew.'

'I wouldn't say he came out unscathed, Mr Athreya. The scars are there, but below the surface. He doesn't let them show. But yes, he is doing everything he can for Manu's cousins. Even for Richie, despite the young man's impudence. Mr Fernandez is very fond of the two young women.'

'Of course, I've not been here for long, but Dora seems devoted to him.'

'She is. So is Manu. Dora demonstrates it openly. Her affection is very visible. Manu, on the other hand, is a reserved person. He doesn't show much emotion outwardly. But he is devoted to his father. He won't go against his father's word. Mr Fernandez, on his part, doesn't make Manu do anything he doesn't want to do. He never imposes anything on him.'

'Mr Fernandez seems to be pretty hard-nosed. Very practical and clued-in. Thoroughly grounded in reality, he is.'

Sebastian nodded, and Athreya went on.

'Yet, he believes that eleven is an inauspicious number for the family.'

'We all have our beliefs, Mr Athreya. His father and mother also held the same belief against the number eleven. It's a family thing.'

'I guess so,' said Athreya, nodding. 'I saw Michelle and Dora agreeing with him.'

'I don't know if you have realized it yet, but we have a bigger problem now, Mr Athreya,' Sebastian said quietly.

'What problem?'

'With Father Tobias joining us, we are now thirteen.'

If Bhaskar was uncomfortable that thirteen people were at dinner, he didn't show it. Cheery and voluble, he invited his guests to sample all the dishes, and talked at length about his preference for British authors over American when it came to crime fiction. Sebastian, Athreya, Dora and Manu joined in enthusiastically, even as Varadan poked logical and legal holes in the plots, trying to demonstrate that fiction was not as credible as readers liked to believe.

Phillip shot wry one-liners that had Dora, Michelle and Jilsy in stitches. Richie and Abbas were in a conversation of their own, as a drunken Ganesh concentrated on transporting food from his plate to his mouth without mishap. Father Tobias blinked and smiled at anyone who looked his way, and held desultory conversations with his neighbours at the table.

At a little past eleven, the satiated diners rose and stood talking, before they split up into smaller groups and continued chatting. Richie and Jilsy escorted a wobbling Ganesh through the mist to the annexe. After speaking with the others for a little while, Manu and Dora went away to the rose garden, and Michelle and Abbas sauntered away to Sunset Deck.

Sebastian had a room prepared in the annexe for Father Tobias, and escorted the cleric to it once Bhaskar had retired for the night. Varadan and Phillip sat chatting in the drawing room. Left alone, Athreya decided to take a stroll along the walkways before going to his room. He went around in a circle, enjoying the novelty of being near-sightless in the fog. When he began his second round and passed the rose garden, he heard Dora talking softly.

'Uncle said he is willing to help me with twenty-five lakh,' she said. 'But instead of giving me the money, he wants to set up the business himself, with him and me as co-promoters. Upon his death, the entire business will become mine. He said he would talk to you about it. This is crazy, Manu. Why is he tying everything to his death?'

'Did he say *why* he wants to take this approach?' Manu asked.

'I am too fond of Richie, he says... and I will give away the money to him if Uncle transfers it into my bank account.'

'He has a point, doesn't he? You do find it incredibly difficult to say no to your brother. You know it's true, Dora. And knowing Richie, he will start nagging you as soon as he learns that you have money.'

'Maybe. But I want to run my business my way, Manu. The fashion industry is very different. I want to choose what risks I take and what moves I make. Uncle doesn't understand fashion. He'll only be in the way. This could be my big break, Manu. Zofus is willing to offer me a contract—'

'Really? That's great!'

'Isn't it? I will have to take some risk. That's the way Zofus operates. I can't have Uncle tying my hands.'

Their voices grew indistinct as Athreya moved out of earshot. But a few moments later, he overheard another conversation, this time at Sunset Deck. The murky night seemed full of private conversations.

'Did you talk to your uncle about my proposition?' Abbas's voice demanded.

'I did,' Michelle replied timidly in contrast. 'But he rejected it right away.'

'The *kanjoos* old devil!' Abbas hissed. 'Why can't he be a little generous for a change? Is he going to take the land with him when he dies? Or is it that he doesn't trust me? Thinks I'll walk away with his precious land?'

'Abbas—'

'To hell with the bloody cripple! Let him keep his land and take it with him when he dies. I'll have to work this out another way, much as I would like not to. Meanwhile, talk to that lawyer fellow and find out what you can about those bloody wills—'

'Shh!' Michelle cut in fiercely. 'Someone's coming.' Athreya spun around and quickly retraced his steps.

Halfway to the mansion, he met Sebastian, who was returning from the annexe, and they entered together. On his way through the hall, Athreya glanced at the wall clock. It was 11:50 p.m.

Back in his room, he opened his sketchbook and gazed at the second sketch he had made while listening in on the conversation between Michelle and Bhaskar. It was of a sari-clad woman carrying an engraved metal pot. He had no need to label the sketch, for he knew exactly what his mind's eye had seen, and why. The woman was Draupadi from Indian mythology, and the vessel she was carrying was the *Akshayapathram*: Krishna's gift to her, which provided a limitless supply of food, so that she could dole out meals to as many guests as required.

Not unlike Bhaskar, who was doling out money to his nieces and nephew. For a moment, Athreya wondered how Manu felt about his father's generosity.

8

When Athreya woke up the next morning, it was to a brighter day. Although wispy mist drifted past his windows in the breeze now and then, it had thinned out from the previous night. The sun had just risen, making the hedges and bushes of the rose garden clearly visible. The upper half of the annexe could also be seen from Athreya's window, albeit not as clearly. The hilltops beyond were just being lit by the first rays of sunlight. It was a much better day for a morning walk.

Ten minutes later, Athreya was out on the walkway, just as he had been twenty-four hours earlier. Nobody was about, neither inside the mansion nor outside. Apart from Bhaskar, who had been the first to retire last night, Athreya must have been among the earliest to go to bed. But, curiously, the front door again had not been locked. The two large bolts on the inside, glistening faintly from recently applied lubricant, were drawn fully back.

A steady wind had sprung up, sweeping the shredded mist along the valley and rustling the tall eucalyptus trees. With visibility much better today, Athreya set out at a brisk pace along the walkway. When he passed the chapel, he saw its half-open door blow gently open in the wind. As he turned right and continued, the sound of a window banging reached his ears.

The intermittent noise continued to follow him as he walked around the inner lawn and the rose garden. By the time he had passed the silent annexe and returned to finish one circuit, the sound was beginning to bother him. When he passed the chapel a second time, he noticed that one of its windows was open. That was the source of the noise. He retraced his steps to enter the chapel and secure the offending window.

He pushed the door open and stopped uncertainly. Something had caught his subconscious attention. But he knew not what. He retreated from the door, closed it and opened it again. There it was… something gnawed at the back of his mind. He was expecting something that wasn't quite there. After a fruitless mental search, not able to put a finger on what was bothering him, he went in and switched on the lights.

The chapel looked just as it had the previous day, still and empty. The aisle and the pews looked the same, as did the open space in front of the dais on which the altar stood. The doors at the left and right ends of the open space were in relative darkness, as the lights he had switched on were over the aisle and the dais. However, from where he stood, both doors seemed to be shut. Only the window beside the door on the right was open. That was the one that was making the noise.

Athreya went down the aisle and turned right to close the window, noting mechanically that it had no bars. After latching it, he turned around to leave, but then stopped. Something definitely seemed different about the chapel. But what? He checked the door beside him and found it bolted. Whoever or whatever had opened the window had not opened that door.

He swept the chapel with his gaze. Just like the spot he was standing in, the door at the far end of the open space, across the breadth of the chapel was in darkness. As he looked around a second time, his eyes halted at the altar, and he realized what had changed. The candlesticks had been moved. When he had seen them yesterday, the five candlesticks had been distributed evenly along the length. Now, three of them were bunched together at the far end of the altar, the remaining two at the near end.

He approached the altar cautiously and studied it. The thin layer of dust that covered the altar stone had been disturbed in several places. There were long streaks on it where the dust had been removed, and a large patch that gleamed dustless. After inspecting this for a long moment, Athreya went around and climbed the three steps on to the dais on which the altar stood.

Behind the altar were more clues. Two large floor mats had been shifted from their original place and were lying askew. Something or somebody had been here. Either during the previous day, after Manu had shown him around the chapel, or sometime at night. Turning around, he noticed a small scrap of cloth caught on one of the wooden benches that ran along the wall on either side of the mural portraying Jesus. He went down on his haunches and examined it.

Caught on an exposed splinter of wood was a small strip, perhaps half an inch long. Carefully, Athreya removed the dark-blue scrap with his thumb and forefinger. It was of a thickish material, of the type used in apparel. Had somebody's trousers caught on the splinter and ripped?

He rose and surveyed the rest of the dais, trying not to disturb the mats or touch anything. Having scrutinized the area, he descended the three steps on the far end. As Athreya turned to check if that door was bolted, he froze mid-stride.

In the dark corner beside the door, where the chapel wall met the dais, was Bhaskar's wheelchair with its back to him. Slumped on it was a man with a grizzled mane and a salt-and-pepper beard. His hands rested limply on his lap. A large, reddish-brown patch had spread over much of his shirt's right shoulder.

Taking care not to touch or disturb anything, Athreya went up to the wheelchair and peered at the man. Two seconds later, his fears were confirmed. The man's throat had been slit.

Death had returned to Greybrooke Manor.

For a moment, Athreya contemplated rousing the household. No sooner had the thought risen in his mind than he dismissed it.

The dead man was beyond all mortal help now, and had been so for hours. Nothing was to be gained by creating a ruckus. On the other hand, there was everything to be lost once people rushed into the chapel. Whatever little evidence there was would be trampled over and destroyed. It was best to examine the chapel before alerting the others.

The corner where the wheelchair stood was one of the two darkest spots, the other being the corresponding corner near the door at the other end. The wheelchair was placed such that the dead man was facing the corner. It looked as if he had been wheeled there after being killed, perhaps to keep the murder from being discovered inconveniently early.

Using the light of his mobile phone, Athreya found the front of the victim's shirt completely drenched maroon. Blood had flowed down to the hands that rested on his lap. The throat presented a gory sight—it was slit from ear to ear, and the cut seemed very deep.

Athreya retreated from the wheelchair and searched for the light switches. A few seconds later, all the lights in the chapel were blazing. He pulled out his mobile phone, and clicked dozens of pictures from different angles and shot videos of the entire chapel. Ten minutes later, when the battery of his overheated mobile phone was three-fourths gone, he put it away and studied the scene once again.

The floor in front of the altar was covered with rectangular mats, each measuring about four feet by eight feet. They had been arranged neatly across the entire area, and all of them were of the same type and size. Similar mats were spread over the aisle and in the space for people to stand behind the pews, on either side of the chapel entrance. On the mat under the wheelchair were two round spots of blood, each about an inch across.

Athreya's thoughts were disturbed by a thumping sound that

seemed to be coming from a distance. It had been audible for perhaps half a minute, but, because his attention was focused inside the chapel, it had not registered. Now, as it intruded upon his consciousness, he looked up and cocked his head to one side, listening. The sound seemed to be emanating from the mansion.

He hurried out of the chapel, frowning as he closed the door. The same subliminal feeling gnawed at him again. Dismissing it once more, he hurried to the source of the thumping, which was at the rear of the mansion. As he approached the back door, it opened and Sebastian came out, looking groggy. Behind him was Manu, looking annoyed. Both men were still in their pyjamas.

For a moment, the three men stared uncomprehendingly at the closed door of the staff quarters. The noise was coming from behind the door, which had been bolted from the outside. Someone had locked the staff in.

Before Athreya could stop him, Manu hurried down the steps and slid the bolt. The door opened, and inside stood Murugan, a stout middle-aged lady whom Athreya took to be Bhuvana and three young women.

'What—' Manu began, when Murugan interrupted him.

'Somebody locked us in, sir,' he said in Tamil. 'I'm sorry to wake you up, but we had no other choice.'

'Who?' Manu demanded. 'Who did this?'

'I don't know, sir.'

Athreya stepped forward and took charge.

'Murugan,' he instructed briskly, 'before you or anyone else comes out of the staff quarters, I want you to go back inside and make a list of everyone who is inside now. I need you and your wife to physically check if everyone is there, and tell me if anyone is missing. Don't take anyone's word for it. Check with your own eyes that each person is accounted for.'

'What—' Manu began again, but Athreya cut him off.

'I'll explain shortly.'

Soon, Murugan and Bhuvana returned with six young people in tow, and the news that everyone was accounted for. Every member of the staff who was expected to be on the premises was inside their quarters.

'OK,' said Athreya, nodding. 'When did you discover that the door had been bolted from the outside?'

'About fifteen or twenty minutes before you came, sir.'

'But you began banging the door only five minutes ago. Why was that?'

'I tried to get one of the boys to climb out though a ventilator, sir. So that he could open the door from outside. I didn't want to wake up the household after the late party last night. But the ventilator hole was too small. We had no option but to call for help.'

'Did you or anyone else hear the door being bolted?'

'No, sir.' Murugan glanced enquiringly at his wife, who shook her head.

'Talk to the others later and find out if any of them heard anything—either during the night or early in the morning. I also want to know if they heard any unusual sounds.'

'Yes, sir.'

Athreya pulled out his mobile phone and nodded at Murugan.

'Ask the staff to come out one by one,' he said. 'Nobody is to stay inside. Once I have photographed them, you are free to go about your work.'

Athreya shot a video as Murugan, Bhuvana, three young women and three young men filed out of the staff quarters. He returned his mobile phone to his pocket, and gestured at Sebastian and Manu to follow him.

'Try not to touch anything,' he said softly as they approached the chapel.

'What's happened?' Manu asked, now clearly alarmed. 'Why are all the lights in the chapel switched on?'

Athreya did not reply. The feeling that had been bothering him was growing clearer. He strode towards the chapel door, and stretched out his hand to stop Manu and Sebastian as he reached it.

He stood by the closed door for a second and then opened it. It opened smoothly... too smoothly. He realized what had troubled him. The door had creaked when Manu had opened it the prior morning. Today, it opened soundlessly. He stepped up closer to the door and studied its hinges. They were all shiny, and tiny rivulets of clear liquid flowed down from each of the six hinges.

They had been oiled. Less than twenty-four hours ago. Athreya stepped back and took a deep breath. He turned and looked at the two troubled men behind him, watching their expressions. Sebastian was clearly alarmed, and was trying to peer around Athreya into the chapel. Manu was restraining himself and was trying to be polite in the face of Athreya's bewildering behaviour.

'What is it?' Manu asked. 'Why are all the lights on?'

'I switched them on,' Athreya replied.

'Why? What happened?'

'Murder. Your father's fears have materialized.'

'Murder! Where?'

Athreya stepped back and pointed towards the corner where the wheelchair stood, now clearly visible because the full set of lights were on.

'There. In the wheelchair in the corner.'

'Wheelchair?' Manu cried. A second later, he recognized it and the grizzled mane of the bearded man in it.

'Dad!' It was a plaintive wail. 'No! Dad!' Manu pushed past Athreya and ran down the aisle.

'Can't be,' Sebastian called after Manu, following him quickly, 'Manu, your father was in his room when I came out. The sound of Murugan banging on the door had awakened him.'

'Thank God.' Manu paused and threw a look over his shoulder. Relief had flooded his face. Immediately, puzzlement followed and he resumed his sprint towards the wheelchair. 'Then who?' he asked of nobody in particular. 'This is Dad's wheelchair.'

A yard or two from it, he stopped and recoiled at the gory sight. His face had gone white.

'It's Phillip!' he whispered hoarsely. 'But how? Why?'

'I must inform Mr Fernandez,' Sebastian said, turning towards the door. 'He will be waiting for a report.'

'In a few minutes, Sebastian,' Athreya interrupted, laying a hand on his shoulder to stop him. 'Before we let more people tramp all over the chapel and destroy any evidence, please look around and tell me if anything is out of place. You both know the chapel well; I don't. Let's start with the dais and work our way towards the entrance.'

'The candlesticks,' Manu said immediately, as they climbed on to the dais. 'They have been moved.'

'And these floor mats,' Sebastian added, pointing to the floor behind the altar where two mats were askew. 'They were not like this last evening.'

'Are you sure, Sebastian?' Athreya asked.

'Absolutely sure. Dora and I were here. The candlesticks were in their places too.'

'What time were you here?'

'About half an hour before the party began… or forty-five minutes. Dora wanted to check something in the storage cupboards.' He gestured to the two large cupboards at the ends of the dais.

'What were you wearing?' Athreya asked.

'Wearing?' Sebastian looked perplexed.

Athreya nodded. 'Try to remember.'

'Oh, I remember perfectly. I was wearing a pair of shorts and a T-shirt.'

'Colour?'

Sebastian's face grew more puzzled. 'Khaki shorts,' he said, nevertheless. 'You could call it fawn, I suppose. And a red T-shirt.'

'And Dora? What was she wearing?'

'Her usual light-blue jeans and a woollen pullover. It was black. Why do you ask?'

'Just curious,' said Athreya. 'Anything else out of place?'

'The dust on the altar has been disturbed,' Manu replied. 'Someone has definitely been here, and has done more than just move the candlesticks.' He looked up enquiringly at Athreya and asked, 'What brought you to the chapel so early this morning?'

'That window,' Athreya said, pointing towards the one he had closed earlier, 'was open and banging in the wind. And the front door was swaying too. I came in here to latch the window.'

Frowning absently, Sebastian hurried to the window. He opened and closed it, and examined the floor below it. Not satisfied, he opened the door and inspected the ground outside. Athreya noted that the door's bolt was misaligned, and had been difficult to open. It had also creaked when opened, but the window had not. He went over to the window and looked at the hinges. They, too, had been oiled recently.

They shut the door and methodically went over the rest of the chapel. They found nothing between or under the pews. The aisle yielded nothing either. But when they reached the space behind the pews, Manu pointed to the floor at one end. It was bare.

'Didn't this area have mats too, Sebastian?' he asked.

'Two mats,' Sebastian confirmed. 'Four by eight feet in size— same as all the other mats.'

'Were they there last evening?' Athreya asked.

'I can't say for sure; we didn't come over here. We went down the aisle to the dais and back to the door. I did glance around, but I didn't see anything amiss. Mind you, it was already getting dark, and we had only switched on the lights over the dais and aisle.'

'Is the chapel always left unlocked?' Athreya asked.

Sebastian shrugged. 'Mr Fernandez wanted the chapel to be available to everyone at any point in time. Sometimes, people make private visits here and pray alone, especially when their minds are in turmoil. Mr Fernandez believes that they should be free to do so, without having to ask someone for a key.'

'How often is the chapel cleaned?'

'Every day, usually in the morning. One of the boys does it.'

'Does he also oil the doors and windows?'

'Whatever for?' Sebastian threw a baffled glance at Athreya.

'Is the front door of the mansion also kept unlocked?' Athreya asked, switching tack.

'No. Murugan usually locks up before retiring. But last night was different. With so many guests in the mansion and the annexe, we left it unlocked. People were going in and out after dinner, and several of them were taking strolls in the garden till late. We wanted to let them have complete freedom to come and go as they wished.'

'And the back door? Was that left unlocked too?'

'Not really. Murugan would have locked it with his key before retiring to the staff quarters. Thereafter, it would not be possible to open the door from the outside without a key. But from the inside, you could turn the knob and open it.'

'How was it when you woke up this morning?'

'As usual. The lock had been clicked into place. I opened the door by turning the knob.'

'One final question, Sebastian. Where is the wheelchair kept at night?'

'Next to the back door at the very end of the gallery. In the corner, where the rear wall meets the wall of Mr Fernandez's room. You will find a set of electrical outlets there for charging the wheelchair batteries at night.'

The chapel door flew open and a voice thundered through it.

'What's going on here?' it demanded. 'Sebastian! Manu! Are you here?'

Athreya spun around and his eyes flew wide open. Bhaskar was standing on his feet, unaided! Except for a walking stick, he had no support. As Athreya watched, the man he had thought was wheelchair-bound walked in, rocking from side to side on unsteady legs, and stood glowering at the three men.

9

As soon as Bhaskar was apprised of the situation, he took charge. Standing with a pale and drawn face, using the support of his walking stick with one hand and holding the wall with the other, he barked out orders. Sebastian was dispatched with instructions to say nothing to anyone and to fetch a padlock to secure the chapel. Nobody, Bhaskar declared, would enter the chapel, except on legitimate investigative business. He would permit no morbid ogling at the crime scene or the dead man.

Simultaneously, he sent Manu to fetch a spare wheelchair. He himself stepped out of the chapel after peering at Phillip from across the length of the building.

'Everyone is a suspect now,' he said to Athreya, once Sebastian and Manu had left. 'Including me. I haven't been inside the chapel for days, and don't want to enter now and leave telltale signs of my being there. The key will be in your custody, Mr Athreya, and yours alone. Any spare keys to the lock will also be given to you.'

'Why do you rule me out as a suspect?' Athreya asked mildly. 'After all, I have no corroborated alibi for last night, and I was the one who discovered the body. I had a full fifteen minutes alone inside before Manu and Sebastian came.'

'Be that as it may, you are the only outsider. You didn't know Phillip or me when you came here. You are the least likely to have a motive, even if you had the opportunity.'

'What motive do the others have to kill Phillip?' Athreya countered.

'I admit I don't know that. But I can't overlook the fact that Phillip was sitting in *my* wheelchair. Our builds are similar, and he too has—had—a greying head and beard.

'But all that is beside the point. I am handing over charge to you, as far as the investigation is concerned. At least till the police arrive. The rest of us, bar none, will do as you say.'

'OK. For now, let's not tell anyone about the murder. I want to see their reactions when they hear it for the first time.'

'Good idea.'

Bhaskar sighed as Manu returned with another wheelchair, a simple, non-motorized one. 'Now if you'll excuse me, I'll return to my room. I don't think I can stay on my feet for much longer.' He carefully lowered himself into the chair as Manu held it in place. He looked up at Athreya with a faint smile. 'By the way, I noticed your surprise when I came in. Seeing me in a wheelchair, people assume I can't walk. I walk four times a day, quarter of an hour each time. The legs need some exercise if they are not to atrophy.'

'Manu,' Athreya said as Manu began to wheel Bhaskar away. 'Can I borrow your bicycle?'

'Certainly. I'll have Gopal—one of the boys—bring it to you.'

By then, Sebastian had returned with a padlock. Athreya locked the chapel and pocketed the two keys. Then, with Sebastian in tow, he made a quick circuit covering Sunset Deck, the annexe, the inner lawn and the rose garden. They found nothing out of place.

'If you'll excuse me,' Sebastian said, 'I need to call the police, and see how I can bring the inspector at least here.'

'What about the landslide?'

'We have a cross-country motorcycle for just such situations. I will have to find a way around the landslide. I can bring one person back with me.'

'You may need the police doctor as well.'

'I'll see what I can do.'

As Sebastian hurried away, Dora appeared at one of the drawing room's French windows. Her puzzled look followed Sebastian, who had restricted his greeting to a curt 'good morning', without slowing down or meeting her eyes.

'What's happened?' she asked Athreya. 'Bhuvana told me that the staff had been locked in. And now Sebastian is uncharacteristically unsociable.'

'Your room is on the first floor, right?' Athreya asked. 'Did you just come down?'

'I came down about fifteen minutes ago. And I found Bhuvana nervy and unforthcoming.'

'When did you retire last night?'

'Around 12:30 or so. I glanced at my watch when I entered the mansion. It was 12:27 a.m.'

'Did Manu come in with you?'

'No. He said he wanted to take a walk and unwind before going to bed.' She peered shrewdly at Athreya. 'Why all these questions? Something has happened, hasn't it? What?'

'Murder.'

Athreya watched her face as he uttered the word. For a moment, her puzzlement deepened. A moment later, the shock hit her. Her eyes widened and her mouth opened mutely.

'Who?' she croaked.

Athreya was ready with his response, and had pulled out his mobile phone. He showed her the picture of the dead man in the wheelchair.

'Uncle!' she gasped. 'No! Tell me it isn't true!' Tears flooded her eyes.

'Who do you think it is?' Athreya asked.

'It looks like Uncle. It's his wheelchair. The hair and the beard look like his. Tell me it isn't him!'

'It isn't, Dora.'

She gave him a piercing stare.

'You wouldn't be playing with me, would you, Mr Athreya? That would be cruel.'

'I'm sorry, but I had to see your reaction. No, it isn't Mr Fernandez. Take another look. Who do you think it is?'

Dora looked at the picture again and zoomed in with her fingers.

'Phillip?' she asked. 'Is it Mr Phillip?' Athreya nodded.

'Where?'

'In the chapel.'

Dora groaned and buried her face in her hands.

'I wonder when it happened,' she said through her fingers. 'I saw Mr Varadan and him chatting in the drawing room after dinner. Most of us had gone out to the garden. On my way back to the mansion, I ran into Mr Varadan on the walkway. Mr Phillip seemed to have left too, because no one was in the drawing room when I got back.'

'What were you doing in the garden?'

'Talking to Manu for almost an hour about how Uncle is planning to help me with my little fashion business. I had some issues with Uncle's approach, and was discussing it with Manu to see if we could convince Uncle to do it differently.'

Here she was speaking openly about a conversation that could potentially pin a motive on her. She couldn't know that he had overheard part of it. Yet, she was being forthright. He gazed at her silently for a moment. Her eyes were wide and innocent, and her face bore a frank expression. Either she had nothing to hide, or she was an excellent actress.

'OK,' he said aloud. 'Is anyone else up?'

Dora shook her head. 'Didn't see anyone, except Bhuvana.'

'I want you to keep what I told you under your hat. Don't tell anyone that there has been a murder. I need to see people's first reactions to the news.'

'I don't envy you, Mr Athreya. You are going to hurt people.'

'I know. I've learned to live with the guilt. Nice guys seldom solve crimes. Now, I need to run.'

Athreya walked away briskly. A moment later Dora came trotting after him.

'Can I come with you?' she asked. 'Gopal has got Manu's bicycle ready for you. I have mine.'

Athreya stopped and considered her request. On the one hand, it was not good practice to let a potential suspect join the investigation. On the other, her presence might help in the next task.

'OK,' he replied. 'Join me this time. But if I say no in the future, you must respect it.'

'Certainly.'

'And no saying anything to anybody.'

'Of course.'

'Including Manu or your uncle. And Richie.'

For a moment, fear flashed in her eyes. But she quickly nodded and led the way to the bicycles.

A short while later, clad in a zipped-up jacket he had fetched from his room, Athreya was at the gate of the Misty Valley Resort with Dora. Recognizing her, the guard at the gate threw them a salute and grinned, showing crooked, discoloured teeth. This is why Athreya had brought Dora along. She greeted the guard warmly and indulged in some small talk.

'Were you on duty last night?' she asked in Tamil.

'Yes, madam,' said the guard, nodding animatedly. 'My duty is from eight to eight.'

'Then you are the right man.' Dora smiled at him in her friendly manner.

'For what, madam?'

'Somebody from here came looking for this gentleman last night,' she lied, gesturing to Athreya. 'But he didn't leave his name. We wanted to know who it was. We think it may have been one of your guests.'

'We only have two guests now, madam. One is Michelle Madam's husband, Murthy Sir. The other is a younger man. I don't know his name.'

'Only two guests?'

'Manager Sir said that some more guests were expected yesterday, but couldn't come because of the landslide.'

'That's a pity. Did Murthy or the other guest go out of the resort compound last night?'

'Yes, madam. Murthy Sir went towards your mansion. But all of you there know him. You would have recognized him.'

'The person who talked to him was a new employee,' Dora lied again. 'He may not have recognized him. Besides, it was very foggy last night, wasn't it?'

'Yes, madam. I couldn't see five steps in front of me. It was scary! We decided to keep the gates closed after 10 p.m.'

'After Murthy went to the mansion?'

'No, no. He went at about 11 p.m. He went out through this gate only.'

'And when did he return?'

'I don't know the exact time...'

'You don't know?' Dora repeated. 'You were at the gate, weren't you?' She grinned conspiratorially. 'Or did you fall asleep?'

'No, madam. I didn't sleep. But he didn't return through the gate.'

'Is there another way? I thought the compound was fenced.'

'There is a small gate there.' The guard pointed vaguely towards the left of the main gate. 'It is kept latched from the inside, but if you know how to do it, you can open it from the outside too.'

'How do you know somebody opened it from the outside? You said you couldn't see five paces in the fog.'

'But sounds carry well in the mist, madam. I heard the gate open. I went quietly, and saw a man enter. When he reached the lights of the main building, I saw that it was Murthy Sir.'

'What time was it?'

'Somewhere between 1:30 and 2:00 a.m., I think. I can't be sure. I didn't look at the clock until later.'

'Can you show us the gate?'

'Of course.'

Two minutes later, they were at a small wooden gate built into the resort's fence between two wooden pillars. It was hinged to one of the pillars and latched to the other. The guard unfastened the latch and opened it.

'See?' he said, as the hook made a flat noise and the hinges creaked. 'You can hear it from the main gate.'

He repeated his action a couple of times, demonstrating that the gate was always noisy. Athreya asked the guard to step back. He held the top bar of the gate with one hand and lifted it an inch or two. Having done that, he slowly opened the hook without letting it fall. When he had fully opened the gate, he gently let the hook down, a millimetre at a time. Still exerting an upward force on the top bar, he gently pushed the gate open, moving it an inch at a time. When it was half open, he let the gate down gently. It had made no noise at all.

'Sir is very smart!' the guard grinned.

On returning to the main gate, Dora thanked the guard and turned to Athreya, her face tight and pale. She hadn't missed the significance of Michelle's husband having been out of the resort on the night of the murder.

'You go inside and speak to the staff about the other guest,' Athreya said. He didn't want Dora with him for the next activity he had in mind. 'I'll have a look around and come back here in fifteen minutes.'

Athreya mounted the cycle and pedalled towards the two identical cottages across the mud road from the resort gate. The name boards on the gates showed the one to the right to be Phillip's and the other one as Ganesh's. He locked the cycle and entered the right-side gate.

At the front was a covered veranda that was about three yards wide. Bisecting it was the front door. It was bolted from the outside, and a mid-size padlock hung from it. The four windows that pierced the front wall were closed and curtained from the inside.

After studying it for a moment, Athreya went around the cottage. All the windows were shut and curtained. The back door was also shut, and seemed to have been locked from the inside. Once he had completed a full round, he mounted the steps of the veranda and approached the front door.

From his jacket, he pulled out a flat leather pouch and opened it. In it were a set of twenty-four pieces of metal with flat handles and thin, elongated protrusions with differently shaped and sized tips. Along with it were several L-shaped pieces of different sizes.

Lock picks.

Athreya selected one and an L-shaped piece of metal and got to work on the padlock. Less than a minute later, it opened. Athreya pocketed his tools and entered the cottage, quietly closing the door behind him. From another pocket, he pulled out a small torch that cast a highly focused beam.

No sooner had he closed the door than he noticed a wet smear on the floor, a few feet from the front door. He lowered himself on to his haunches and studied it. He could make out a part of a footprint. He touched it with his finger. It was still wet. Someone had been here no more than six hours ago. With a small camera, he photographed it. A couple of feet further into the cottage was another wet smear, which he also photographed.

He stood up and looked around the sparsely furnished sitting room, which clearly belonged to a bachelor. Books, papers and painting supplies lay untidily about. In one corner on the floor were a number of cardboard tubes with metal caps. In another corner was a small music system. At the far end was a small dining table with two chairs.

Three doors led from the room, one to the kitchen and two to bedrooms. He made a quick survey of them, but found nothing noteworthy. One bedroom was used as Phillip's work room, where he did his painting. The rug on the floor carried countless paint blotches and drops of different hues. The other bedroom had a double bed and a couple of cupboards with clothes in them. A small locked steel almirah stood in one corner, which Athreya didn't attempt to open. That was best left to the police.

A short while later, he was back on the veranda, and the padlock was back in its place. Just as he approached the gate, he saw Dora returning from the resort's main building to its gate. He hurried towards her on his cycle.

All she had learned was that Murthy was still fast asleep, and the other guest—a young man, as the security guard had said—was sleeping it off after being stoned for much of the previous day and all of the night. He hadn't stirred from his room since 4 p.m.

When they returned to Greybrooke Manor, they found Bahadur, the Gurkha guard, at the rock garden, scrutinizing the lawn with obvious disapproval. On hearing the approach of the two cycles, he looked up and threw them a salute, grinning from ear to ear.

'*Namaskar*, madam! *Namaskar*, sir!' he called.

'Good morning, Bahadur,' Dora replied. 'What are you looking at?'

'Cigarettes, madam. Someone has littered the place with cigarette butts.'

Athreya leapt off his cycle and joined Bahadur. Scattered on the grass were half a dozen cigarette butts. Some of them were regular cigarettes with white bodies and yellow filters. But a couple of them were thinner and dark brown in colour. Two people had smoked here. Judging by the number of butts, they must have been here for a while. On the stone bench was an empty packet of Gold Flake cigarettes.

'Weren't these there last afternoon?' Athreya asked.

'No, sir. The gardener swept the entire lawn last afternoon. *Bada Saab* likes the garden neat and clean during parties.'

'Who could it have been?' Dora asked as she joined them. 'All of us were around the inner lawn—the rose garden, Sunset Deck and thereabouts. I wonder if anyone came here. Did you see anyone, Bahadur?'

'No, madam. But it was so foggy that I could have missed someone sitting here.'

'Two people,' Athreya said. 'There were two people here. There are two kinds of cigarettes.'

'Abbas smokes the thin, brown one. "More", I think it is called.'

'Who else smokes, Dora?'

'Nobody in the family, except Uncle, who occasionally enjoys his pipe or cigar. He doesn't touch cigarettes.'

'Richie?' Athreya asked.

Dora shook her head. 'Both of us hate cigarette smoke. Sebastian doesn't smoke either. I don't know about Mr Varadan.'

'Phillip?'

Dora looked up sharply. 'Funny that I didn't think of him... now that he is dead. I haven't seen him smoke, but that doesn't mean that he didn't.'

'Ganesh? Jilsy?'

'Oh, Ganesh smokes like a chimney. Especially when he drinks. You would have seen him puffing away last evening. But I wonder if he was in a position to walk on his own here in his drunken state.'

'Yes… provided he was truly drunk. What about his wife?'

'She doesn't, as far as I know. She hates it when he blows smoke in her face. That leaves Father Tobias. I wouldn't expect priests to smoke.'

'The priest told me to give you his thanks,' Bahadur interrupted on hearing the cleric's name. 'He left early in the morning, when it was still dark. About 5 a.m.'

'Father Tobias has left?' Athreya asked, surprised.

'He has a morning service to conduct,' Dora explained. 'It'll take him a couple of hours to reach his church if he has to go around the landslide. He said last night that he would be leaving very early.'

'Did he say anything to you, Bahadur?' Athreya asked in Hindi.

'He talked to me for two minutes as I opened the gate for him, sir. He asked me how my family back home was, and asked me to pray for them. He also asked me to pray for my employers, who have given me food, shelter and money.'

'Was he carrying anything when he left?'

'No, sir. Nothing.'

'OK. Did you see anyone else during the night or in the morning?'

Bahadur shook his head. 'Only Sebastian Sir. He's gone out on his motorcycle.'

'Did you hear anything or anybody in the night? Anything unusual?'

Bahadur shook his head again. 'The gate was locked all night. Nobody came in or went out.'

'Thanks, Bahadur.' Athreya turned to his cycle. 'Come, Dora, let us go indoors. People must be up and about by now.'

117

They were. When Athreya and Dora entered the hall, they were confronted by a group of six anxious people.

'Where have you been?' Michelle demanded. 'What's happened?'

'Why?' Dora asked.

'Manu and Uncle are nowhere to be seen. Sebastian has gone off on his bike. You two were missing. Gopal and Murugan gave some yarn about them being locked in, and avoided questions thereafter. What's happening here?'

Dora didn't answer, and instead looked at Athreya for guidance. Six other faces—Michelle, Richie, Abbas, Varadan, Jilsy and Ganesh—turned towards him. Athreya stepped forward.

'I have bad news,' he said. 'There has been a murder.'

The six people reacted very differently. Michelle gasped loudly, while Jilsy cringed and grabbed her husband's arm. As Ganesh gaped stupidly at Athreya, Varadan's intelligent eyes narrowed a trifle. Next to a poker-faced Abbas, Richie flared up angrily.

'Is this a joke?' he demanded. 'Or a game for a weekend party? If so, it is in very poor taste.'

'I'm afraid not, Richie,' Athreya replied calmly. 'There is a dead man in the chapel right now... slumped in a wheelchair. Killed during the night.'

'Uncle!' Michelle cried.

Her eyes snapped to Abbas, who, seeing her gaze, paled and stepped back. His impassive face crumbled as a look of horror took over. Varadan's piercing gaze was on Michelle's face. Ganesh's mouth fell open and his wife closed her eyes tightly. Her lovely face was marred by lines of terror. Richie was glaring at Athreya, his anger mounting.

'Mr Fernandez has been killed?' Varadan asked sharply, swinging his gaze around to Athreya.

For a moment, Athreya didn't answer. He looked around at the ring of faces twice. Then he responded.

'No,' he said. 'Not Mr Fernandez. But in his wheelchair.'

'Who?'

Athreya was about to answer when Richie cut in.

'Phillip!' he said. 'He is the only one missing other than the priest, who must have returned to his church.'

'Is that right, Mr Athreya?' Michelle asked, almost imploring him to agree. Relief seemed to be flooding her face.

'Yes, Michelle.' Athreya's eyes swept over the six faces once again. 'Phillip was found dead in your uncle's wheelchair. In the chapel, as I said.'

Abbas had a look of utter confusion on his still-ashen face. Ganesh's witless face might have been that of a stone ogre. Jilsy's frightened eyes had snapped open. Varadan was not amused—he seemed to have taken exception to Athreya's chicanery in leading them to think that Bhaskar had been killed. Richie too had seen through the trickery, and his face was flushed with anger.

Shifting his gaze, Athreya saw Murugan and Gopal standing halfway up the staircase leading to the first floor, listening intently. Gopal's mouth was half open in morbid fascination. Murugan seemed stricken. As if he had just realized that the person who had locked him in was, in all probability, the murderer. Athreya wondered how much he suspected. His thoughts were interrupted by Varadan's hard voice.

'If you knew it all the while,' he asked drily, 'why this drama, Mr Athreya? Why didn't you tell us straight away that Phillip has been killed?'

'I know,' Richie snarled. 'He thinks one of us killed Phillip.'

'And he is probably right,' rumbled a voice from the mouth of the art gallery. Bhaskar had emerged from his room, propelling his unmotorized wheelchair with his arms. His pallid face was deeply lined. Manu came behind him. 'Sebastian has gone to fetch the police.'

10

'We don't know when the police will come,' Athreya said, smoothly taking charge. 'Meanwhile, every hour that passes takes us further away from the time the murder was committed. We must find out as much as we can before time and the killer erase the evidence.' He turned to Michelle. 'Can you examine the body and estimate the time of death? Only a doctor can do that.'

'I know... but I am just a general practitioner, not a coroner or a forensic pathologist. I don't have much experience in this kind of a thing.'

'I understand that, but with each passing hour, a coroner's ability to accurately determine the time of death also reduces. We must do what we can with what we have. Your estimate will be better than mine or anyone else's here.'

Michelle hesitated for a moment, then nodded.

'Give me a moment to fetch my medical bag from my room.'

As she went up the staircase, Athreya turned to Manu.

'We must search for the murder weapon,' he said. 'I have an inkling where it could be, but I am in no position to reach the place.'

'Are you sure he would have thrown away the weapon?' Manu asked.

'Well, a sensible murderer wouldn't run the risk of keeping it in his or her possession. He or she would do one of two things as soon as possible: get rid of it in a way that doesn't lead back to them, or plant it on someone else.'

'Plant it!' Richie exclaimed brusquely. 'You are not a very trusting soul, are you?'

'Perhaps not.' Athreya turned and looked Richie full in the face. 'I see no reason to take the murderer at his or her word.

Before you ask, let me also say this: I will not automatically believe what you or anyone else tells me. I will listen, but not necessarily believe. My friend, I may not be very trusting. But you will find me trustworthy, if you know what I mean.'

'So,' Richie sneered, 'you hope to solve this murder, do you?'

'Like to lay a wager, Richie? I hope to not only solve the murder, but I also intend to suss out smaller crimes and transgressions along the way.'

He turned away, seeming to dismiss Richie. He looked up the staircase impatiently. Michelle had not yet come down. Athreya turned to Manu.

'You may want to bring along a couple of boys to help us,' he said. 'We need to search the stream. It is an ideal place to dispose of a murder weapon. It's right next to the crime scene, and the running water would erase fingerprints and any other telltale signs. I'll join you as soon as Michelle finishes her bit.'

Fifteen minutes later, Athreya and Michelle stood inside the chapel, speaking softly. She had examined the body and done the usual things as he watched. She now looked calm and collected, having performed her professional chore.

'Before I give you my estimate, I want to reiterate that I have very little experience in this sort of thing. I might be wrong.'

'I understand,' Athreya nodded. 'What's your best estimate?'

'Death occurred between 2 a.m. and 3 a.m., give or take a little. If I had to pick a time, I'd say 2:30 a.m.'

Athreya nodded and led the way out of the chapel. He locked the door, and the two of them went behind the building. There they stood watching the brook from above. About a hundred feet to their left, Gopal and another boy had let down a ladder under Murugan's directions. A small knot of people stood behind Murugan, watching the activity.

'That's where the stream bed is closest to us,' Michelle explained.

'There is a depression on the bank that is about five feet deep. It is the best place to climb down to the stream. Dora and I used to do that as kids. We loved collecting pebbles.'

They watched as, having changed into shorts and rubber slippers, Manu followed Gopal and the other boy down the ladder. Starting from that spot, they began walking up the stream, scrutinizing every inch of the rock bed, acting on suggestions from the people above, who had a bird's-eye view.

Initially, anything slender caused excitement, be it a stick or sliver of stone. But gradually, they learnt to distinguish between stones, sticks and foreign objects. Manu repeated Athreya's instruction time and again, reminding the searchers not to touch anything with their hands. If they found the weapon, Athreya had said, they were to pick it up with a pair of tongs and drop it into a transparent plastic bag.

The searchers reached the chapel and passed the point where Athreya and Michelle stood, making their way towards Sunset Deck. Dora joined the two watchers on the bank. Halfway between the chapel and Sunset Deck, Manu suddenly called out, 'I think I've found it!'

Athreya hurried along the bank and peered down when he reached where Manu was pointing into the water with a stick. Wedged between two rocks, half buried under blackish-brown sand, was the handle of what looked like a dagger. The blade was already under the coarse sand that was being swept along by the water, which was about two or three feet deep.

'Use the tongs, Manu,' Athreya reminded him.

Clutching the tongs firmly in his right hand, Manu dipped it into the water and closed its arms around the dagger's handle. When he was sure that he had secured a firm grip, he held the tongs tightly with both hands and pulled it out. Gopal was waiting beside him with an open bag.

The keen metal glinted menacingly in the morning light as Manu dropped it into the plastic bag. It turned out be a crude, country-made dagger, with a slim blade that was an inch wide at the base and about six inches long. The short handle comprised two wood pieces, bound together by what looked like leather.

There was no hope of retrieving any fingerprints from the weapon. Athreya doubted if DNA information could be retrieved either. All he could do now was to try and find out if someone could identify it.

Back in the drawing room, Athreya showed the dagger—still in its protective bag—first to Bhaskar. The older man studied it for a long while, then silently shook his head.

'It seems vaguely familiar, but I can't place it,' he said as he handed the bag to Manu. 'It's certainly not from my collection of antiques, nor does it seem like it belongs to the kitchen. It's a rough, crude weapon. Can you place it, Manu?'

Manu had been frowning at the dagger just as his father had, and he too, after careful thought, shook his head. Athreya then asked all the others to look at the weapon and recall if they had seen it anywhere. Everyone—the Fernandez family members as well as the guests—drew a blank.

'The next thing I need to do is to talk to each of you—' Athreya began when Bhaskar cut him off.

'Let me spare you the unpleasantness, Mr Athreya. I know where you are heading. Allow me to say it instead of you.'

Bhaskar looked enquiringly at Athreya. After a moment's thought, the latter nodded.

'Now listen, everyone. There has been a murder, and each one of us here is a potential suspect. In addition, there may be, by my reckoning, at least three other potential suspects who are not in this room. That makes it a dozen of us in all.

'Of these, eleven are innocent. One is not. Justice demands that the cloud be lifted from these eleven. To my mind, that is far more important than finding the one who killed Phillip. But to clear the eleven, we *must* find the one. Unless we do so, the cloud will hang over us forever.

'Most of you are young, and have too much of your lives ahead of you to allow that to happen. There is nothing worse than to have a shadow of suspicion hang over you. Take this advice from a man who knows, one who has suffered because of it.

'I was once suspected of being a fence, of having passed off a stolen antique sculpture. The shadow of suspicion dogged me for two years, and it ruined my business and reputation. People looked askance at me wherever I went. They whispered behind my back. Invitations to parties and weddings stopped coming.

'Until, by happy chance, the real culprit was found. My business bounced back, and my friends returned. But I never forgot how I was treated during those two years. I don't wish such a fate upon any of you. I want a resolution to the mystery of Phillip's murder, and will seek it with all the energy and resources at my disposal. That is why I have commissioned Mr Athreya to investigate.

'For those of you who don't know, there is nobody better in the country for the job. So please, do yourselves and your loved ones a favour. Do me a favour. Cooperate with him. Help him do his job.

'Now, I suspect he wants to speak to each of us in turn, in private. He will want to know about our movements last night. Please do not consider it an insult. Please do not be affronted by his having dared to suspect you. The way it works is that everyone is a suspect until proven otherwise.'

Bhaskar turned to Athreya and asked, 'Is that what you were going to say? That you'd like each one of us to tell you about his or her movements last night?'

'Yes, Mr Fernandez. That's precisely what I wanted to do, although I lack your eloquence.'

'It's decided then. Use the study or the library for your discussions, whichever suits you. If there is anything else you need, tell Manu or me. Sebastian will be away for most of the day, I suspect.'

'Thank you.' Athreya swept the anxious faces with his gaze. 'I would like to speak to each of you in the study. I have no preference for the order in which I speak to you. For now, I need you to tell me about your movements last night as accurately as you can. Take your time if you want to gather your thoughts. I'm happy to wait, but I'm now ready to start with the first person.'

A long, pregnant silence followed. People looked nervously at each other, but nobody said anything. After a few awkward moments, two people spoke up simultaneously.

'I—' Varadan began, but stopped since Dora had also started to speak at the same time. He glanced at her and gestured to her to continue.

'I don't know about the others, but I want to speak in public,' she said. Her usually affable face was puckered in unpleasant rumination. 'I agree with what Uncle said. There is nothing worse than the suspicion of my being a murderess hanging over me. I'm on this side of thirty, and have a life to live. I still have to make my name in the world. I can do without a cloud hanging over me.

'I am therefore *insisting*—I repeat, *insisting*—that I speak in public. I have nothing to hide, and want to talk about my movements openly. Anyone—not just Mr Athreya—is welcome to question me. I promise that I will take no offence.'

'Now, girl,' Bhaskar barked, 'there is no call for—'

'With respect, Uncle, allow me to interrupt you. Being the youngest, I have seldom claimed privileges. I mostly do as I am told. I fall in line; you know that. But this is a privilege I do wish to claim. I insist that I go first and tell everyone what I have already told Mr Athreya. May I, sir?' she asked, turning to him.

'Please,' he said.

'If I remember right, dinner finished at around 11 p.m. last night. We hung around till about 11:15 p.m., after which we split up into smaller groups. After exchanging small talk for a while, Manu and I went to the rose garden a little after 11:30 p.m. I don't know the exact time, as I didn't look at my watch.

'We talked for close to an hour, and I returned to the mansion at 12:27 a.m. I remember the time because I looked at my watch. I met Mr Varadan on the walkway outside the front door. He had just come out, and I was going towards the door. On entering, I went straight up to my room and went to bed a short while afterwards.

'Some noise woke me up at about 7 a.m. this morning. I now realize that it was the thumping of the staff quarters' door. I freshened up and came down at around 7:15 a.m. After speaking to a distressed Bhuvana, I went outside at 7:30 a.m., where I met Sebastian and you.

'Some of the timings are approximate and some are precise. I'm sorry, I can't make it more accurate than this. Do you want me to tell you what Manu and I talked about?'

'Not now, Dora. Maybe later. This is consistent with what you had said earlier in the morning. Were you in your room from 12:30 to 7:15 a.m.? Did you leave your room at all?'

She shook her head firmly. 'No. I was in my room the entire time. I didn't step out even for a second. All the rooms have bathrooms attached. So no need to leave the room.'

'Did you hear anything unusual during the night?'

'Nothing out of place. I've been thinking about it, but I don't remember hearing anything unusual.'

'No sounds of doors opening or closing?'

'That, I did. I often do. I am a light sleeper. But there is no way I can remember any of it, or the time. Such sounds just don't register deeply enough for me to recall them in the morning.'

'Thank you, Dora. That's all for now.'

But Dora was not done. She looked around at the circle of faces and asked, 'Any questions? Seriously, I won't take offence. Ask me.'

When nobody responded, she shrugged and looked deflated.

'I guess I'm done then,' she said.

'With your permission, Mr Varadan, can I go next?' Manu asked. 'Because what I have to say corroborates with what Dora just said.'

'Sure, Manu.' Varadan nodded. 'Go ahead.'

'Thank you, sir.' Manu turned to Athreya. 'I endorse all that Dora said about our chat last night. I can go further and confirm the time we went to the rose garden because I happened to look at my watch then. It was 11:35 p.m.

'What I have to add is this: After Dora returned to the mansion, I went for a walk to clear my head and to wind down before going to bed. The others will tell you that I often do that. I must have walked around for about fifteen minutes, and then entered the mansion through the front door. My best estimate of when I returned is about 12:40 a.m.

'I went straight to bed. I noticed that there was no light under your door or Sebastian's. I assumed that both of you had retired by then. I checked Dad's door too, as I always do. His light was also off.

'Unlike Dora, I am a deep sleeper. I didn't wake up during the night, and didn't hear anything, either. I woke up only when Murugan started banging on the door of the staff quarters, which was around 7 a.m. I went to the back door immediately, and saw Sebastian opening it. I remember noticing that Dad's wheelchair was not in its usual charging point beside the back door.'

He stopped and looked at Athreya enquiringly.

'Questions, sir?'

'None. Thank you, Manu. That was quite comprehensive and concise. Who would like to go next? You don't have to do it here just because Dora and Manu chose to do so. We can talk in the study.'

'Perhaps Mr Varadan would like to go next,' Manu suggested. 'It seemed as though he wanted to go first, but Dora and I stalled him.'

'That's quite all right, Manu,' said Varadan, smiling. He turned to Athreya and went on in his own slow, precise manner. 'Anticipating this interview, I prepared a note for you and the police. Shall I read it out to you? I am perfectly willing to have this in the public domain. In fact, I'd prefer that.'

'Yes, Mr Varadan.' Athreya nodded. 'Please proceed.'

'My contribution to the investigation is limited,' Varadan began as if he were giving evidence on a witness stand. He had opened a folded piece of paper. 'The timings I have detailed are my best estimates. I am prepared to swear to them in court if need be, but only after some additional contemplation. I left the mansion at 12:27 a.m. and reached my room in the annexe at 12:55 a.m. As Dora mentioned, I met her on the walkway outside the mansion after I had come out of the front door.

'Much of the twenty-eight minutes between my leaving the mansion and entering my room was spent talking to Michelle. I met her en route, and we walked around the rose garden a few times, talking. I am not at liberty to disclose the contents of our discussion at this time.

'Once I reached my room, I changed into my nightclothes and retired for the night. Like Manu, I too am a sound sleeper. I heard nothing, and I doubt if I would have woken up in the middle of the night after the wonderful feast and wine.

'As I said, these are my best estimates at this time. I can give you this paper if you wish. It has the details of what I just said.' He handed the paper over to Athreya.

'I understand you were talking to Phillip before you stepped out of the mansion. You may well have been the last person he spoke to. Can you tell me what you talked about?'

Athreya could see that the lawyer's mind was working furiously. He had perhaps not realized that he was the last person Phillip had spoken to.

'We spoke mostly about Phillip's abilities as a painter,' Varadan said. 'His main point was that he was an artist with no creativity—a strange animal by his own assessment. His fingers could paint exceedingly well, to the extent that they could produce almost identical copies of a landscape before him or of the works of the masters in front of him.

'But, by himself, he was unable to imagine a picture to paint. So, he was, he repeated several times, a painter with zero creativity. "What else can you say of an artist who can't create a painting of his own?" he asked. I was forced to agree with the logic of his argument. That's what we mostly talked about. He felt sad about it, and considered himself less for it. The tag of an artist, he felt, was ill-deserved.'

'How was his mood?' Athreya asked.

'Pensive. Subdued.'

'Did he seem out of sorts?'

'Difficult for me to say; I hardly knew him.'

'Yet, he opened up to you, didn't he?'

'Yes,' said Varadan, nodding. 'I wonder why. I am not a person who normally inspires such confidences. Perhaps he just wanted someone to talk to. I noticed that he said little during the party except when the subject was painting. He seemed a lonely man.'

'Thank you, Mr Varadan,' Athreya concluded. 'That was useful. Who wants to go next? We can adjourn to the study.'

But with Dora and Manu having set the precedent, nobody wanted to appear less forthcoming. After a long pause, Michelle spoke up.

'I'll go next,' she said.

'Go into the study, girl,' Bhaskar rumbled. 'Don't let Dora's and Manu's choices affect yours.'

'I'm fine, Uncle,' Michelle responded with a wan smile. 'I'd rather say my piece here. What's there to hide? I may have my problems, and I may have my timings mixed up, but I know that I didn't kill Phillip.

'Mr Athreya, I am not as sure about my timings as Mr Varadan or my cousins are. I seldom look at my watch, except when I am taking a patient's pulse. I'll do my best, but please don't hold it against me if I make a mistake.'

'Do your best, Michelle,' Athreya said encouragingly. 'That's the most anyone can ask of you.'

'I will, thanks. I think I stepped out of the mansion a little after Dora and Manu did. I say this because I remember seeing them go out. I must have come out ten minutes or so after they left. That makes it...' Michelle stumbled and referred to a piece of paper on which she had scribbled something, 'about 11:45 p.m. I strolled along the walkways for some time, and when I passed Sunset Deck, I saw Abbas there. I sat down with him and we chatted for a while.'

Athreya remembered seeing Michelle and Abbas walking out together the previous night, shortly after Manu and Dora had left. He wondered why Michelle was giving him a slightly different version of events. Was she misremembering? Or was it deliberate?

'For how long?' Athreya asked aloud.

'Oh, I don't know. Maybe for half an hour? After that, I walked some more and met Mr Varadan. He said that he had stepped out

130

of the mansion at…' Michelle consulted her paper again, '12:27 a.m. From what he said, Abbas and I must have spoken for… twenty-five minutes or so.

'I won't repeat what Mr Varadan has already said. After chatting with him, I returned to the mansion and went up to my room. So I must have come back to my room just short of 1 a.m. I brushed my teeth and went to bed. I didn't hear anything at night. When I woke up, it was 8 a.m. I must have come down at quarter past eight, after which I spoke to Murugan and Gopal. We were quite perplexed and worried when you and Dora came in. After that, you know the story.'

Athreya had a number of questions to ask, but he decided not to do so in public. He would speak to her separately later.

'Thank you, Michelle,' he said. 'If you remember anything else, please do tell me.'

'I know that my account is vague and my timings imprecise,' Michelle persevered. 'But, honest to God, I had nothing to do with Phillip's death. Do you believe me, Mr Athreya?' It was almost a plea.

'How do you expect him to answer that question?' Bhaskar interposed gently.

'But I am telling the truth, Uncle.'

'I'm sure you are, Michelle. But don't embarrass Mr Athreya by asking questions he can't answer.'

'We'll go next,' Ganesh butted in to everyone's relief. 'Jilsy and I. There isn't much to tell, but I'll go first and Jilsy will add to it. That OK?' he asked his wife.

She nodded silently.

'Honestly, I don't remember when or how I got to my room,' Ganesh went on. 'I must have had a drink too many. That doesn't happen often, you know. I can hold my rum. It must have been the cognac I had after dinner. But it was a wonderful cognac, Mr Fernandez. I must try it again tonight.'

Jilsy nudged him. For a moment, he gaped at her uncomprehendingly. Then he continued.

'As I was saying, I don't know when or how I reached my room. The last thing I remember is enjoying the cognac. The next thing I knew I was waking up and looking at the clock. It was close to 8 a.m. I had slept like a log. Good food and good drink have to be matched with good sleep. Thankfully, I'm blessed in that department. Sleep like a baby, I do.'

He grinned and turned to his wife, gesturing to her to add her bit.

'There isn't much more,' she said in a small voice, her eyes on the floor. 'Richie helped me get Ganesh to our room. After that, I locked the door and went to bed. I woke up a little before Ganesh, but I just lazed about in bed, and got up when he did. Then we came here.'

She looked up briefly and flashed an imploring glance at Athreya. It seemed to him that she was entreating him not to cross-question her. He obliged and nodded. After a pause, Abbas cleared his throat and spoke.

'That leaves Richie and me, I guess,' he said. 'Let me go first. Listen, I never once looked at my watch all evening or all night. What's the point of attending a party if you are going to be a prisoner to time? That's not my style. I'm not going to pretend that I know what I did when or what time I went to bed, for the simple reason that I don't.

'I went out of the mansion about fifteen minutes after we broke up, and must have walked around for an hour or so. I was feeling full after the feast, and had to walk around a little bit before hitting the sack. Sometime in between, I met Michelle at Sunset Deck, and we chatted for a while.

'After she left, I wandered around for a little more and smoked a ciggy or two before returning to my room. It was a great party,

Mr Athreya, and I enjoyed myself thoroughly. It's truly unfortunate that Phillip has been killed, but there is nothing I can do about it. A nice man, he was. My neighbour, you know. He lived across the mud road from the resort. I'll miss him.'

'Where did you wander, Abbas?' Athreya asked mildly.

'Oh, here and there. All over the place. It's not a huge place, you know, and the fog was impenetrable. I stuck to the walkways because I knew that they would lead me back to my room, even if I could see nothing else.'

'Never stepped off the walkways?'

'Don't think so.'

'Did you happen to overhear any conversations? We have just learnt about two conversations, apart from the one you had with Michelle.'

'If I did, I don't remember. Listen, there were voices here and there, but I didn't eavesdrop.'

Which meant he did, Athreya thought.

'Your cigarettes,' he asked, 'do you have them on you now?'

'Sure.'

Abbas pulled out a packet of More cigarettes and showed it to Athreya. The cigarettes were slim and dark brown in colour.

'Did anyone borrow your cigarettes?' Athreya asked.

'No, why do you ask?'

'Just curious.'

'The only other person who smokes is Ganesh, but he prefers stronger stuff.'

'Do you know if Phillip smoked? I thought you might know as he was your neighbour.'

'No, he didn't. Said he had been a chain-smoker in his younger days, but he cut the habit seven years ago when he moved here.'

Abbas's eyes were searching Athreya's face, but the latter kept it pleasantly expressionless.

'Thank you, Abbas,' he said and turned to Richie expectantly.

'I have nothing to say, Mr Detective, if that's indeed what you are,' the younger man drawled. He was leaning back nonchalantly in his chair, with one leg draped over an armrest. 'You offered me a wager, and I have decided to take it. Then why should I help *you* win?'

'Richie!' Bhaskar snapped.

'I know what you are going to say, Uncle,' Richie responded, turning towards Bhaskar. 'But I have no information of any value for Mr Athreya. After escorting Ganesh to his room, I returned to the mansion and went to bed.'

'You?' Bhaskar demanded. 'To bed so early?'

'Why not, Uncle? It had been a busy day. Besides, I had no intention of falling into the stream and breaking my neck in the fog. Like that Englishman who died.'

'And you stayed in your room for the rest of the night, Richie?' Athreya asked mildly.

'Of course.'

'Never left it?'

'Why should I?'

'Just asking. If you wish to change your testimony, do let me know.'

'That leaves only me,' Bhaskar said. 'I probably have the least to tell you, despite the fact that my room is the closest to the chapel. As you know, I was the first to retire, and once I got off the wheelchair, I was more or less bound to the bed. It had been a tiring day for me. I'm afraid I have little to offer.'

'That's fine. Did you happen to hear anything during the night?'

'I hear things every night, Mr Athreya, real and imagined. I don't know which is which. After the intruder's attack, I seldom sleep deeply. I keep my automatic under my pillow, you know.

134

The slightest sound disturbs my sleep. Sometimes, I find that the sound was only inside my head.'

'Did you hear anything last night?'

'Yes... people walking, laughter, voices in the mist, doors closing and opening, Murugan locking up for the night, Sebastian retiring, many things. But now that I think about it, I think I did hear the whir of my wheelchair sometime during the night. I can't say when. I thought I had imagined it, and decided that the noise was only inside my head.'

'Why did you think you had imagined it, Mr Fernandez?'

'Who would touch my wheelchair, Mr Athreya? It's been around for a while, and it gets charged every night. It's never been touched before. But it turns out that I was wrong. Somebody did take it.'

Athreya sat back and considered the facts. Everyone had returned to his or her room by 1 a.m. Each one of them had claimed that they had not left their room after that. By 2 a.m., they would have all been fast asleep. Yet, the murder took place between 2 a.m. and 3 a.m.

Who was lying?

11

'The next thing I'd like to do,' Athreya said, 'is to understand the deceased. Please tell me what you know about Phillip. What kind of a person was he? What work did he do? What were his interests? Does he have any relatives nearby? Who is the next of kin? Anything that can help me understand him.

'Some of you may have personal views on him, both positive and negative. I recognize that you may not want to air them in public. Please feel free to hold those back and tell me later. Let's start with his age. Dora told me this morning that he was going to be sixty next year. Is that right?'

Bhaskar nodded. 'That's right.'

'What work did he do?'

'He painted for a living. You've seen some of his work.'

'When did he come to the valley? Where was he before he came here?'

'He came about seven years ago and wanted to rent that cottage,' Bhaskar replied. 'I don't know where he came from.'

'Any relatives nearby?'

'Not to my knowledge. I think there is a sister somewhere—in Pune or Nagpur, someplace like that.'

'He has a sister in Pune,' Jilsy confirmed. 'He mentioned her to me a few times. But where in Pune, and what her name is, I don't know.'

'I recall him saying that his sister was a few years older than him,' Abbas added. 'And that she was involved in some sort of social work in Maharashtra.'

'Name? Address? Phone number?'

Abbas shook his head.

'Won't it be on his mobile phone?' Manu asked. 'Do you know where it is?'

'In his pocket,' Athreya said. 'Whatever evidence it carries will keep till the police arrive. I would rather let the police deal with it. They are touchy about such matters.'

'But we retrieved the dagger,' Manu countered.

'If we hadn't, it would have been covered by sand by the time the police got here. Estimating the time of death was similarly an urgent task. We had to do it.' He turned to Jilsy. 'Phillip was your neighbour. What can you tell me about the kind of person he was?'

'A very nice man.' Jilsy's eyes brimmed with tears. 'Soft-spoken and courteous. He never raised his voice. He was always willing to help Ganesh or me with a chore. He used to come over for dinner sometimes.'

'What did he talk about when he visited you?'

'That's the funny thing about him. He spoke very little, but was always willing to listen to my ramblings. A brief word here and a one-liner there would keep me going. I have so few people in the valley to talk to, Mr Athreya that I ended up talking to him quite often. He could listen for hours without getting bored. I'm going to miss him terribly.'

She fished out a tiny kerchief from her handbag and dabbed her eyes.

'Did he have any... enemies? That's perhaps a strong word, but you know what I mean. Was there anyone who might have wished him ill?'

'I can't imagine,' Jilsy replied, shaking her head. 'He kept to himself and had very few friends. He said nothing controversial, and he was not the kind of man to pick fights. Abbas, you want to add anything?'

'He used to come to the resort and play carom with the guests and the staff. He occasionally would drop by for a drink with me or with my father. He had a standing invitation to join us for any meal, any day. The resort kitchen cooks for so many people, one more makes no difference. And Phillip didn't eat much.'

'Let me add to what Varadan said earlier about Phillip the painter,' Bhaskar said. '"A painter with zero creativity", Phillip called himself. That is even truer than I have suggested. Remember the large painting of the mountain scene on the wall near the front door? The one that was painted by Phillip?'

'Yes, I remember.' Athreya nodded. 'The one showing the hills at the far side of the vale.'

'I had let you assume that Phillip sat on a hill and painted the scene before his eyes. That is not true. That painting is a scaled-up version of a photograph that was taken with a high-resolution camera. Phillip drew a grid on the photo and reproduced it on canvas, square by square, making each square four times larger as he painted it. If you remove the painting from its frame, you will see the markings of the grid at the edges of the canvas. So that was Phillip the painter, for you. He could reproduce paintings and photos perfectly. Yet, he could compose nothing.'

Ganesh and the others soon chimed in, and the picture of a reserved, taciturn man emerged—a man who was a threat to nobody and was at peace with his neighbours. None of them could think of anyone who may have wanted to harm him. They could think of no motive, not even the feeblest.

'What stumps me,' Manu said, 'is what he was doing in Dad's wheelchair.'

'When we answer that question,' Athreya replied, 'we would be close to solving the crime.'

'A related question is whether he was killed when he was in the wheelchair, or he was put there *after* he was killed?'

'Another good question, Manu. One for which we don't have an answer yet.'

'And why was he in the chapel?' Dora asked. 'Was he killed there, or was he wheeled there after he was killed? Was he put in the chapel merely to delay discovery?'

'That certainly is a possibility, Dora.'

'If that is the case, *where* was he killed? Was he killed where you found him or somewhere else? Is that why the murderer borrowed the wheelchair? It would be far easier to transport a dead body on a wheelchair than to carry it,' she said.

'That brings us to the question of who the murderer could be,' Manu said. 'He—I am assuming it was a man—knew where the wheelchair was. He knew how to unplug it in the dark without making noise or switching on the light. It couldn't have been an outsider. It *must* be someone familiar with this house and the way things are done here.'

Abrupt silence descended on the room. They had been harshly recalled from their fond memories of Phillip to the cold reality of a murderer being in their midst.

'Remember last evening's bizarre conversation?' Michelle asked in a hushed voice. 'The one about women preferring poison, and men preferring blades and other violent means. Do you agree with Manu, Mr Athreya? Do you think the killer is a man?'

'You are a doctor, Michelle,' Athreya said. 'You have seen both the wound and the weapon. What do you think? Was it an act that was beyond a woman?'

Michelle looked down at her large hands and sinewy arms. Slowly, she shook her head.

'No,' she whispered. 'I think I could have managed it… if I took him unawares. It would be easier if he was sitting.'

'Keen on digging your own grave, girl?' Bhaskar growled.

'I don't think she is, Mr Fernandez,' Varadan said. 'It's quite apparent that she and Dora have the strength to do it.' He glanced at Jilsy, who was nervously crushing her kerchief in her hand. 'Jilsy may be a little different, though.'

'Coming back to the question of motive,' Dora went on, 'isn't there a fundamental question here? Did the murderer kill Phillip knowing that it *was* Phillip? Or did he kill him by mistake? Did he think he was killing someone else?'

'Meaning me?' Bhaskar rumbled.

'Isn't that a possibility, Uncle? After all, he *was* in your wheelchair and wearing a shirt similar to the one you were last evening. The two of you don't look very different from behind. Remember, it was a foggy, foggy night. Besides, heaven knows there are enough people with a motive, your two wills notwithstanding.'

'What's with the girls of this family today?' Bhaskar snapped fiercely. 'Why do you two insist on putting your necks into nooses? Most women would have tried to make the case that it was an outsider who killed Phillip.'

'We are not putting our necks into nooses, Uncle,' Dora said. 'Mr Athreya is a very sensible man. He would not be swayed by such talk. In fact, it may work the other way. If we made a specious case for an outsider being the murderer, he would smell a rat.'

'I give up.' Bhaskar groaned and rubbed his beard vigorously with both palms. 'And they used to call *me* venturesome! I never shot myself in the foot. You girls are something else. May heaven protect you from yourselves.'

It was only when Athreya returned to his room did he realize that he had not bathed, changed or had breakfast. He had gone out for an early stroll in his track pants, and had remained in them throughout the morning. Other than to collect his lock picks and jacket, and then to return them, he had not been to his room. As he entered it now, devouring the sandwich the cook had thoughtfully provided, he noticed his clean laundry lying on his bed. What had been collected the previous morning had been returned, neatly folded and ironed. As he stared at it, a thought flashed through his mind. Simultaneously, a knock sounded on his door. It was Gopal.

'I've come to pick up your laundry, sir,' he said.

'Do you do laundry every day, Gopal?'

'Yes, sir. When we have guests.'

'Do all the guests give you laundry, like I did yesterday?'

'Yes, sir. There are more guests today. We are collecting everyone's laundry. They are just returning to their rooms.'

'I assume you wash the clothes right away. When do you iron them?'

'As and when they dry, sir. The thicker clothes are mostly done late at night or early morning.'

'And you always return them the next morning?'

'Yes, sir.'

'Thank you, Gopal. Give me a moment. I'll also give you the clothes I am wearing.'

After Gopal had gone, Athreya plugged in his mobile for charging and took a slow and preoccupied shower, his mind on the discussion he had just had with Gopal. Then, he brushed back his uncommonly fine hair. It was beginning to grey—except for the silvery tuft in the front, the rest of his head was still largely black. His fine-haired beard, too, was mostly black, except at the chin where a small patch of silver matched the tuft on his head.

Tall and lean, he was sometimes compared by his friends to a weeping willow, especially when he let his hair grow. At other times, his beard, which made his already long face look even longer, was compared with that of a Bearded Collie.

A short while later, he was on the phone, talking to his friend Rajan, the retired IPS officer in Coonoor. He briefed him on what had happened, and sought his help in finding out as much as possible about Phillip, Abbas, Ganesh and the people at Greybrooke Manor. He asked him to speak to the retired postmaster and his wife, and to anyone else who might be able to throw light on their backgrounds. He also asked him to tap the police network in Ooty and Coonoor if he could.

He then went to the art gallery and photographed all of Phillip's paintings. He returned to his room, called a Delhi number and spoke on the phone briefly. After hanging up, he sent the photographs via WhatsApp to the person in Delhi.

Then he went upstairs to Phillip's room and unlocked it with the key Sebastian had provided him earlier. Athreya examined the room thoroughly without leaving fingerprints or smudging any that were already there. With a pencil or the tip of his shoe, he opened the cupboards. But he didn't find anything out of place. A few clothes hung in the cupboard and Phillip's bag lay open in one corner of the room. The bathroom had nothing other than his toiletries.

After a fruitless search, he opened the door and found Dora waiting for him at the top of the stairs.

'Can I speak to you?' she asked softly.

'Certainly. Where would you like to talk?' Athreya asked as he relocked Phillip's room. 'The study?'

'Let's take a walk outside, if you don't mind.'

'I don't mind at all.'

They went down the stairs and out of the front door together, then along the walkway towards the rock garden.

'I remembered one or two things from last night. I don't know if they are relevant. I don't even know if they really happened or I imagined them. I thought I should tell you about them. I can't swear by them, but I kind of think I didn't imagine them. Is that OK?'

'It's perfectly fine. Tell me.'

'As I said earlier, I returned to the mansion at 12:27 a.m. Of that, I am absolutely certain, and it doesn't change. Besides, Mr Varadan also corroborated it.

'When I shut the front door and turned to go towards the stairs, I thought I heard a small noise from the art gallery. I stopped and peered in the direction of the sound, but I couldn't see anything amiss in the faint light of the night bulb. I didn't see anyone there. I didn't think much about it as it could have been anyone: Murugan, Uncle, Sebastian or any of the staff.

'I am not sure of the next thing I'm going to say. I thought— and I am not certain—that I saw a thin crack of light at the end of the gallery, as if the back door was slightly open. If it was open half an inch, light from the staff quarters would have spilled in, and that's how it would have looked.

'Dismissing it from my mind, I went up the stairs. Now, you need to understand how the rooms upstairs are laid out. The four rooms that are occupied are in a line. I am using the first one, which is the corner room above the drawing room. The next room is occupied by Richie and the third by Phillip. Michelle is using the last one. Is that clear?'

'Yes. Go on,' said Athreya.

'The stairs come out between the second and the third rooms: Richie's and Phillip's. When I reached the top of the stairs, I noticed two things. First, there was no light under Phillip's door. I didn't think that was relevant until I realized that he was talking to Varadan till about 12:25 a.m.

'If Phillip had gone up to his room immediately after that, he would have *just* entered his room when I reached the first floor, and the light would have been burning. Most of us would have our lights on for at least a few minutes after entering our rooms. And as Phillip had *just* entered his room, his light should have been on. But it wasn't. Again, I am not sure if it is relevant or not, but I thought I should tell you.'

'You did the right thing, Dora,' Athreya said, his mind churning. 'I can't be sure yet, but it could turn out to be very relevant. You said that you noticed two things. What was the second thing?'

'I noticed Richie's light was on. The line of light was clearly visible under his door, and I also heard him humming a tune.'

Athreya stopped and looked Dora full in the face.

'Now, Dora. Look me in the eye. You wouldn't be protecting your brother, would you? We all know how much you love him, and I have seen you come to his defence at least once before. He continues to disappoint you, but you fight for him. This is not one such case, is it?'

Dora flushed deeply and bit her lip. Tears sprang to her eyes and she looked hurt. After a few moments' struggle, she whispered through a choked throat. 'That was not fair, Mr Athreya.'

'Perhaps not,' Athreya conceded. 'But I'm sure you see why I *have* to ask that.'

Dora nodded mutely and dropped her eyes.

'I am speaking the truth, Mr Athreya,' she said. 'I am *not* making this up. I don't know how to convince you, but I'll swear to it if you want me to.'

'No.' Athreya resumed walking. 'No need to swear. All this about Richie's light being switched on only serves to establish that he was in his room at 12:30 a.m. The murder didn't take place for two hours after that.'

'Yes, I realize that. There is more, but I am on unsure ground here. After entering my room, I locked the door, changed into my shorts and T-shirt and went to bed. It must have been around 12:45 a.m. or so.

'I was just beginning to drift off when I heard a door open and close. I am not in a position to say which door, but I did hear a door open and close on the first floor. Then, after ten minutes or so, I heard the sound of a door again. Opening and closing.

'The two sounds could well have been Michelle and Phillip returning to their rooms. I think Michelle said that she had returned just short of 1 a.m. So the first sound could definitely be her.'

'Possibly. Anything else?'

'No, that's it. I hope it's useful, but it looks like I've only made things murkier.'

'That's how it always is. Things get murkier before they get clearer. It's important to get the right facts. I'm glad you told me this. Ah! Here is Manu. Let's see if he noticed anything. He entered the mansion around fifteen minutes after you.'

He hailed Manu who was hurrying down the walkway from the annexe.

'I've wanted to tell you something, but I didn't get the chance,' Manu said as he joined them. 'The dagger we recovered from the stream... it seemed vaguely familiar, but I couldn't put my finger on it. I think I have it now, but I am not a hundred per cent sure. You see, I only saw it once, and fleetingly.'

'That's all right. Where?'

'It looks like the dagger the intruder brought with him.'

'The intruder who broke into the mansion and tried to kill your father?' Athreya asked.

'Yes. He dropped his dagger when Dad shot him. Murugan picked it up and showed it to us. It had a narrow blade and a leather-bound hilt very similar to the one we found in the stream today. So similar that I think it is the same dagger.'

'What happened to the dagger after Murugan picked it up?'

'That's the annoying part... I don't know. I think my attention was on the intruder and not the weapon. I don't remember seeing it again.'

'Someone would know, I guess?'

'I'll ask Murugan, if you wish.'

'No. Don't mention this to anyone, yet. I'll speak to your father alone and take it further. Meanwhile, I have a question for you about last night. Did you notice anyone or anything in the art gallery when you returned to the mansion through the front door after your stroll?'

'No.' Manu shook his head firmly. 'As you know, I have to go through the gallery to reach my room. Also, I walked almost up to my father's door to see if his room's light was on. I saw nothing in the gallery.'

'Would you have seen if someone was there?'

'I think so... unless he or she heard me coming and hid behind the totem pole or the suit of armour.'

'Ah, of course! Another question: Was the wheelchair in its place when you returned?'

'I'm afraid I can't say, Mr Athreya. The totem pole and the suit of armour are placed just in front of it. They stand between Dad's door and the charging point. I wouldn't have noticed it, one way or the other.'

'I see... all right, the final question: Was the back door shut?'

'Yes,' Manu said with certainty. 'I remember glancing at it. Now, if you'll excuse me, I need to run. Sebastian called to say that the police are coming shortly. He is bringing an inspector and a police doctor. I need to take a car to our side of the landslide and wait there. He'll bring the police around that far on his motorcycle.'

As Manu hurried away, Athreya spoke to Dora in an undertone.

'I want you to help me with the investigation,' he said. 'There are things that you can do without attracting attention that I can't. Will you help me?'

'But I am a suspect, Mr Athreya.'

'That may be so, but I know that you did not slit Phillip's throat.'

'At the risk of putting my neck in the noose as Uncle said, let me ask this: How can you be so sure? I thought we established that Michelle and I have the strength to do the job.'

'You do have the strength... but you are left-handed.'

'So?' Dora stopped and swung around to face him.

'Phillip's throat was slit from behind. It was a very deep wound—too deep to have been inflicted from the front. Frontal slashes tend to be shallower as the victim reflexively rocks back when the blade bites. Especially where the slash ends, the wounds are almost always shallow; they start deep and end shallow. But in this case, it is the opposite; the wound gets deeper as it progresses to the side of the neck.

'In this case, we can make out the direction of the knife because the weapon was a crude dagger, which wasn't as sharp as more professional weapons. Torn skin bordering the wound shows the direction the blade was pulled.

'The wound starts very low on the left side of his neck and ends high on his right. As I said, it gets deeper as it progresses. That suggests that the killer pulled the dagger towards himself as he cut. The nature and the direction of the slash could mean only one thing: the killer cut Phillip's throat with his right hand.'

Athreya reached out to lift Dora's right hand.

'Not only are you left-handed, but your right hand is still raw from the injury. Cutting with a dagger exerts a lot of pressure on the palm. Had you used your right hand, your wound surely would have bled.'

'Wow.' Dora grinned. 'You mean it? You don't suspect me?'

'Well, at any rate, you didn't commit the fatal act.'

'Thanks,' Dora shot back with a mock bow. 'That's a comfort... however small it may be. But what if I am an accomplice?'

'That's possible, but I have taken that into account.'

'Really, Mr Athreya.'

'So will you help me?' he repeated.

'If I can, I would love to. What do you have in mind?'

'Laundry.'

12

Inspector Muthu turned out to be an intimidating hulk of a man, over six-and-a-half feet tall, with powerful limbs and shoulders. His uniform stretched tight over his body and seemed to be a size too small for him. When he walked, it was with a swagger born of an unshakeable confidence in one's physical prowess. His hair was close-cropped and jet black. His mobile phone looked like a toy in his hand.

Watching him from the far end of the drawing room as he came in, Jilsy took an involuntary step back, half-hiding herself behind her husband. Dora eyed him warily, and Michelle grew visibly nervous.

Sebastian made the introductions quickly and with minimum words. He had been brought up to speed with what had transpired in his absence, and had, in turn, updated the inspector and the police doctor. Bhaskar had asked everyone to gather in the drawing room, so the two officials could meet all of them in one go.

Muthu glowered at each one of them in turn, trying to intimidate them into conceding the upper hand to him. But he met with little success, except with Richie, who had suddenly gone sullen and shifty-eyed.

When Muthu's eyes fell on Ganesh, his back straightened and he threw the major a quick salute, which Ganesh returned. Uniform, it appeared, admired uniform. With Varadan, Muthu remained cautious, limiting himself to a quick nod. When Abbas's turn came, the inspector's scowl deepened, but Abbas remained placid and polite.

Bhaskar seemed to take an instant dislike to Muthu, though it was not clear to Athreya if it was something he carried over from the past, perhaps from when the break-in was investigated. Muthu had already met Manu and Sebastian on their way to Greybrooke Manor.

The ladies the inspector glossed over, appearing to consider them irrelevant. His eyes lingered over Athreya, whom he studied the longest.

'You are the one who discovered the body?' he asked belligerently.

'I am,' Athreya answered evenly.

'How long were you alone with the body before you called the others?'

'Fifteen minutes or so.'

'Why didn't you call them immediately?'

'So that I could study the crime scene. I didn't want people coming in and contaminating the evidence. In any case, Mr Phillip was long dead.'

'But *you* contaminated the evidence!' Muthu snapped fiercely.

'I didn't touch anything after I discovered the body, except the body itself, which I touched to gauge its temperature.'

'You touched something *before* you discovered it, then?'

'Yes. I closed an open window that was banging in the wind. That's what I had entered the chapel for. And, of course, I touched the chapel door.'

'So, you left your fingerprints on the window and the door. That's contamination. Then you studied the crime scene, you say? What did you find?'

'I have made a list, which I will give to you. I have also spoken to everyone here and made a note of their movements during the night.'

'You? Who gave you the authority to talk to the witnesses?'

'I did,' Bhaskar cut in sharply. 'I asked him to investigate the crime.'

'A suspect investigating the crime?' Muthu demanded without taking his eyes off Athreya. 'Are you a policeman?'

'No,' Athreya answered calmly.

'Then?'

'Let's say I have a little experience in such matters. Would you like me to share my findings?'

'A civilian's findings?' Muthu looked incredulous. 'Let alone a suspect who discovered the body? I will make my own investigations. Now, Mr Sebastian says that you have the murder weapon in your possession. Hand it over.'

'Gladly.' Athreya produced a key ring with two keys.

'This is the key to the padlock on the chapel. Two identical keys. The dagger is in a sealed plastic bag inside the chapel. Nobody has touched it.'

'Why did you meddle with the evidence?'

'For God's sake, man,' Bhaskar thundered, 'if he hadn't found it, it might have been buried under the sand and gravel in the brook by now. Can't you see that he did you a service by recovering it?'

'How did you know it was there?' Muthu persisted, eyeing Athreya again.

'I thought there was a good chance that the killer might have thrown it there.'

'You want me to believe that?' Muthu attempted to thunder as Bhaskar just had, and failed miserably.

'That's your choice, Inspector.'

'Lord in heaven, Inspector!' Bhaskar exclaimed. 'Do you know who he is?'

'It wouldn't matter if he was the prime minister. He is a civilian and a suspect. That's all that matters. The law,' he concluded loftily, 'applies equally to everyone.'

Athreya gestured Bhaskar to back off.

'Mr Sebastian told me that one of you is a doctor,' Muthu went on. 'And that the person has estimated the time of death. Who was it?'

'Me,' Michelle said timidly. 'I am only a GP, and I don't know much about it. I did my best.'

'That is fine, madam,' Muthu conceded magnanimously. 'It's always a good thing to estimate the time of death as soon as the body is discovered. As time passes, the accuracy drops. So, thank you, madam. You have saved us one task.

'Now, the police doctor and I will go see the body. I want everyone to remain here. You—' he pointed to Athreya, '—you come with me. I want you to tell me how exactly you discovered the body.'

Flashing a quick smile at a bristling Bhaskar and a horrified Manu, Athreya followed the inspector out through the French windows.

'The chapel is to the left at the end of the walkway,' Sebastian called out after Muthu, who grunted in response and turned left.

The police doctor, a small quiet man, had been staring at Athreya during his exchange with the inspector. As Muthu strode forward on his long legs, pulling away from Athreya and the police doctor, the latter fell in step with Athreya.

'I think we have met, sir,' he said deferentially.

'We have, Doctor. I remember it well. It was the double murder in Ooty three years ago, wasn't it?'

'Yes, sir. I'm surprised that you remember me.'

'I just happen to be blessed with a good memory for faces. That's all.'

'Don't mind the inspector, sir. He is always like that. He doesn't know who you are. I'll tell him later when we are alone.'

'Don't bother, Doctor. I'm sure he will discover it by himself within twenty-four hours. Has the landslide been cleared up?'

'They have almost finished clearing one lane of the road. I think the police wagon will be here to collect the body in an hour or two.'

'Excellent. There is something I need you to do.'

'What?'

'You need to perform an autopsy as soon as possible and examine the contents of the stomach.'

'Any specific reason?' the doctor asked.

Athreya told him.

Athreya sat alone on a stone bench beside the walkway, sifting through what had been said in the drawing room in the morning, and what Dora and Manu had added later on the walkway. While most of the testimonies had fitted with each other—like those of Michelle and Varadan—the overall picture was as murky as last night's fog. The various accounts had offered no indication that any of the suspects were out and about at the time of the murder. Surely, someone—or more than one person—had stayed out later than they had admitted. Or they had gone out again after retiring by 1 a.m.

While the people who were staying in the mansion itself would have run the risk of being seen by others, the people in the annexe ran no such risk as each room there opened on to the walkway. They could have stepped out into the thick mist without anyone seeing them.

And what made the picture even murkier was the complete lack of knowledge about what Phillip had been up to from the time he and Varadan finished talking till the time he was killed. Of course, Athreya still had three potential suspects to talk to. Maybe one of them had a clue. As if on cue, footsteps sounded on the walkway, and he looked up to see Sebastian approaching.

'I'm sorry about the way the inspector spoke, Mr Athreya,' he began as he sat down beside Athreya. 'I should have explained who you were before I told him about our searching the chapel.'

'Don't give it another thought, Sebastian. I don't take offence so easily. I've dealt with even more hostile police officers before. I will be surprised if Muthu doesn't back off in the next day or two. I made some calls earlier this morning, and the news will reach him sooner or later.

'Instead, let's turn to more useful things. I've spoken to most of the others about their movements last night and asked them if they saw or heard anything that was out of place. As we wait for the inspector to finish his examination of the chapel, why don't you tell me about your movements and whatever you noticed?'

'That's what I came for. Mr Fernandez sent me.'

'Excellent. Let's start.'

'I'm not sure if I have anything significant to say. You will remember that we entered the mansion together. It was a little short of midnight.'

'11:50 p.m., to be precise,' Athreya interjected.

'That sounds right. I came in, checked if Mr Fernandez was asleep, and then retired at about midnight or a few minutes after.'

'Was Mr Fernandez asleep?'

'He was.'

'Did you see anyone in the gallery?'

'No.' Sebastian turned a startled face towards him. 'Was someone there?'

'I don't know. Had there been someone, would you have seen him or her?'

'I think so… unless he was flat against the wall, next to the suit of armour.' He shook his head suddenly. 'No, that's not right. How stupid of me! I plugged in the wheelchair to charge. I would have seen if there was anyone in the gallery, even behind the suit of armour.'

'Is that your routine every night?'

'Yes. Once Mr Fernandez retires, I plug in the wheelchair.'

'OK. And was the back door locked?'

'It was. I checked it. The spring lock could have been opened without a key from the inside, but not from outside.'

'What did you do after that?'

'Went to my room, changed into my pyjamas and went to bed.'

'Did you hear anything in the night?'

'I would be lying if I said I hadn't. The fact is that I am a light sleeper; more so after the break-in happened. I heard some voices drift in through the window. I also heard a couple of doors opening and closing. One of them must have been Manu's door, I guess. But I didn't think much of it. Voices and sounds of doors were expected last night.'

'Talking about doors, would you have heard the chapel door open?'

Sebastian sat bolt upright.

'Yes,' he said, his eyes flashing. 'The door creaks, and creaks loudly. I would have heard it.'

'Yet, you didn't.'

Sebastian nodded. 'I wonder why. Did I sleep sounder than usual? I didn't drink much.'

'The interesting thing is that none of us four who slept on the ground floor—you, Mr Fernandez, Manu and me—heard anything. Yet, the wheelchair was taken. Yet, the chapel door was opened. Yet, Phillip was killed.'

'Are you trying to suggest something, Mr Athreya?'

'I don't know. It just seems to me that some prior planning was done for last night.'

'You mean it was premeditated?'

'Either that, or someone had intended something else. And things went wrong.'

The conversation was interrupted by Muthu opening the chapel door and beckoning Athreya to come in. Sebastian followed Athreya to the door and stopped there, looking at the hinges. From the aisle, Athreya threw a glance over his shoulder and thought he saw a perplexed look on Sebastian's face.

A couple of hours later, after enduring a belligerent interrogation by Muthu, Athreya was back at the Misty Valley Resort. The inspector had chosen to grill Athreya first, making use of the study for his questioning. He had made Athreya repeat his narrative several times, trying to find inconsistencies. Athreya had patiently repeated his account without the slightest deviation.

At length, a frustrated Muthu gave up and dismissed him. Throughout the gruelling hour, Athreya had answered all of the inspector's questions promptly, but had offered nothing—views or information—proactively.

As Athreya brought his borrowed cycle to a halt at Misty Valley's gate, he was surprised to find the same security guard as in the morning. On seeing Athreya, he threw a salute and grinned as he had done earlier, showing uneven, stained teeth.

'Still here?' Athreya asked. 'I thought your duty ended at 8 a.m.?'

'The manager asked me to stay, sir,' the guard said conspiratorially. 'Something has happened at the mansion, he said. I may be wanted.'

'Smart man, your manager,' said Athreya, nodding in approval. 'Tell me, do you know if Mr Phillip has a maid or someone who helps him keep the house clean?'

'Yes, sir. Mrs Carvallo. She goes there every day and tidies up his house.'

'Where can I find her?'

'Here, sir. In the resort. She works here and part-time for Mr Phillip. Do you want me to call her?'

'Yes, please.'

Five minutes later, Athreya was talking to a kindly widow of about sixty, who was wearing her cross prominently. He had left the cycle with the security guard and was walking with Mrs Carvallo on the mud road between the resort and Phillip's house.

'Is Mr Phillip all right?' she asked, as soon as she joined Athreya on the road. 'They say something has happened to him.'

'All in good time, Mrs Carvallo,' he replied. 'I wanted to ask you a few questions first. When were you inside Mr Phillip's house last?'

'Why, sir, four hours ago. I cleaned the house.'

Athreya swung around and stared at her. She had cleaned the house, so whatever evidence there might have been would now be lost.

'You cleaned the house?' Athreya repeated after her stupidly.

'Yes, sir. I have a key. I clean it every day. Even when he is not at home. I usually go there earlier, but as he is away, I went today at about noon.'

'Did you find anything out of place?'

'No, nothing. Everything was as usual.'

'Nothing missing?'

It was Mrs Carvallo's turn to be astonished.

'No, sir,' she exclaimed. 'Missing? Good Lord, no. This is a safe place.' She peered at Athreya shrewdly. 'So, something *has* happened to Mr Phillip.'

'I'm afraid so.'

Athreya told her the minimum he could get away with, without telling her outright that Phillip had been murdered. She shed copious tears and spoke about how the Lord always took back the best of His flock. In response to a question, she declared that Phillip had been a very good and kind man who couldn't have had any enemies. Athreya steered the conversation towards his dealings with neighbours.

Yes, there had been a few altercations, she said, but then who didn't have some disagreements in this day and age? There were bound to be misunderstandings between people, but the right thing to do was to talk it over and sort it out. Take Thursday's quarrel with Ganesh, for instance. There had been raised voices between Phillip and the retired major, who had been upset with the painter.

Someone had overheard Phillip call someone else a mongrel, and the major had got it into his head that it was him that Phillip had been referring to.

But Phillip had been patient and had explained that he had not called Ganesh a mongrel. If he had indeed called someone a mongrel, it would certainly not have been a man who had fought for the country. After about ten minutes, the major had left, and as far as Mrs Carvallo knew, the matter had been sorted out.

Was she sure that she had heard it right? After all, 'mongrel' was an English term that didn't translate well to Tamil. No, sir! Mrs Carvallo was affronted. She had, in case Mr Athreya didn't know, studied in an English-medium Catholic missionary school. She knew English well, and even read novels.

After apologizing for his error and tasking her with the Herculean burden of not telling anyone about Phillip's death, Athreya went into the resort in search of Murthy, who turned out to be a handsome, moustachioed man, a little on the short side. His long, luxurious hair was brushed back at an angle to reveal a lean face. Athreya could see how he might hold some appeal for women. This Adonis-like charm, Athreya couldn't help thinking, was a common quality that united Abbas, Richie and Murthy. Perhaps the three men had more in common, too.

Murthy nodded warily as Athreya introduced himself; he showed no surprise at seeing him. Michelle had had all the time in the world to relay the developments to him.

'On what basis do you believe that I was at Greybrooke Manor?' Murthy asked Athreya, as they sat in his room, facing each other. An open packet of Gold Flake cigarettes lay on the table. 'Did anyone see me? Did anyone hear me? Michelle will tell you, if she hasn't already done so, that she didn't see me all day yesterday.'

'Couldn't anyone else have seen you?' Athreya asked.

'Who?' Murthy countered. 'I am not on speaking terms with Bhaskar, and do not enter the mansion. I have not met anyone else from the family recently, except Richie. I met him here, at the Misty Valley Resort.'

'Are you absolutely sure that nobody saw you?' Athreya asked.

'Name one person who could have seen me,' he challenged, without answering the question.

'Abbas.'

'Did he say that he saw me?' Murthy shot back. 'Don't try to pull the wool over my eyes.'

Athreya said nothing, and stared at Murthy, whose forehead had a thin film of sweat. Short of asserting that he had not been at Greybrooke Manor, Murthy had done everything to lead Athreya to believe he had.

'Are you telling me that you were not at Greybrooke Manor last night?' Athreya asked.

'You heard what I said,' Murthy shot back a second time. 'Why do you want me to repeat it?'

Athreya sighed and rose.

'You may want to rethink your story, Mr Murthy,' he said. 'You were seen at Greybrooke Manor and you were talked to. Despite the fog, you were also seen returning to the Misty Valley Resort in the wee hours.

'Be aware that the police inspector is not a man to take kindly to disingenuousness. He tends to see things in black and white—innocent or guilty. If someone conceals evidence from him or lies to him, he is likely to assume that the person is guilty of murdering Phillip.'

'But I didn't kill Phillip!' Murthy exclaimed angrily even as his face paled. 'Don't try to hang that around my neck.'

'Did I say you killed him?' Athreya enquired mildly with a hand on the door knob. 'All I am telling you is what the inspector is likely to think. I know what I know, which is probably more than what you think I know. If I were you, I'd be careful.'

As Athreya stepped out of Murthy's room, he felt his mobile phone buzz. It was his contact in Delhi, to whom he had spoken in the morning.

'Your photos are generating interest in certain quarters,' the person said when Athreya answered the call. 'You said this painter retired to the Nilgiri Hills?'

'That's right. A short drive from Coonoor. What kind of interest are his paintings generating?'

'A couple of them seem to be copies of little-known works of well-known painters. Excellent copies, from the looks of it. And the signature "Philipose" rings a bell too with a couple of people. Can you send me better photos of the paintings? High-resolution close-ups to study the brushwork. I need to send them to some people who know more about this matter, and see what else we can find out.'

'OK, I'll see what I can do. What can you tell me about Philipose?'

'There was a painter in Austria by that name who seems to have vanished a few years ago. He first appeared in Europe in 2008, and is said to have come from India. Apparently, he was very good at converting photographs to paintings. Very good paintings, I'm told. But despite the painter's obvious skill, works that were not original did not sell for much. As a result, Philipose found it difficult to make both ends meet, especially in Europe, where the cost of living is pretty high.

'Wanting to take advantage of his unusual skill and sorry financial state, art sharks began commissioning him to make copies of famous paintings, which they then sold to gullible, wannabe art collectors for a huge profit.'

'Fake art, eh? That's interesting.' Athreya recalled Bhaskar's description of Phillip—an artist with little creativity but his fingers could weave magic on canvas.

'Yes. Philipose himself is said to have received little for his efforts, but it at least provided a steady income that enabled him to put by some savings. It is unclear if he knew that his copies were being passed off as originals.

'One of the men I spoke to believes that Philipose might have begun suspecting this in his later years. Rather than risk the wrath of dangerous men by refusing to work for them, he may have decided to disappear quietly. He seems to have been caught in an unenviable situation. If he continued to work for the art sharks, knowing that his copies were being sold as originals, he would become an accessory to their crimes. On the other hand, if he refused to work for them, they might have killed him.'

'An unenviable predicament, if ever there was one,' Athreya said. 'What did he do?'

'And so,' the man went on, 'in the year preceding his disappearance, he had apparently worked day and night to earn extra money. Once he had accumulated enough to leave Austria, he vanished.'

'Were there any significant art thefts around the time Philipose disappeared?' Athreya asked.

'That thought occurred to me too, and I checked. No significant thefts took place, and absolutely none in the cities around where he lived.'

'When did he disappear?'

'2012.'

'That fits. Phillip came to the valley in 2012. Do me another favour, will you? Can you make a list of art-related crimes that happened around Vienna in 1994 and 1995? Thefts, deaths, anything significant, even if it is not a crime.'

13

When he returned to Greybrooke Manor, Athreya found a buzz of activity around the chapel. A police wagon and a clutch of policemen had arrived in his absence. While the wagon waited in the driveway for the body, a forensics team was busy at the chapel collecting physical evidence. Relentless in his pursuit, Inspector Muthu had ordered a man to collect the fingerprints of all the people at Greybrooke Manor—residents, guests and staff.

'Where have you been?' he asked Athreya on his return. 'We need to take your fingerprints.'

'At the Misty Valley Resort,' Athreya replied. 'I've just discovered that the victim's housekeeper cleaned his house earlier today. Whatever evidence—'

Athreya broke off as Muthu let loose a colourful curse. He summoned two policemen and sent them to Phillip's house with instructions to prevent anyone from entering it. He also sent orders that nobody should leave the Misty Valley Resort.

He then hailed the fingerprinting man and told him to take Athreya's prints. On seeing Athreya, the man threw him a salute, flummoxing Muthu in the bargain.

'You want to take *his* prints?' the fingerprinting man asked in surprise. 'He is one of us. He's the one who solved the Ooty double-murder case.'

'Eh?' Muthu stuttered. 'Eh?'

'It's all right, my friend,' Athreya cut in. 'You have to take the prints of *all* the people who were here during the murder. How else will you identify all the prints you find? My prints are already there on the chapel door and on one of the windows.'

'But, sir—' the fingerprinting man protested, only to be cut off by Athreya again.

'Do as the inspector says. Also take the prints of the dead man and everyone else who was here. Do you have a complete list?'

'I have a list of all the residents, guests and staff.'

'Add two more names to the list: Mr Murthy, who is staying at the Misty Valley Resort, and Father Tobias. You may want to check up on some of the others staying at the resort, including the staff, too.'

'Yes, sir.'

Athreya continued, 'I hope someone is dusting the chapel for prints? Make sure they pay close attention to the wheelchair and the altar. You need to dust every square inch of the wheelchair and identify every print on it, full or partial, clear or smudged.'

'Leave it to me, sir. If you'll come with me for a moment, I'll take your prints.'

'Oh, Inspector Muthu,' Athreya said as he turned to go with the fingerprinting man, 'I need to go out for an hour or so. I will report to you as soon as I return.'

Leaving a baffled Muthu behind, the other two went into the mansion. A short while later, Athreya was being driven by Dora to Father Tobias's church. They found the cleric fussing over his altar and preparing it for the next morning's service.

'Ah!' he said, as he straightened up and peered myopically at the newcomers. 'Hello, Dora. Welcome, sir.' He didn't seem to recognize Athreya.

'We met last night at Greybrooke Manor,' Athreya reminded him.

'Yes, of course. Mr Athreya, isn't it? Welcome, sir.' After greeting the priest, Dora had gone straight to the altar, before which she knelt and offered silent prayers. Watching her, Father Tobias seemed to sense that something was amiss.

'What is it?' he asked Athreya gently. 'Something is troubling the child.'

'Mr Phillip has been killed,' Athreya replied. 'In the chapel.'

Father Tobias blinked and stared at Athreya. He remained silent for a long moment and then nodded.

'He died under Christ's eyes,' he mumbled, referring to the mural in the chapel. 'He is blessed. Excuse me.'

He went to the altar, where he knelt and removed his glasses. He closed his eyes, bowed his head and concentrated hard on a long, silent prayer. Only his lips moved. Minutes passed, during which Dora completed her prayers and rose. As they watched Father Tobias silently, a solitary tear dropped from his eye to the ground. With that, he rose and put on his glasses again.

'A prayer for Phillip's soul,' he explained softly. 'The best prayer is one that comes from the heart and brings tears. The pain that Phillip must have suffered before his death deserved a tear.'

'Pain?' Dora asked.

'Death is often painful, my child, even if the suffering lasts for a brief time. Unless one passes away in their sleep, of course. Phillip must have endured pain for a few moments.'

'I have two requests for you, Father,' Athreya interposed. 'We need your help.'

'At your service, Mr Athreya. What can I do for you and the stricken household at Greybrooke Manor?'

'Phillip was killed sometime during the night, and I am making enquiries to see if we can find anything that points to how and why he was killed. I have spoken to everyone at the mansion, and I thought I must speak to you too.'

'Certainly.' Father Tobias blinked rapidly, and gazed at him with muddled benevolence. 'How can I help?'

'You spent the night at the annexe. Did you happen to hear

or see anything during the night that might help us understand this crime?'

The cleric bowed his head and stayed silent for a long moment, trying to remember.

'Sebastian very kindly showed me to my room after dinner,' he said at length. 'Once there, I removed my cassock, washed and said my thanks for the night before retiring to bed. One of the blessings I enjoy is that of deep, undisturbed sleep. I slept soundly till about five this morning, when I rose out of habit, said my prayers and left the estate.

'Unfortunately, I didn't hear anything during the night, neither from the chapel nor elsewhere. Poor Phillip. He must have had no time to shout. I'm sorry, Mr Athreya, I wish I had some information that could throw light on this tragedy. But don't be disheartened. Our prayers will be answered, and light will dawn on this affair.'

'Did you see or hear anyone when you left early in the morning, Father?'

'Only Bahadur at the gate. Nobody else.'

'Did you hear any voices or sounds from the rose garden or the rock garden?'

Father Tobias shook his head.

'Did you pass anyone on the road?'

'No... it was still dark when I left. The few people who might have been about at that time would have been in their houses today. It had been an unusually murky night.'

'It was,' Athreya agreed. 'And you had lost your way until you saw the lights of Greybrooke Manor. Did you pass anyone or hear any voices yesterday when you were approaching the estate?'

'Once again, I am forced to answer in the negative. I'm sorry I can't throw any light on this tragedy. But, as I said, the Lord will show the way, don't fret. Light will shine on the misdeeds of men. All will be revealed.'

'Thank you, Father,' Athreya replied with a bowed head. 'With your blessings, I'm sure it will. My other request is to ask you if you recognize any of these things.' Athreya opened a cardboard shoebox with a number of items and showed it to the cleric. On top was a dark-blue silk scarf, which Father Tobias picked up and examined.

'No,' he said. 'I don't recognize it.'

He dropped the scarf into the lid and picked up the next item. It was a silver cigar case with intricate carvings depicting the three kings visiting the infant Jesus on the night of His birth. The gleaming silver box was coated with clear lacquer to keep it from tarnishing.

'Ah!' the cleric exclaimed, as he picked it up appreciatively and opened it. 'A beautiful piece. This is from Mr Fernandez's collection, isn't it?'

'Are you sure, Father?'

'Yes, I've seen it in the display case next to the dining-room door. And this next one—' he dropped the silver box and picked up a glass paperweight '—is from Mr Fernandez's study.'

The paperweight had small purplish bubbles frozen in the glass, and at the centre was a splash in an eye-catching shade of bright red.

'You are an observant man, Father,' Athreya commented. 'I am hoping you would recognize this, too.'

He pulled out his mobile phone and showed the priest the photograph of the dagger they had recovered. After gazing at it for a long moment, Father Tobias shook his head.

'No, what an evil thing it is. Is it the murder weapon?'

'Yes.' A disappointed Athreya pocketed his phone and closed the shoebox. 'Thank you, Father.'

'I will come to the estate after the Sunday morning service tomorrow,' Father Tobias said, turning to Dora and blinking rapidly.

'If there is anything I can do to ease the pain, I will be delighted to do it. And we must hold a service for poor Phillip.'

'If you could let me know when you wish to come, Father,' Dora said, 'Manu or I will come and pick you up.'

'Thank you, my child. Meanwhile, if you need me there at any time, do tell me. I will come immediately. Please ask your uncle when he would like to hold a memorial service.'

Back at Greybrooke Manor, Athreya strolled through the dining room into the kitchen, where dinner was being prepared. He complimented the cook and the girls helping her on the previous night's excellent dinner. Having missed lunch, he sat down and snacked on some of the dishes they were preparing.

As he munched, he struck up a casual conversation, which Bhuvana and her girls were more than willing to participate in. They had heard about his interviewing the others, and showed an unholy interest in anything he had to say.

It turned out that one of the girls had heard the whir of the wheelchair sometime during the night, but was unable to pinpoint the time. Murugan, who was also in the kitchen, dismissed it as a combination of fertile imagination and morbid curiosity.

'Sebastian tells me that the front door had been kept unlocked last night,' Athreya said to him. 'Is that right?'

'Yes, sir. Those were Mr Fernandez's instructions. Guests were to be completely free to come and go as they pleased.'

'I see that you keep the doors in good condition. The bolts of the front door are lubricated with just the right amount of oil. Not too much, not too little.'

'Yes, sir,' a pleased Murugan nodded. 'The house has many old teak doors. They need to be taken care of properly. That's why I don't let anyone else attend to them.'

'I noticed that all the doors here are mostly noiseless. My bedroom door too.'

'Mr Fernandez is a light sleeper, sir. Creaking doors wake him up, especially after that horrible break-in we had. I make sure that none of the doors or windows in the house make noise.'

'The chapel too?'

'No, sir. It doesn't matter if the chapel doors creak. In fact, you have to struggle with one of the side doors to open it. If I hear a creak, I know that someone is there.'

'Did you hear a creak last night?'

Murugan was stumped. He stopped what he was doing and stared unseeingly across the kitchen. The girls watched him wide-eyed.

'No, sir,' Murugan said at length. 'I didn't hear the door creak.' He swept the kitchen with his imperious gaze and barked in Tamil, 'Did any one of you hear the chapel door make noise?'

All the staff in the kitchen shook their heads, including Gopal and another boy who was cleaning the grinder.

'Where do you keep the oil dispenser?' Athreya asked, studying a piece of cauliflower Manchurian appreciatively.

'There, sir.'

Murugan pointed to an open cupboard near the back door of the kitchen, where a number of tools were neatly arranged. Athreya went over to it and picked up a small plastic oil dispenser with a round body and a long, slender snout. Oil had spilled out, and had made the surface of the dispenser greasy. It had also left a ring on the shelf. He touched the oil with the tip with his finger and smelled it. It smelled the same as the oil on the chapel door's hinges.

Murugan hissed when he saw that the dispenser was greasy. He strode up with a piece of cloth and offered it to Athreya.

'I'm sorry, sir. I always wipe it after the work is done. Not everyone does that,' he said, shooting Gopal a dark look.

'Not me, sir,' Gopal yelped. 'I didn't use it.'

'Then who did?' Murugan demanded when the other boy also shook his head. 'None of the girls are allowed to touch the tools. And I wiped it the day before yesterday after I oiled the front door.'

'I don't know, sir. Honest.'

'Leave the poor boy alone,' Bhuvana called from her stove, furiously stirring the contents of a large vessel. 'He didn't do anything. That oil dispenser was borrowed yesterday.'

'Borrowed?' Murugan asked, turning around. 'By whom?'

'Richie.'

From the kitchen, Athreya went in search of Bhaskar and found him in the library, reading a collection of short stories from the nineteenth century. He was haggard and pale in his old wheelchair as he looked up from his book.

'Come, Mr Athreya,' he said and closed the book after inserting a bookmark into it. 'I had hoped that we would meet in this library under pleasanter circumstances to chat about this treasure trove I have here.'

He waved his arm, gesturing to the tall bookshelves covering the walls of the library.

'We still can,' Athreya replied. 'After this affair is resolved.'

'I certainly hope so. But your visit to Greybrooke Manor is already serving another purpose, notwithstanding that oaf of an inspector. I must apologize for his behaviour—'

'There is no need for you to apologize, Mr Fernandez.'

'He was pretty nasty the last time around too,' Bhaskar went on as if Athreya hadn't spoken, 'when the intruder broke in and tried to kill me.'

'That was what I wanted to speak to you about,' Athreya cut in, seizing the chance. 'Manu tells me that the dagger we found in the stream may be the same one the intruder had dropped when you shot him.'

Bhaskar's eyes flew open, and he sat up straight.

'That's right!' he exclaimed. 'Remember I told you that it looked vaguely familiar? That's it! Manu has hit the nail on the head. The dagger you found in the stream looks very similar to the one the intruder dropped.'

'Are you sure, Mr Fernandez?'

'Hmm… am I sure?' Bhaskar frowned deeply. 'I think so. But could I swear to it? Probably not. You see, we didn't pay much attention to the dagger that day. Murugan picked it up, and by the time we thought about it, there were many sets of fingerprints all over it. But after that day, I haven't seen it. It's been awhile now, and I can't be sure if it is the same dagger.'

'Where was it kept after that day? Do you remember?'

'I'm afraid not. Perhaps Murugan will know.'

He reached out and pressed the button of a portable bell. Somewhere deep in the mansion a bell chirped. A minute later the door opened and Murugan came in.

'Yes, sir?' he asked.

Bhaskar asked him about the dagger the intruder had dropped.

'I remember putting it in the top drawer of the table that stands in the hall,' he said. 'That was soon after I had picked it up and everyone had examined it. I didn't see it after that.'

'Go check the drawer, Murugan,' Bhaskar said. 'See if it is still there.'

Less than a minute later, Murugan was back, shaking his head. Sebastian trailed in behind him.

'No, sir. It isn't there.'

'Was that the last time you saw it, Murugan?' Bhaskar asked. 'When you put it in the drawer?'

'Yes, sir.' Murugan had paled. He seemed to have made the connection. 'The dagger that was found today, sir… it looks very similar to that one.'

'Could it be the same dagger?'

Murugan nodded silently.

'I think so too,' Sebastian added. 'Murugan is right. We put it in the drawer and forgot about it.'

'Then,' Athreya said, 'anyone could have taken it, I suppose?'

'Yes.'

'Who all were at the mansion when the intruder broke in?'

'Mr Fernandez, Manu and Mr Phillip. Also Murugan, the staff and me. Richie and Dora came the next day.'

'And when did this intruder break in?'

'Let's see… about three months ago.'

'There is something I haven't told you about the intruder,' Bhaskar said. 'When I described the man, Inspector Muthu seemed to recognize him. The intruder was a short, wiry man who moved about very rapidly and belligerently. I didn't see his face, but his mannerisms reminded me of a small, pugnacious street dog.'

Something stirred at the back of Athreya's mind. Bhaskar's description had reminded him of something he had heard recently. Very recently.

'But we kept the description of the intruder a secret. Muthu's boss—the assistant commissioner of police—had said that there was a known offender of that description who prowled across Tamil Nadu and Karnataka. Once every few months, he said, he was seen in these parts. They would apprehend him the next time they came across him. They wanted to question him on one or two other matters too. It was best not to put him on his guard by letting his description out.'

'The ACP also said that this offender had a nickname,' Sebastian added. 'I don't remember what it was.'

'Mongrel,' Bhaskar filled in. 'He is known as the mongrel.'

The penny had dropped in Athreya's mind—that was the term Mrs Carvallo had used. She had said that she had overheard Phillip call someone a mongrel.

Before he could voice his thought, the library door flew open and Inspector Muthu walked in. He seemed pleased with himself, and was bursting to share some news.

'Guess whom we found at the Misty Valley Resort?' he asked. 'The mongrel! He was hanging around with Ismail, one of the resort staff.' His face split into a wide grin as he regarded Bhaskar and Sebastian. 'And you know what? His left thigh has a recent bullet wound.'

'Who is this mongrel, Inspector?' Athreya asked.

'He is many things, sir.' Athreya noticed the change in how the inspector was addressing him. 'We don't have proof to nail him, but we know that he is a thief. And, more importantly, he is a blade for hire.'

'Then,' Sebastian said, his eyes ablaze with fury, 'anyone could have hired him to kill Mr Fernandez. Anyone.'

Meanwhile, as Athreya was talking to Bhaskar, Dora had gone to the service area adjoining the kitchen to carry out the assignment Athreya had given her. This was the time when a lot of the ironing would be done. While the cook and her girls were busy preparing dinner in the kitchen, the boys would be busy ironing clothes in the service area. A perfect time to do a little snooping.

She sauntered into the kitchen as she often did, and began chatting with the staff. She was very well liked by them, and they took the liberty to joke with her in a way they did with none of the other residents.

As she spoke with them, she found her way to the service area where two boys were ironing clothes. They had just begun and were indulging in small talk to lighten their chore. She joined in as they talked about daggers in general and the one they had retrieved from the stream in particular. One of them was telling about how tribals around his village made their own weapons for hunting, including daggers, bows and arrows.

Keeping up the banter, Dora went through the heap of unironed clothes, looking for something made of thickish dark-blue cloth. She found three candidates, and picked up each of them in turn and held them up to study the fabric.

Unsure, she dropped them and sauntered away, pushing her hands into her pockets. From her left pocket, she pulled out the scrap of cloth Athreya had given her and studied it. She put it back in her pocket and drifted over to the pile of clothes. Athreya had told her to identify the apparel from which it had been torn, but not why. Nor had he told her where he had found it.

She then re-examined the three pieces that were dark blue in colour. One of them, a shirt, was made of cloth that was much thinner than the scrap. She discarded it.

The second was a pair of trousers made of a thick material, but seemed to be cotton or linen, and it lacked gloss. Her scrap was clearly synthetic.

The third turned out to be the one closest to what she was looking for. But by this time, Bhuvana was looking at her suspiciously. There was no point in being surreptitious any longer. Boldness was the only way forward.

'Hey, this is a nice piece,' she exclaimed and picked up the garment. 'I haven't seen one like this in a while.'

It turned out to be a nightgown with embroidery at the hem and the lapels. It was indeed a striking gown. As she held it up, she noticed a tear about a foot and a half from the hem. It was an inch-long rip, into which the scrap in her pocket would have fitted well.

'Whose is it?' she asked casually.

'Don't know,' one of the ironing boys said. 'Look at the room number on the tag. Here, show it to me.'

He straightened the tag attached to one of the buttonholes and peered at it.

'Room number three,' he said presently, and began to iron the nightgown.

'Three?' Dora repeated. 'Can't be. That's the room Phillip was staying in.'

'Not upstairs, Dora,' Bhuvana said, still eyeing her. 'Room number three in the annexe.'

Dora was about to ask who was occupying the room, when she decided against it. That was a piece of information she could easily obtain elsewhere, and Bhuvana was looking at her more and more doubtfully.

Dora seemed to lose interest in the dark-blue nightgown and shifted the conversation to what was being prepared for dinner. Ten minutes later, she walked out of the kitchen.

Athreya hurried out of the library and into the drawing room, where the other residents were to gather before dinner. There, he buttonholed Ganesh and strolled out through one of the French windows with him and Jilsy.

'You had an altercation with Phillip on Thursday,' he said quietly, once they were out of earshot. 'Can you tell me about it?'

'It was really nothing, Mr Athreya,' Ganesh replied guardedly. He shot an annoyed glance at his wife. 'Just some silly misunderstanding. It was sorted out and forgotten.'

'That's good. But I'd still like to hear about it.'

'Really, Mr Athreya, it was nothing,' Jilsy pleaded. 'It's got nothing to do with Phillip's death. It was not really a fight between Ganesh and Phillip. We were very good friends with him.'

'At this point,' Athreya countered firmly, 'we can't tell if it had anything to do with Phillip's death or not. We just don't know enough about his murder to tell what may be related to it and what may not be. However, if you fear I am suggesting that the altercation pins a motive on you, rest easy. My intention in asking this question is something else.'

Relief flooded Jilsy's pretty face. The tension slipped out of Ganesh's bearing too.

'You are a good man, Mr Athreya,' he said.

'Now,' Athreya persisted, 'will you tell me about it?'

'Well, it was like this,' Ganesh began. 'Phillip's gate and our gate are side by side, and our cottages are adjacent to each other. I was entering through my gate when I overheard Phillip say, "the mongrel is here". At that point, I didn't think much of it. But within the next ten minutes, Jilsy, who was out in the front garden, heard the term "the mongrel" repeated twice.

'There was no doubt that Phillip was referring to someone. Each time the context was such that Jilsy thought that he meant me. Upset, she came and told me what she had heard. I recalled him saying "the mongrel is here" minutes earlier when I entered.

'I put two and two together, and concluded that he was insulting me. I went over to his cottage immediately and confronted him. He seemed a little shocked that I had heard him use that derogatory term, but denied that he was referring to me. When I asked him whom else he could have meant, he had no satisfactory answer.

'But he insisted—pleaded, rather—to me to forget what I had heard. It was not me he was talking about when he used that word, he repeated. He then cooked up a cock and bull story about someone who was visiting a servant at the resort and whose nickname was "the mongrel". But Phillip seemed so sincere that I decided to let it go.'

'Did he say that the servant's name was Ismail?'

'That's right,' Ganesh exclaimed in surprise. 'How did you know?'

'This was on Thursday?' Athreya asked.

'Yes. The day before we gathered here. Jilsy and I decided to forget about it once and for all.'

'Do you know who Phillip was talking to when he said "the mongrel" thrice?'

'Er...' Ganesh began uncertainly.

'I know,' Jilsy cut in. 'He was talking to two men in his cottage. A pretty serious discussion, I would say, from the sound of it. You remember I was in the garden when I overheard Phillip? I saw them leave shortly after the conversation. That's how I know who he was talking to.'

'Who?' Athreya asked.

'Abbas and Murthy.'

Athreya stopped, and turned to face Ganesh and Jilsy.

'Don't speak of this to anyone,' he said in an undertone. 'We don't know if it is relevant. But if it is, such information can be dangerous.'

'You mean—' Jilsy began but broke off. She had turned pale.

'There is a killer around. It's best to play safe.'

14

The next day dawned foggy and dim, but it was not as murky as it had been on Athreya's first morning at Greybrooke Manor. As had been the case the past two mornings, Athreya was among the first to rise. Soon, he was out in the garden, jogging along the walkways. While the last two days had seen a lot of activity, he hadn't got the exercise his body demanded. This was an excellent time to remedy that.

Looking back, Athreya was a little surprised at how much had happened in one day. The first twenty-four to forty-eight hours after a murder were always critical, but yesterday had been highly productive by any standard. It felt as if he had discovered the murder a long time ago, not just twenty-four hours before. Today too would be crucial. He was hoping that new evidence would emerge, and that his enquiries would bear fruit.

A quarter of an hour into his jog, his phone rang. It was Rajan calling from Coonoor. He had made the enquiries Athreya had requested, and was calling to share his findings.

'By all accounts, Ganesh Raj seems to be a harmless fellow,' he said. 'He is on the denser side, but people seem to like him. An ex-army man who saw a lot of action in the line of duty. Twice, he was wounded badly, but went back to the front line each time. He has a reputation for being courageous and dependable in action. Known as a doer rather than a thinker. A genuine guy, whom his colleagues recall with fondness.

'But being a bit of a dullard, he was overlooked for promotion several times. Lacked the intelligence and tact to rise very high, it seems. But when it comes to integrity and honesty, he is top-notch. Not the slightest blemish on that account in his entire career. A very forthright person, he is, if sometimes thoughtless. Gets into altercations sometimes for calling a spade a spade.

'Now, his wife seems to be a different sort. A bit of a flirt who is not averse to having a quick fling when her husband is not looking. She is seventeen years his junior, and seems bored out of her skull in this middle-of-nowhere valley that Ganesh picked as his post-retirement home. Poor girl, it's not been a great marriage for her.

'I'm told that she spends a lot of time at Greybrooke Manor, more out of nothing else to do, I suppose. Bhaskar humours her and tolerates her feigned interest in his library.'

'That's useful, Rajan. It fits in well with what I have observed. What about Abbas?'

'He's an interesting bloke. There seems to be little doubt that he is a crook of some sort. But what sort is the question. The police have been keeping an eye on him, but have not been able to lay their hands on anything to corner him. His resort loses money hand over fist, but he still runs it. Keeps a staff of about fifteen people, despite having very few visitors. Always deals in cash, it appears, and is never short of it. Something smells fishy there, for sure.'

'Any talk of drugs?' Athreya asked, and went on to narrate what he had overheard.

'Bhaskar may have something there,' Rajan said. 'They don't say anything openly, but what you say seems consistent with the local police's reactions when asked about Abbas. The resort may well be a cover for shady activities.'

'Anything on Murthy and the folks here at Greybrooke Manor?'

'Nothing much other than Murthy and Richie being unsavoury characters. The locals talk highly of Manu and Bhaskar's nieces. Bit of sympathy for Michelle due to her rotten husband. Huge respect for Bhaskar. Huge. And for Sebastian too, but Bhaskar is placed on a pedestal.'

179

'And the staff at the mansion?'

'Only positive feelings for them. The cook is reputed to have a sharp tongue but a heart of gold. Runs the place like an overbearing matron, it seems. What with having young women under her wing, along with some young men? Bit of a disciplinarian.'

'The priest? Father Tobias?'

'Harmless, abstracted bloke. Poor as a church mouse, I'm told. His family has been around in the Western Ghats for a couple of generations. Has a brother in Madikeri.'

'And finally, the victim? Phillip?'

'You'll be surprised at how little the locals know about him. His presence doesn't seem to have registered around here. In fact, some of those I spoke to asked, "Who is Phillip?" when I brought him up. Rarely comes to town, I believe.'

Hardly had Athreya thanked Rajan and hung up when his phone rang again. It was the fingerprinting man. Athreya sat down on a bench at Sunset Deck and took the call. This was going to be important.

'Thought I'd give you whatever information I have at this point,' he said. 'There are several prints on the candlesticks on the altar, but they are not from the night of the murder. The prints of Sebastian, Dora and Murugan are all over them, but dust has settled on top of them in most cases. The same is the case with the altar.

'But there is a funny thing about the altar. Judging by how the dust has been disturbed or rubbed off, I think it has been handled extensively. However, there are no fresh prints.'

'Gloves?' Athreya asked.

'Gloves,' the fingerprinting man concurred. 'And did you know that the altar top is not made of a single piece of stone? It is made of three separate slabs that fit neatly into each other.'

'But isn't that how it always is? Marble, granite and other stones come in slabs of fixed dimensions. They are cut and glued together during installation. That's the case with all counter-tops—kitchens, offices or altars.'

'That's right, but that's not what I am saying. The three pieces here are not *glued* together. They just fit precisely next to each other.'

'Why would they do that?'

'I'm not sure. But there is something else too. The wheelchair.'

'Go on.'

'Parts of the wheelchair had to have been rubbed down after it was wheeled into the corner. There are two handles at the rear of the wheelchair, which are used to push or pull it. If there was one place that should have had prints, it is these handles. But they have no prints. Zilch!'

'Not even old or smudged prints?'

'None. The handles have been wiped clean.'

'If the handles have been wiped clean, it's possible that they were used by someone without gloves. Then, after the job was done, that person wiped the handles.'

'Exactly!'

'The hands that touched the altar wore gloves, but the ones that wheeled the wheelchair didn't. That's interesting.'

'There's more. Parts of the armrests had been wiped clean too. They are full of Bhaskar's prints, as can be expected. But there are some that belong to Phillip, too. The parts that have been wiped clean are probably those someone would hold on to if they were moving the wheelchair.

'The other interesting aspect is the prints on the console and the joystick assembly. What is intriguing is that here, there are no prints at all—not even Bhaskar's. Again, zilch. Wiped clean. I don't think blood spilled on to the console and the joystick.

Some traces would still be there if it had, especially in the natural cracks on the leather covering of the joystick.'

Holding his phone in his left hand, Athreya was listening intently. His right hand was drawing invisible figures and words with its index finger on the stone bench—a sign that the owner's mind was working in high gear.

'One of the staff members says she heard the whir of the wheelchair at night,' Athreya said. 'If that is true, someone drove it. The console and the joystick were used, presumably just before the murder. But later, it was wheeled into the corner and rubbed down. There just may be a pattern here.'

'If there is a pattern, sir, I don't see it,' the fingerprinting man said.

'Thanks for this,' Athreya said. 'It's very useful. By the way, did you do the last piece of work I'd requested?'

'Yes, sir. We'll know the results tomorrow.'

After the call, Athreya sat still as stone at Sunset Deck. For a long while, he didn't move. The only movement came from two fingers of his right hand as they furiously scribbled invisible words and phrases on the bench. Athreya's erstwhile colleagues used to joke that they would have cracked most cases sooner had they known of a way to decipher the invisible shapes Athreya's fingers made when his mind was working hard.

At length, he stirred. He had decided what he needed to do next. He had to spend some time alone in the chapel. Just as he rose, his phone rang for the third time. It was the police doctor. He had done the autopsy the previous night.

'You were right, sir,' he said. 'The contents of the stomach show it clearly. The victim was killed between one and a half and two hours after his last meal. If dinner finished at 11 p.m., he was killed between 12:30 a.m. and 1 a.m.'

Athreya slowly pocketed his phone and made his way back

to the mansion. The case had changed drastically. There were a number of people who had been up and about between 12:30 a.m. and 1 a.m. And his hunch had been right.

Michelle had lied about the time of death.

Athreya went early to the dining room, shortly before breakfast was to start, and stood there for a moment, looking around. He went to the near end of the long table and sat down there, surveying the other chairs around the table. After a brief moment, he rose and adjusted the position of some chairs that were set along the two long sides, then returned to the same end chair.

The head of the table was where Bhaskar always sat, and it was often one of the younger folk who went to the other end. Today, Athreya wanted to sit at the tail end of the table for a reason. As he settled into the chair and began reading a newspaper, Manu walked in.

'Good morning, Mr Athreya,' he said, as his glance lingered on Athreya and his choice of seat.

'Morning, Manu,' Athreya replied.

'Trying a different seat today, sir?' Manu asked with a smile.

Athreya shrugged and returned the smile.

'Not a bad idea,' he continued, as he strolled over and took one of the chairs on the long side. 'Who knows, it may give you a fresh perspective.'

Athreya blinked in surprise. Was it just a fluke, or was the younger man uncommonly perspicacious? Either way, he had got it right.

'Always useful, isn't it?' Athreya replied. 'A new perspective.'

'Good morning, Mr Athreya,' Dora's voice sounded from behind him as she walked in. 'I was looking for you in the drawing room. I saw you jogging early. Hope you have worked up an appetite.'

'Good morning, Mr Athreya,' Sebastian echoed as he wheeled in Bhaskar in the old wheelchair.

'Oh. I'm sorry I didn't see you at this end of the table,' Bhaskar apologized. 'Thought it was someone else. Good morning.'

People began streaming in behind Bhaskar, and within a minute, everyone, including Richie, had come in. They all looked a little more relaxed today than they had been at dinner the previous night. They seemed to be coming to terms with the new reality, and perhaps with the shadow of suspicion hanging over them. Conversation was more natural than last night's, and there was a sprinkling of laughter as well.

Athreya ate quickly as he kept an eye on the progress of the others. He had to make his move when everyone was at the table and, hopefully, concentrating on their breakfast. He didn't want Richie, who ate quickly and didn't have the courtesy to wait for others, to leave the room.

When most people were a little more than halfway through breakfast, he adjusted his position slightly so he could see all the faces around the table.

'I have a piece of news,' he said casually as he picked up his cup of coffee, as if to sip it. 'Fresh evidence has come in.'

As the sparse conversation around the table paused, he went on.

'Phillip did not die at 2:30 a.m. as we first supposed,' he said in a clear, loud voice. 'He was killed at 12:45 a.m.'

He chose to declare a specific time instead of the usual time window for a reason. By conveying certainty and precision, the assertion he was making would have a deeper impact on those listening. As soon as he said it, he began sweeping his eyes over the faces around the table rapidly. As he had hoped, the reactions were varied. Some eyes snapped to him, while some others completely avoided him.

Dora dropped her spoon, which clattered to the floor. For a fleeting moment, Athreya saw dismay shrivel her face before she dived after her spoon in an effort to hide her consternation. It was obvious that she was avoiding his eyes.

Beside her, Michelle choked on her water and burst into a fit of coughing. Even the flush the coughing brought to her face failed to cover the gathering pallor. Her lips were trembling violently when she let go of her glass and buried her mouth in her napkin. All the while, she had kept her gaze away from Athreya's.

Next to her, Richie had frozen. He had been reaching for the butter dish when Athreya had dropped his bombshell. His startled eyes, now suddenly looking haunted, remained riveted to the table. His extended arm, instead of lifting the butter, was pulled back as if it had touched fire.

Beside Richie was Abbas, calm and collected as ever. He betrayed nothing. Except for a momentary halting of his knife, which was cutting his omelette when Athreya spoke, he betrayed no outward sign of having received major news.

Further up the table, and closest to Bhaskar at the other end, Varadan slowly placed his knife and fork on his plate and picked up his napkin. He dabbed his lips carefully as his glazed eyes remained fixed on the table before him. It was apparent that his lawyer's brain was recalibrating events in light of the fresh evidence.

What was common among all the five people on Athreya's right was that they were avoiding looking at him.

But it not so with the others. Bhaskar, Manu and Sebastian were staring at him across the length of the table. Bhaskar's eyes were drilling holes into Athreya's head. He had realized what Athreya was up to. A moment later, Bhaskar's own gaze swept over the faces around the table.

Manu's eyes were dancing as a smile tugged at his lips. *I knew it*, the look on his face said. Sebastian's face had a similar look to what Athreya had seen when the former had discovered that the hinges of the chapel door had been oiled. He appeared bewildered and seemed to have to make an intense effort to comprehend the new information.

Jilsy had a horrified expression on her face. Along with the horror was deep revulsion, as if she were watching a particularly revolting horror movie. So deep was the disgust that it caught Athreya unawares. In a searing flash of insight, he understood the reason behind it. All of a sudden, some of the unresolved questions in his mind found answers.

Meanwhile, beside her, Ganesh's slow brain was just beginning to register the import of what Athreya had said. His mouth had fallen open and his uncomprehending face turned towards Athreya.

'12:45 a.m.?' Bhaskar demanded from across the table. 'Are you sure?'

Athreya nodded. 'The police doctor called. I had asked him to perform an autopsy as soon as possible, and to examine the stomach's contents,' he explained, and went on to repeat what the man had said. 'Phillip was killed between one and a half and two hours after his last meal. If dinner finished at 11 p.m., he was killed between 12:30 a.m. and 1 a.m.'

'*You* asked him,' Bhaskar queried. 'Were you expecting this?'

Michelle, Richie and Abbas were still not looking at Athreya. Varadan was, and Dora was stealing glances at him through the corner of her eye.

'Yes,' Athreya nodded. 'I was expecting it.'

'That changes everything,' Bhaskar said loudly. 'If I recall correctly, people were up and about between 12:30 and 1 a.m. Almost everyone.'

'That's right,' said Athreya. 'At least four people have acknowledged being out at that time in their testimonies. The rest of us could very easily have gone out again after retiring. I, for instance, went into my room at 11:50 p.m., and have no alibi after that. Nothing would have stopped me from sneaking out of the back door at 12:30 a.m.'

Suddenly, a choking sound came from Jilsy. As he had been responding to Bhaskar, Athreya had noticed the sickly look on Jilsy's face going from bad to worse. By now, she had acquired a greyish pallor. She leapt to her feet, clasped her hands over her mouth and fled towards the washroom. Seconds later, faint retching sounds reached the dining room.

Dora threw a distressed glance at Athreya and went after Jilsy. A few long moments later, Ganesh excused himself, rose to his feet and left the room too.

Neither Richie nor Michelle finished their breakfast, and Abbas seemed to have suddenly lost his appetite. Varadan was once again looking at Athreya disapprovingly; just as he had done the previous morning when Athreya had announced that there had been a murder and had led people to believe that Bhaskar had been killed.

Bhaskar and Manu entered into an animated discussion about what the new development meant, while Sebastian listened, contributing from time to time. Without meeting Athreya's eye, Michelle mumbled an apology and rose. Richie was quick to follow, but without an apology.

'Mr Athreya,' Varadan said severely. He was visibly angry now. 'What have you achieved by this needless melodrama? I suspect you planned this one too, as you had planned the previous one. And you chose to speak of the autopsy at the breakfast table. All the three ladies are very upset. So I ask you again: What have you achieved?'

'I did not enjoy this any more than you or Jilsy did, Mr Varadan. But I had to do this. My apologies for taking the liberty, Mr Fernandez,' said Athreya as he turned to face Bhaskar, 'but I have been charged with solving this crime.'

'Then,' Varadan retorted, 'I suppose you have achieved something through this stage show?'

'Yes. A part of the puzzle has fallen into place. As a lawyer, you will appreciate this, Mr Varadan… a lot more is at play here than just a straightforward murder. Unless I strip away the extraneous, I will not be able to see the core clearly.'

15

Half an hour later, Athreya was knocking on Michelle's door. She had sent him a text message, asking him if he would come up to her room. Athreya had agreed, and had strolled up the stairway to the first floor. As soon as he knocked, the door opened, and Michelle asked him to come in and take a chair. Her face was streaked with tears and she was trembling.

'I'm sorry, Mr Athreya,' she sobbed. 'I deceived you. I didn't know what else to do; I am caught in a trap. But before that, I must thank you.'

'Thank me?' Athreya asked, genuinely surprised.

'Yes, I'm grateful to you for not calling out my deception in the dining room in front of everyone. You could easily have accused me then and there, and I would not have had anything to say. That's what the police inspector would have done.

'But thanks to your kindness, they all think that it was just an error on my part. They all heard what I had said yesterday: I am a GP and know little about estimating the time of death. So thank you, Mr Athreya, for preserving my dignity.'

Athreya opened his mouth to respond, but she beat him to it.

'You knew I was lying, didn't you?' she asked.

'Well… let's just say that I thought it was a possibility.'

'You had your own estimate of the time of death?'

'A very rough one based on my own experience. I thought it was around 1 a.m. The time window you suggested seemed too late.'

Michelle nodded and wiped her face.

'You know why I did it?' she asked.

'Your husband was here until almost 2 a.m. that night.'

She let out a moan and sat down on the bed.

'When I asked you to come with me to the chapel to estimate the time of death, you came up to your room to get your medical bag. But you took a very long time. I figured that you had called your husband.'

'What else could I do, Mr Athreya? I couldn't knowingly cast suspicion on him, could I?'

Athreya remained silent, watching her. She stood up, removed her jacket and draped it on the back of a chair. As she did, the loose forearm-length sleeves of her shirt rode up to her elbows. On her lower arms were bruises. Some old and some new. She realized this at once and pulled down her sleeves, but it was too late.

'He can be a hard man sometimes, Mr Athreya. Especially when he is angry.'

'I'm sorry, but anger is no excuse.'

'Anyway, let that be. I wanted to talk to you to… to… ask your advice. I'm stuck, Mr Athreya, stuck like a kitten in a pipe. I can't go forward, and I can't go back. I don't know what to do. I see no way out.'

'Tell me, Michelle, does the phrase "the mongrel" mean anything to you?'

'Mongrel?' she repeated, bewildered. 'No. I mean, nothing beyond the English meaning of the word: a street dog.'

'*The* mongrel?' he asked again.

'No.' She shook her head. 'Nothing.'

'Have you ever heard your husband use this phrase?'

'I don't think so.'

'How about Abbas?'

'No.'

'Are you sure you have never heard it mentioned by Abbas or Murthy?'

'No, never. What *are* you driving at?'

'If you haven't heard it, Michelle, you are better off not knowing. You'll be safer. At any rate, don't repeat this to Abbas or your husband.'

'Safer? You're frightening me, Mr Athreya.'

'I'm sorry, but I had to ask. Tell me, do you believe that there were attempts on your uncle's life recently?'

'Yes.' Michelle's eyes went round. 'The intruder even came into his room to kill him. Thankfully, Uncle had his automatic with him.'

'Who do you think sent him, Michelle? And where do you think he hid after being shot in the leg? There aren't many places around here to hide.'

Michelle's eyes became even rounder. Her mouth opened to form an O. Slowly, she gathered her wits. Athreya watched her silently as emotions flashed across her face.

'Tell me honestly, Mr Athreya,' she whispered at length. 'Do you think Abbas killed Phillip thinking that he was Uncle?'

'I can't answer that yet because I still don't *know*.'

The emphasis on the last word was not lost on Michelle.

'And Murthy?' she asked, her voice barely above a whisper.

'Same answer, Michelle. I don't *know*.'

'Am I in for grief, Mr Athreya?'

'Likely. Quite likely.'

'Uncle says I should leave Murthy—divorce him,' she blurted out, as though taken by a sudden urge to confide in him.

'Does Murthy know that Mr Fernandez said that?' Athreya asked tenderly.

Michelle nodded slowly, realization dawning on her.

'Uncle is right,' she said. 'I'm a trusting fool. I don't know when to keep my mouth shut.'

She looked up suddenly, fierce determination rising in her face. She squared her shoulders and stared straight at Athreya.

'What do *you* think I should do?' she demanded.

'All I'll say is this, Michelle. Know your husband for what he truly is. Know your friends for what they truly are. Let the scales fall from your eyes. Then make your decision. It's yours, and only yours, to make.'

'And as far as Phillip's murder is concerned?'

'Stick to the truth. Don't lie on anyone's behalf. *Anyone*'s. If you did not kill Phillip, you have nothing to fear.'

They were interrupted by a knock on the door. It was Dora.

'Uncle wants us in the library now,' she said. 'The family and you, Mr Athreya.'

Michelle and Athreya were the last to enter the room. Bhaskar and Varadan sat together against a wall, and facing them was a semicircle of five chairs. Manu, Dora and Richie had taken three, leaving two for Michelle and Athreya. Sebastian sat just behind the semicircle.

Athreya pulled the last chair a little away from the rest and sat down. He had a sense of what Bhaskar might have in mind, and wanted to have a clear view of all the faces.

'You already know the contents of the first will,' Bhaskar began. 'I called you all here to tell you about my second will. This is the one that takes effect if I die of *unnatural* causes. There will be a few changes of course, due to Phillip's death. The paintings, which were to go to him, now stay with the mansion.

'I've asked Mr Athreya here for obvious reasons. If I do die of unnatural causes, Mr Athreya will be commissioned to get to the bottom of my death. It is therefore best that he sits in on this short meeting.

'The reason I have chosen to disclose the contents of my second will now is this. There has been a development about last evening that shows that someone has indeed been trying to kill me. The intruder who broke in three months ago and tried to kill me is back in the valley.'

Gasps escaped from Dora and Michelle.

'Where?' Dora demanded.

'Later, Dora. It's not relevant right now. The police are working on it. But coming back to the will: Why am I disclosing the contents of the second will now? Because it is obvious that my ploy of keeping the second will a secret is not working. Why else would the intruder have returned to complete his aborted job?'

'But Uncle—' Dora began.

'Later, girl!' Bhaskar snapped. 'Later. Let me first get to the provisions of the second will.'

Athreya looked around. Michelle and Dora seemed stunned. Richie was listening intently. Manu seemed calm. It was clear that he already knew what was going to be said. Bhaskar would have shared the contents of the will with his son before sharing it with the others. Varadan might have been a wooden statue.

'If I die of unnatural causes,' Bhaskar went on, 'all bequests, except those earmarked for Manu, go into a trust for five years. That means that none of you will be able to access them for five years. The trust will be managed jointly by Manu and Varadan.

'At the end of the five years, each bequest will go to the concerned beneficiary *only* if there is *positive* and *indisputable* proof that the beneficiary did not play a part in my death. *Both* Manu and Varadan must be convinced of this beyond any doubt. The mere absence of incriminating evidence is not sufficient.

'Alternatively, if the person behind my death is identified and apprehended, and both Manu and Varadan are convinced that the right person has been apprehended, the bequests, other than those earmarked for the perpetrator, will be released.

'In the interim, your allowances will continue unchanged, as will a salary to Sebastian, even if Manu chooses not to have him at the mansion. Your bequests, you already know. They are the same as in the first will.'

'Is mine still an annuity for twenty years?' Richie asked.

'Yes, Richie. That will ensure that you will have a steady income for twenty years. After that, when you are older and wiser, the corpus—which is a sizeable amount—will come to you.'

'Can't you reconsider this, Uncle? After all, I could do so much with the money. I could make it grow faster than what an annuity investment would yield.'

'You could, Richie. But, on the other hand, you could deplete it too. My pledge would remain unfulfilled if that were to happen, and my soul wouldn't rest in peace.'

'But, Uncle, you are treating Dora differently.'

'That is because she *is* different.' Bhaskar's tone sharpened, 'Now isn't the time for this discussion, Richie.'

Silence descended on the group. A full minute passed without a sound.

'Well?' Bhaskar asked. 'Any comments?'

When nobody responded, Bhaskar turned to Dora.

'Speak, girl. Say what's on your mind.'

'I don't know how to say this, Uncle, but it seems like… like the three of us are being treated as potential murderers. That's not a nice feeling.'

'Not just you three, Dora. All beneficiaries except Manu. That includes Sebastian, Father Tobias, Murugan, Bhuvana, Bahadur, Gopal, and a bunch of others in Coonoor and Ooty.'

'Still… we are your blood relatives.' There were tears in her eyes. She looked deeply hurt.

'I know it's unfair on the rest of you. But the fact remains that someone is trying to get rid of me.'

'And how do you expect this little speech of yours to change that?' Dora shot back.

'I'm hoping that whoever sent the intruder will now see in black and white that he or she will not benefit from killing me.'

194

'Exactly!' Dora fumed, her eyes afire with fury. 'The person trying to kill you is going to hear what you have said to the three of us. Then that person is either among us three, or someone who is close to one of us. Is that what you think of me, Uncle?'

'Dora—' Bhaskar tried to reason with her, but she cut him off and rose angrily to her feet.

'Isn't the shadow of suspicion already hanging over our heads enough?' she demanded, her voice cracking with emotion. 'Should you pile it on too, Uncle? I am at a total loss. I don't know what I have done to deserve this.' She turned and stormed out of the library.

Athreya entered the chapel and locked the door behind him. The police had finished with the building and, after removing the body and doing a full forensic examination of the crime scene, had returned the keys to him. If Athreya was to find a new clue, it had to be something the police had overlooked. Whatever Muthu's faults may be, he was as tenacious as a bulldog and very thorough.

Athreya stood still about a foot inside the chapel door, narrowed his eyes to slits and tried to mentally travel back in time to when the murder had taken place. He was, of course, familiar with the physical details of the chapel. What he wanted now was to get an intuitive feel of the place, and to put himself in Phillip's shoes.

Why had Phillip come to the chapel?

That, Athreya knew, was the key to the riddle. If he could answer the question, he would take a giant stride forward in the investigation. There was something special about the chapel that had brought Phillip and his killer to it at around 12:30 a.m. that night. What was it?

Phillip would have entered through the chapel door—which Richie had oiled sometime during the day—and would have stood where Athreya was now standing.

The lights would have been off, but Phillip would have silently surveyed the dark chapel. Had he been expecting to find something or someone? Or had he just wanted to ensure that it was empty and he was alone?

Was the wheelchair with Phillip at that time? From the way blood had spilled all over the front of his shirt down to his waist, Athreya was inclined to believe that Phillip had been sitting in the wheelchair when someone came from behind and slit his throat.

But where had the wheelchair and Phillip been when the killer had struck? Surely, such a deep ear-to-ear gash would have severed both the jugular vein and the carotid artery, and made blood gush out. Some of it *must* have spurted out on to the floor.

Where? There hadn't been the slightest trace of blood anywhere in the estate outside the chapel—not on the grass, the walkways or in and around the mansion. It then stood to reason that Phillip's throat had been slit in the chapel.

Even inside, there was very little blood on the floor or the mats. The mat at the corner where the wheelchair had been found had only two small spots of blood on it. Nowhere near the amount that should have been there.

Had Phillip been killed somewhere else in the chapel and then wheeled to the corner? Likely. Very likely. Then, wherever he had been killed, the mats must have soaked up a fair amount of blood. But they had found no bloodied mats. That's because the killer must have removed them. But they would have left telltale signs on the floor underneath them!

Athreya spun to his right and strode along the space behind the pews until he came to the end where two mats were missing. He switched on his torch and crouched, studying the floor.

Five minutes of examination yielded no result. There was not the slightest trace of blood or discoloration. Athreya straightened up. This meant that the two mats from here had been taken to replace the bloodied mats somewhere else in the chapel.

He could get two policemen and have them lift every mat in the chapel and examine the floor. Alternatively, he could guess where Phillip had been killed. A possible answer leapt at him. The one spot that was different from every other in the chapel was the altar.

He strode down the aisle and stopped in front of the altar, studying the mats there. Two showed less signs of wear than those beside them and the ones on the aisle. He bent down, picked up the corner of one mat and pulled it up. Immediately, he saw it.

On the floor was an irregular patch of discoloration the size of a football.

He picked up the other mat and moved it aside. Under it was another patch, a smaller one. A closer examination revealed that it was blood—blood that had soaked through and stained the floor. He replaced the mats and stood with his hands on his hips.

So, Phillip's throat had been slit in front of the altar. Visions of medieval blood rituals and human sacrifices rose to his mind. Suddenly, he recalled the words of Sarala, the wing commander's wife, whom he had met on the toy train on his way to Coonoor. She had talked about devil worship and human sacrifice at Greybrooke Manor.

Whether that was true or not, what was certain was that something evil and malevolent had happened at the altar after midnight. Candles had been moved around, unlit. Someone wearing gloves had done something on the altar. The mats behind the altar had shifted under the weight of a body or bodies. And then, someone without gloves, possibly the person who had slit Phillip's throat, had wiped down the wheelchair.

What a gruesome night. An involuntary shiver ran down Athreya's spine.

He was sure now that more than two people had been at the chapel that night. Not just Phillip and his killer, but others too. But not one of those present had admitted to it. Before he could investigate further, a series of loud knocks sounded at the chapel door. It was Inspector Muthu and two policemen.

'They told me you were here, sir,' he said, his attitude towards Athreya having undergone a sea change. 'Did you find anything new? Our forensics team went through the chapel with a fine-tooth comb.'

'I'm sure they did,' Athreya said. 'What did they say about the blood spots under the mats?'

'Blood spots?' Muthu scowled more out of habit than from any disrespect to Athreya.

'The ones in front of the altar. Under the mats.'

'Show me.'

Two minutes later, Muthu was berating a forensic man over the phone. Athreya slowly walked out of the chapel, his face set in grim lines. He had to call out several bluffs now. Just as he had said to Varadan, he had to strip away the extraneous. Only then would he be able to look at the core.

Athreya found Dora at Sunset Deck, sitting alone and contemplating the ripples in the stream below. He went and sat beside her.

'Do you think I was unjustified in what I did, Mr Athreya?' she asked.

'Not really,' Athreya replied, picking his words carefully. 'Being under a cloud of suspicion is never a pleasant thing. It gnaws away at you, makes you tense and makes you irritable. People in situations like yours have said worse things than you did today.'

'I couldn't stand what Uncle implied. It was too hurtful.'

'That, I cannot argue with. The implications were clear. You had the courage to call it out. The others didn't.'

'Do you think they have something to hide?'

Athreya let out a long sigh. 'There were thirteen at dinner that night,' he said. 'One died. That leaves a dozen of us. Most of the dozen have something to hide. They have either lied or are withholding information.'

'Mr Athreya,' Dora said slowly. 'You do realize the implications of what you are saying, don't you?'

Athreya turned to face her.

'I do, Dora,' he said equally unhurriedly. 'And I hope you do too.'

Dora remained silent. When she didn't speak for a full minute, Athreya went on gently.

'The time for hiding things is past. You do everyone more harm by hiding things. But, most of all, you harm yourself.'

Dora remained silent, neither acknowledging Athreya's allegation nor denying it.

'It is about what you heard and saw after you retired that night, isn't it?' Athreya continued, staring at the stream along with Dora. 'You heard the sound of two doors opening. One was Michelle's. But you know about the other one too. That's what you are hiding. Did you also see him go down the stairs?'

'Yes…' Dora whispered through a choked throat. 'Yes.'

'It must have been between 12:50 and 1 a.m. Am I right?'

Dora nodded again, and turned her face to Athreya.

'What would you have done in my place, Mr Athreya?' she croaked. 'He is my brother.'

'You can't shield Richie forever, Dora. I have one more question to ask you. You remember Thursday evening, the first dinner I had here? Richie came in late?'

She nodded.

'There was a sudden silence when he came in, and tears came to your eyes. I think I know the reason for it. Will you confirm it for me?'

16

Father Tobias had been true to his word. After completing the morning service at his church, he had come down to Greybrooke Manor. When Athreya and Dora returned to the mansion, they saw him in the drawing room, talking to Bhaskar and Sebastian. They were discussing details of the memorial service that was to be held that evening. Sebastian was making a list of people to call.

'Would you like to call Mrs Carvallo?' Athreya asked. 'Phillip's housekeeper.'

'Of course,' Sebastian nodded and made a note. 'I believe she works at the resort. She was fond of him and kept a tidy house, despite Phillip's idiosyncrasies.'

'Idiosyncrasies?'

'The painter in him really messed up the house, you know,' Sebastian said with a slight smile. 'You must see the room he used as his painting studio. There are so many spills and blotches of paint on the rug that you can't make out its original colour. Phillip would leave paints, canvases, brushes and all sorts of things all over the place. If Mrs Carvallo didn't come one day, you could make it out from the state of his house.'

'A bit of a dreamy man, Phillip,' Father Tobias agreed, no less absent-minded himself. 'Forgetful and erratic in his habits. But he was kind and generous. Always willing to help out his fellow men. The few times he did come to the church, he would always drop something into the collection box.'

'Have the police traced his sister?' Athreya asked. 'Jilsy said he had a sister in Pune or somewhere.'

'I believe so,' the priest nodded. 'They found her phone number on his mobile phone, the inspector told me. He had come to ask me if I knew her, and if I could break the sad news to her. Unfortunately, I don't know her. It's always such a shock to receive such news. Especially over the phone.'

'They got her address from her letters they found in his house,' Sebastian added. 'Muthu was thoughtful enough to have a local policeman deliver the news to her husband. I believe they are coming here tomorrow.'

'Ah. That's good.' Father Tobias bobbed his head in a relieved manner. 'There is the matter of his interment. They will have to decide where to bury him.'

The cleric glanced at Bhaskar, but Bhaskar ignored him and remained steadfastly silent. Was Father Tobias expecting Bhaskar to offer the family cemetery to a friend?

'That's, of course, for the family to decide,' the priest went on after a brief pause. 'I hope they have the money.'

'I believe the police found a fair bit of cash in Phillip's house,' Sebastian clarified. 'Phillip only dealt in cash. I don't know if he had a bank account. I've never known him to go to a bank in Coonoor, but he used to pay his rent promptly. Always in cash.'

Athreya wondered what Phillip's source of income had been. Was it only the money he had saved in Austria, or did he have a local source too? He must have invested his savings somewhere. He made a mental note to ask Inspector Muthu about it. On a day-to-day level, how had Phillip replenished his cash supply if he was not in the habit of going to a bank?

The discussion went on to the details of the memorial service. Dora became involved, and Athreya, finding that he couldn't contribute, decided to keep out of the way of those who were organizing it.

He had not completed his examination of the chapel, but there was no chance of continuing it today. He would have to do it tomorrow morning, when the rest of the household was asleep.

He had confronted Michelle and Dora regarding their deceit. There was one more person to confront at the earliest possible moment, but now was not the time for it. Let the memorial service be the sole activity for the day, he decided.

The planning for the service continued during lunch, with Father Tobias, Dora and Manu taking the lead. Sebastian was the one organizing it, and his lunch plate was surrounded by pieces of paper with lists on them.

Athreya retired to his room and checked with his contact in Delhi to see if he had learnt anything new about Phillip. Apart from having developed a greater confidence that Phillip was indeed the Philipose who had disappeared from Austria seven years ago, he had nothing. The high-resolution photographs Athreya had sent him had only confirmed his suspicions.

With his investigations temporarily stalled, Athreya decided to take stock. He sat and wrote down the timings at which various people had been outside the mansion on the night of the murder.

According to the autopsy, the murder had taken place sometime between 12:30 a.m. and 1 a.m. But experience had taught him that these estimates were not cast in stone. Coroners went by averages derived from empirical estimates, which were based on diverse studies. Case-specific variations had to be taken into account over and above that.

Some people digested food faster than others. If that had been true for Phillip, the murder could have taken place before 12:30 a.m., except that Varadan had seen Phillip at around 12:25 a.m. Similarly, if Phillip had been a slow digester, he might have been killed as late as 1:30 a.m.

This meant that Athreya had to operate with the time window of 12:25 a.m. to 1:30 a.m. With that in mind, he went down the list of people and their time logs.

Dora had returned to the mansion at 12:27 a.m., and had been seen by Varadan. Unless she had gone out subsequently, she seemed to be in the clear.

Varadan had gone out at 12:27 a.m., and then conversed with Michelle till about 12:50 a.m. Unless they were both lying, they provided alibis for each other for the early part of that time window. But Varadan was alone after that and would have had the opportunity to kill Phillip.

Michelle had said that she had gone to her room a little before 1 a.m., but there was no evidence to corroborate that. Dora hearing Michelle's door at 12:50 a.m. didn't mean much. It could have been another door. Even if it had been Michelle's, it did not mean that she had entered and stayed in her room.

Richie had stepped out of his room at some time between 12:50 a.m. and 1 a.m. He too would have had the opportunity to kill Phillip. There was little doubt in Athreya's mind that Richie had oiled the chapel door in anticipation of nocturnal activity. He was sure that Richie was one of those who had visited the chapel that night.

Abbas had ended his discussion with Michelle at 12:25 a.m. at Sunset Deck. Nothing was known about his movements after that, although Athreya did suspect him of meeting Murthy sometime later in the rock garden, where they had smoked together. So, Abbas too had the opportunity. Besides, his last admitted location—Sunset Deck—was close to the chapel.

Murthy had been skulking around Greybrooke Manor till about 2 a.m. He too had been in a position to kill Phillip.

Then there was the whole matter of the mongrel. He had been at the resort on the night of the murder, having returned to complete his aborted mission of killing Bhaskar. He would have conducted extensive reconnaissance of the estate, and would have known his way about in the fog. In fact, the fog would have aided him.

And, if Jilsy was right, he was already hand in glove with Abbas, Murthy and Phillip. The question that remained was whether the mongrel had killed Phillip by mistake, taking him to be Bhaskar.

That left Bhaskar, Manu, Sebastian, Ganesh, Father Tobias and Jilsy. None of them had alibis, and all of them, with the possible exception of Jilsy, could have slit a throat. Nothing could have stopped any of them from stepping out into the fog and killing Phillip.

Bhaskar and Manu had their own private French windows through which they could have passed unnoticed. So could Sebastian, if Bhaskar was asleep. Ganesh and Father Tobias were in the annexe, and would have been completely hidden by the fog. Nobody knew precisely where Bahadur was at any point in time.

The list of suspects was still too long. He had to find ways to eliminate some names from it.

With a start, he realized that his right hand had been sketching while his mind had been churning. It was a crude picture of Jesus on a cross, looking down upon a man in a wheelchair. Between the two of them was a broken altar.

The memorial service turned out to be a long, sombre affair that was attended by between thirty and forty people. Athreya hadn't known that there were so many people in the vale. The chapel had been full. All the pews had been taken, and people were standing in the area behind them.

Bhaskar had asked Mrs Carvallo to sit in the first row, with Dora beside her. The family had taken the first row on the right side, and invited guests had sat in the other rows in front. But Jilsy had refused to go anywhere near the spot where Phillip's body had been found, preferring to take the last row on the right.

Athreya had stood in a corner at the back and watched Father Tobias conduct the service with grace and empathy. His tone was just right for the occasion, solemn but clear. He invited people to speak about Phillip, and was kind and encouraging to Mrs Carvallo, who spoke wistfully between bursts of emotion.

Ganesh's loud voice boomed through the chapel as he recalled his relationship with his neighbour. Michelle and Dora said short, quiet pieces, and Bhaskar finished it off with a brief, erudite speech.

Outside the chapel, the mist was gathering again, promising to be as dense as it had been on the day of the murder. At the end of the service, people melted away in groups, most of them going down the path towards the Misty Valley Resort. Not wanting him to risk getting lost in the thickening murk, Bhaskar asked Father Tobias to stay for the night.

When they sat down for dinner, it was a dozen of them—the same group as before, with the exception of Phillip. Bhaskar was back in his motorized wheelchair, which had been cleaned. It had been stripped down to its metal frame, and all the bloodied parts, including the upholstery, had been thrown away. The replaceable sections—the seat, back and armrests—had been replaced with new ones.

'How is your investigation coming along, Mr Athreya?' Ganesh asked amidst a long, awkward silence, trying to spark conversation. 'The revised estimate of the time of death has thrown a spanner in the works, hasn't it?'

'Not really,' Athreya answered. 'Earlier, nobody had an alibi. Now, with the revised time frame, some people seem to have one, at least on the face of it.'

'Any idea of the motive yet? From what we heard at the service today, Phillip seemed to be a well-liked man.'

'A case of mistaken identity may well have prompted the murder, Major. But, just as we have multiple suspects, we're looking at a host of possible motives too, some quite esoteric. Did you know that Phillip spent many years in Austria as an artist, converting photographs to paintings and copying the works of others?'

'Really?'

Several heads jerked up, as the diners transferred their gaze from their plates to Athreya's face.

'Austria?' Manu asked. 'Wow, I didn't realize that he had lived overseas. Usually, that shows up in the way people speak and in their choice of words.'

'He was a reserved man who spoke little,' Dora said. 'Taciturn, really. Maybe that's why it didn't show. In all the years I've known him, I don't think I would have exchanged more than a few dozen sentences with him.'

'That's true, Dora,' Manu agreed. 'He was a quiet man. I wonder who would want to kill such a man. He kept largely to himself.'

'It must have been someone from outside. I just can't see anyone we know wanting to kill him.'

Father Tobias had been watching the exchange across the table as if he were watching a tennis match from the sidelines. His head turned this way and that, from one speaker to the other. With each utterance, he seemed to be getting more confused.

'Pardon me,' he interrupted, apologetically blinking his eyes. 'I don't understand. Why are we talking as if we don't know who killed Phillip?'

'What do you mean, Reverend?' Bhaskar asked, his eyes drilling into the cleric's. 'Of course, we don't know who killed Phillip. Do you?'

'Oh dear.' Father Tobias's face flushed red. 'I must have made a mistake then. I *must* have misheard the inspector.'

'The inspector?'

By now, everyone at the table was staring at the priest, who was clearly feeling awkward under the combined scrutiny.

'Oh dear,' he mumbled again. 'How stupid of me.'

'Tell us what you think you heard, Reverend,' Bhaskar urged.

'Well, Inspector Muthu was very pleased when he came to see me. He said that he had solved the case, and that he had done it without the help of any fancy specialist, whatever that meant.'

The meaning must have been obvious to everyone in the room other than Father Tobias.

'Solved the case?' Bhaskar echoed.

Father Tobias nodded vigorously and went on.

'Apparently, he has already apprehended the man who had broken into this mansion three months ago and attacked you. The dagger that killed Phillip was his, too. And he had been hiding among the staff of the Misty Valley Resort the night Phillip was killed.'

As a stunned silence engulfed the room, Athreya glanced at Abbas. This time, the suave resort owner faltered. He had stopped eating, and his face had begun to blanch. Michelle and Richie also glanced at Abbas.

Into the shocked silence, Father Tobias threw another unwitting bomb.

'Apparently, the arrested man is a well-known criminal, and has been recognized as the one who had tried to kill Bhaskar. He has a nickname. I believe he is called "the mongrel".'

Michelle's eyes flew wide open, and her head snapped to Athreya. By contrast, Jilsy, frightened out of her wits, shut her eyes and fists tightly, as if she wanted to cut out the world. A second later, Ganesh's mouth dropped open.

'The mongrel?' he echoed. 'Phillip was heard talking about the mongrel.'

'What!' Manu exclaimed. 'Phillip knew the mongrel? Are you sure, Major?'

'Very sure.' Ganesh's head bobbed up and down, even as Jilsy kept her eyes shut. 'I heard him talk about the mongrel. Clearly.'

Suddenly, it dawned upon the major that he might have erred seriously. His despairing eyes sought out Athreya. But it was too late. Ganesh shut his mouth with a snap and picked up his glass of rum and Coke. Fortunately, nobody asked him whom Phillip had been talking to when he mentioned the mongrel, and how it was that he had overheard him.

Abbas had paled further, and was looking ashen. With an unsteady hand, he picked up his wine glass and brought it to his lips, keeping his eyes on the table the entire time. Michelle was staring at Abbas, her lips compressed and her nostrils flaring. Her eyes were glistening with moisture. An expression of incredulity came over Richie's face. Dora, Sebastian and Varadan were also staring at the resort owner.

When Athreya took his eyes off Abbas, he found Bhaskar staring at him. He returned the gaze unflinchingly and nodded slightly, telling Bhaskar that he had known about the mongrel's association with Phillip.

'So,' Manu hissed. 'Phillip had known the mongrel, eh?' He looked uncharacteristically angry. 'That answers a few questions, doesn't it?'

'What questions?' Dora asked. She was still stunned at the sudden turn of events.

'First, how did the mongrel get into the mansion that evening, three months ago?' Manu asked. 'Murugan had locked up the house. He and Sebastian were in the storeroom in the staff quarters. Only three people were in the main mansion: Dad, Phillip and me.

'Dad had retired for the night, and his wheelchair had been plugged in for charging. I was in bed, reading. Phillip was in the room you are now staying in, Mr Athreya. All the doors and windows were locked, both Murugan and I had checked them just fifteen minutes previously. And, after the break-in, we checked each door and window again—none of them had been forced open.

'So, you see what I am getting at? The mongrel couldn't have got in... unless someone *let* him in!'

'Jesus!' Sebastian exclaimed. 'Murugan and I were in the store-room when we heard the gunshot. We had begun our stocktaking immediately after locking up the main house.'

'Second question,' Manu went on. 'Who took the dagger from the drawer in the hall? Where did it go? Did Phillip take it? Did he return it to the mongrel?'

'Third question,' Sebastian cut in, his face intense with anger. 'You remember the time when Mr Fernandez went to Coonoor, and the car's brakes failed after we had visited the bank?'

'What about it?' Bhaskar growled.

'Phillip had come with us on the outbound journey, but had decided to stay and return later. He had no friends in Coonoor, and didn't even bank there. All his purchases were made by others. Why then did he opt to stay?'

'Sebastian,' Bhaskar said. 'Do you remember where you had parked the car that day in Coonoor? Some by-lane, wasn't it? Because you couldn't get parking near the bank.'

'Yes. You had to wait for five minutes for me to bring the car. It was three or four streets away on a side road.'

'An ideal opportunity to tamper with the brakes!' Manu finished. 'Where was Phillip during that half hour we were at the bank?'

'We don't know. We didn't know what he did or where he went.'

'What do you think, Mr Athreya?' Manu asked, his face shining. 'Could Phillip have been behind at least some of the attempts on Dad's life?'

'Possible, Manu,' Varadan interjected before Athreya could respond. 'But we must keep in mind that all this is circumstantial evidence.'

'Mr Varadan is right,' Athreya said. 'I would not jump to conclusions without further consideration.' He turned to Bhaskar and asked, 'You and Phillip talked a lot about paintings, didn't you?'

'Yes. That was possibly the only topic he was keen to talk about.'

'Did he ever talk about stolen paintings?'

'Stolen paintings!' Manu cried. 'What on earth?'

Athreya didn't answer him, and kept his gaze on Bhaskar. The older man's face had frozen. He seemed to be thinking, mentally going back in time. At length, he lifted his eyes and nodded.

'Yes,' he said haltingly. 'When I talked about crime and read out some escapades to him from my books in the library, he asked if I had any stories—true or fictional—about crime in art. About stolen paintings. He wanted to know how easy or difficult it was to sell stolen art. I had a few books that I lent him. I also recommended a couple of stories in which priceless stolen paintings were concealed by painting over them with a type of paint that was easily removable.

'This was done in real life too during the Second World War, to hide precious art from the Nazis. The idea was to fool them into thinking that certain paintings were ordinary, so they wouldn't steal or destroy them. Once the Nazi threat had receded, the top layer of paint would be removed to reveal the original painting.

'There were also cases where a precious painting would be hidden behind the canvas of an ordinary painting. The two canvases would be mounted together so that the precious canvas was hidden behind the ordinary canvas. The only way to discover this was to weigh the mounted paintings or to use curved outside callipers to measure the thickness of the canvas. If there were two canvases instead of one, it would show up.'

'Dad!' Manu cried. 'Outside callipers… is that an instrument with two curved arms joined together at a pivot? Like the curved claws of a crab?'

'Yes. And it has a knob and a scale at the pivot for measurement.'

'Dad... Dad,' said Manu, choking. He coughed a few times and recovered. 'Dad... I've seen Phillip with one,' he said in a strangled voice. 'I saw him measuring the thickness of some of the larger paintings in the gallery here, as recently as last week.'

'The paintings he sold you, Mr Fernandez,' Athreya asked sharply. 'Did he sell them to you as canvases or as mounted paintings?'

'Mounted paintings,' Bhaskar whispered. 'Always mounted. He was very good at mounting them. He even mounted some of my other paintings.'

'If Dad had died that day,' Manu said fiercely, 'the entire painting collection would have gone to Phillip. The undeserving betrayer!'

17

As they adjourned to the drawing room after dinner, Bhaskar drew Athreya into the library. The discovery of Phillip's treachery had shaken him, as it had affected the rest of the family. They had discussed their nasty discovery repeatedly, and had grown increasingly convinced of Phillip's betrayal.

Three times could not have been a coincidence. And the first occasion—when the intruder had been let in by somebody—brooked no other explanation. That Bhaskar had been kind to him, and had financially supported him by buying his paintings, only made it more difficult for them to accept the revelation.

'The mongrel has made me an offer,' Bhaskar said quietly, once they were alone in the library. 'Varadan has been to town and has seen him at the police lock-up. He had asked to speak to my representative privately, which Muthu had allowed for five minutes. As you know, his conviction may well hinge on my identifying him as the intruder who had broken into my house and tried to kill me.

'The offer is simple. If I agree to not recognize him, he will tell me who commissioned him.'

'Cunning,' Athreya said. 'He may look an ordinary ruffian, but he is no fool. I take it that Muthu got no whiff of this offer?'

'None. He is playing it by the book. He insists that I should identify the little man only in a line-up, as mandated by law. That way, the prosecution's process will be watertight. He could easily have brought the rascal here, at least informally. But that might play into the hands of a smart defence lawyer.'

'Muthu is playing his hand well. I wonder how convinced he is that the mongrel killed Phillip.'

'You don't think he did?' Bhaskar countered, studying Athreya's face.

'He might have, but that would only be a part of the answer. It throws no light on the other major question.'

'Which is?'

'What was Phillip doing in your wheelchair in the chapel in the middle of a murky night?'

'It doesn't, I agree,' said Bhaskar, nodding. 'Coming back to the scoundrel's proposition, what do you think?'

'Don't you already know who commissioned him, Mr Fernandez?'

Bhaskar let out a tired sigh. 'Perhaps I do, Mr Athreya… perhaps I do. The heart is more willing to accept one part of what the brain says. But there is another part that I wish wasn't true.'

'Murthy?' Athreya asked.

Bhaskar nodded pitiably.

'Imagine what that would do to Michelle, Mr Athreya. She will be broken.'

'It may also be for the best,' Athreya said softly. 'I think the scales are falling from her eyes.'

'She lied about the time of death to protect him,' Bhaskar retorted. 'That was a mere thirty-six hours ago.'

'Much has happened since, and the events have left Michelle emotionally wrung out. There is a possibility that she may follow your advice.'

Bhaskar stared hard at him, but didn't ask how Athreya knew about his advice to her.

'So,' he said, returning to the original question, 'should I accept the offer?'

'How do you know he will keep his word? Once you examine the line-up and say that you don't recognize anyone, there is no going back.'

'True. What do you suggest I do?'

'Postpone the decision. Let matters play out.'

'One more question… you spoke about Phillip being in Austria. What name did he go by there?'

'Philipose. At least, that's how he signed his paintings. If he had another name too, I don't know it yet.'

'Jacob,' Bhaskar said in an undertone. 'Does the name Jacob Lopez ring a bell?'

'No. But I'll see what I can find out.'

'I returned from Austria in 1996. Phillip seems to have been there much later. Do you know when?'

'Between 2008 and 2012, I believe.'

'Jacob Lopez was released from prison in late 2007. Like Phillip, he too was of Indian origin.'

When Athreya returned to the drawing room, he found Jilsy waiting for him. Ganesh, Varadan, Manu and Father Tobias were talking together in one corner, while Dora, Michelle and Richie were whispering to each other in another. Abbas was nowhere to be seen, and Sebastian had gone to talk to Bhaskar in the library.

'Can I talk to you, Mr Athreya?' Jilsy asked in a small, frightened voice.

'Of course, Jilsy.' Athreya smiled. 'Where would you like to talk?'

'Somewhere private. Where nobody can hear or disturb us.'

'We can go to my room or to yours, whichever you prefer. We might be interrupted in the study. Or else, we can walk outside.'

'Outside?' Jilsy gasped.

She took one look at the dark, gloomy night and shook her head. The fog was as thick as it had been on the night of the murder. Memories of that night were all too fresh in her memory.

'Can we go to your room, if you don't mind?' she asked. 'I'll tell Ganesh and then come.'

Soon, they were in Athreya's room, sitting in chairs facing each other.

'What should we do, Mr Athreya?' she asked as soon as they were settled. 'You told us not to speak about the mongrel, but Ganesh blurted it out. He is afraid too. More for me than for himself.'

'Nothing,' Athreya replied. 'Do nothing. Don't talk about it, but don't avoid the subject either, at least in an obvious manner. If someone asks, Ganesh can say that he doesn't remember when he had heard Phillip mention the mongrel's name. He can probably say that he might have heard him speak over the phone to someone. That way, you will avoid the question of who Phillip was speaking to when he mentioned the mongrel.'

'You think that will work?' Jilsy asked doubtfully.

'That's the best you can do now. If you try avoiding the subject, people may think that you know more than you are letting on. That could be dangerous.'

'I guess you're right.'

'And Ganesh should not say that you too overheard Phillip.'

'Yes.' She nodded animatedly. 'We understand that. Ganesh won't make a mistake again. Thank you, Mr Athreya.'

'If you have another fifteen minutes, I want to speak to you on another matter—here alone and totally in private.'

Jilsy stared at him with large, round eyes and nodded.

'Now, for your sake, and that of your husband, I want you to not get up and run away in the middle of the conversation. It's going to be a difficult one… perhaps harder than any conversation you've recently had. Understand?'

She nodded mutely, anxiety etched on her face.

'Please understand that I am trying to help you. I know that you did not kill Phillip.'

Her eyes became saucers. She stared at Athreya dumbstruck.

'Jilsy,' he said tenderly, 'I know that you went into the chapel on the night of the murder.'

A stifled cry escaped her and she recoiled, shrinking into the chair, trying to disappear into it. She stared at Athreya as if hypnotized, unable to tear her eyes away from his. He stared back at her. A full minute passed.

'You went there a little after 1 a.m., didn't you?' Athreya asked gently.

That broke the spell. With a soft whimper, Jilsy buried her face in her hands and began sobbing silently. Her shoulders shook and her hair fell forward over her hands and face, hiding them.

'Let me tell you a story, Jilsy,' Athreya said in an avuncular manner. 'You don't need to look up at me. Just listen to what I say. It's a story about a young, vivacious city girl; a girl who loved being with people, enjoyed being in the midst of things. She had a large circle of friends in Pune, and spent much of her time with them. She loved parties, travelling, shopping... everything that a lively young girl of her kind liked.

'After she got married, she continued to enjoy herself. As an army wife, there was endless socializing to do, if she desired it. And she did. Life was a lovely, merry party.

'But when she moved and settled in a place that was the back of beyond, life changed abruptly. There were no friends to speak of, no girls of her age or disposition. There was nowhere to go. No shops, no movies, no concerts, no gatherings, no malls... in short, no city. She got bored out of her skull, living day in and day out in this monotonous place.'

Jilsy had stopped sobbing, and was listening with her face still buried in her hands and her long tresses covering both.

'Then, one day, out of sheer boredom, she grew venturesome. She broke the rules of marriage. She did something imprudent, risky. Something she would never have done had it not been for the boredom. She repented it immediately and was mortified. "Never again", she told herself.

'But boredom is a powerful thing. It is relentless. It slowly, but surely, crushes you. There came a time when she was tempted again. She succumbed, and broke the rules of marriage once more.

'Again, she felt embarrassed, but this time it didn't last for as long. She succumbed to temptation for a third time. It was becoming easier. Thrice she had broken the rules, and thrice, she had not been caught.

'Alas, she took refuge from the unrelenting boredom in her little escapades, convincing herself that they were only temporary. She could stop it any time she wished, she told herself, and things would go back to how they were. But she was wrong.'

Jilsy lifted her face an inch or two from her hands, but did not look up. Her eyes looked downwards even as her ears took in every word Athreya said.

'What she hadn't realized was how people talk loosely. The ones she thought were her confidantes were anything but. Soon, the valley knew about her escapades, and rumours of her dalliances spread to the nearby town too.'

Athreya fell silent. He rose and went to the window. He remained there, looking out, with his back to Jilsy. A minute passed. Jilsy stayed bent forward. Another minute passed. Eventually, she lifted her face. Athreya stayed where he was, with his back to her, not wanting to embarrass her by looking at her.

She must be feeling wretched, humiliated beyond measure. Her secret had been blown open by a stranger—a man. The only saving grace, if any, was Athreya's age.

'If you are thinking that this is none of my business, you are partially right,' he said. 'Had it not been for this murder, I

217

wouldn't have intruded. But, as fate would have it, your activities are closely tied with those of the murderer. I hope you will understand. I hope you will forgive me. Your secret is safer with me than with those who betrayed your confidence.'

Athreya fell silent. Jilsy was sitting up now, wiping her face.

'It was Richie, wasn't it?' Athreya asked eventually. 'I need to know because I must eliminate possibilities. Only then can I catch the murderer.'

'Yes,' said a low, broken voice from behind him.

'Behind the altar?' he asked gently.

'Yes… how did you know?'

'The mats behind the altar had shifted under the weight of bodies. And your blue nightgown caught and ripped on one of the benches, leaving a scrap of cloth behind.'

'Oh, God. What have I done!'

'Another question, Jilsy… did you enter through the chapel door or the window?'

'Window.'

'What time was the rendezvous?'

'1:10… 1:15.'

'And when did you leave the chapel?'

'About 1:45.'

'Through the window?'

'Yes… I didn't want to risk using the door… it's visible from the mansion.'

'You were there from 1:15 to 1:45 a.m.… didn't you see Phillip's body in the corner?'

'No! You must believe me… I didn't.'

'I believe you, Jilsy. That's why you threw up, I know. You were disgusted at the thought of the body lying there all the time when you—'

'Please, don't go into that! I beg you!'

'I won't, but the next question is important. During that half hour, did anyone come in?'

'No. Thankfully… no.'

'And when you left… did you hear or see anything?'

'No.'

'And Richie left immediately afterwards?'

'I guess so.'

'The candles on the altar… did you see how they were placed?'

'No. No. It was too dark.'

'Thank you. I'm sorry that I had to put you through this. Now, take your time and compose yourself. I won't turn from the window until you leave the room. I have embarrassed you enough. I'm sorry.'

The room fell silent for another two minutes. Athreya kept his word and stared steadfastly out of the window. Then to his surprise, she spoke.

'Mr Athreya?' she said softly.

'Yes, Jilsy?'

'Turn around… please.'

Athreya blinked in surprise. 'Are you sure?' he asked.

'Yes, I am.' Jilsy's voice was steady. 'I want to see your face.'

Athreya slowly turned to see her standing in the middle of the room, looking at him through pensive eyes. Her face had been rubbed clean of make-up. She looked lonely, vulnerable.

'You have been far more decent than you needed to be,' she said. 'You didn't call me out for what I am.'

'You are nothing but an unfortunate young lady who has erred.'

'Thank you… you are too kind. But that's not what I wanted to talk about. I wanted to ask about one of the things you said. Does the whole valley really know?'

Her eyes were full of shame. Athreya nodded silently.

'Bhaskar? Manu?' she asked.

'Yes. Others, too. Dora is aghast and ashamed at Richie. She agonizes over what he does and sheds tears.'

'My husband…' she began wretchedly, but couldn't finish. Her words hung in the air.

'He doesn't, as far as I know. He is one of the few who doesn't. Also because he trusts you. He will not think ill of you.'

Her voice shook. 'He deserves better.'

Jilsy gnawed at her lower lip for a long moment, thinking furiously. Athreya waited. At length, she looked up.

'If I promise to never do this again, Mr Athreya—*never*—will you help us leave this valley?'

'In what way?'

'With what has just happened, I am going to tell my husband that it is dangerous for us to remain here. There is no telling what the mongrel could do to us after being released from jail. After all, we were the ones who tipped you off about him.

'I'm going to tell Ganesh that we must leave this place as soon as we can. This will become a closed chapter; I will never return to this place. We can settle happily somewhere else. I promise that I will *never ever* be so stupid again. Will you help me, sir? Will you back me up when I tell Ganesh that we need to leave this place forever?'

'I will.'

'Thank you, sir. I couldn't have asked for more.'

It was going to be an uneasy night. Athreya could sense the disquiet among the guests when he returned to the drawing room. There had been thirteen at dinner on Friday, and Phillip had been killed. Now, a dozen remained, and the night was disconcertingly similar to Friday. Grey coils of mist, heavy and damp, swirled in the valley, reducing visibility to a few feet. Low clouds hung overhead, shrouding the world in inky darkness. It was only the light spilling from the French windows and the feeble glow of a few lamps along the walkways that challenged the night's reign.

Talk was desultory and faces wary. Yet, people seemed reluctant to break up the gathering. They were drawing comfort from being together in a group, putting off the loneliness of the bedroom for as long as they could.

Ganesh took refuge in his rum and Coke as Jilsy sat beside him, preoccupied and silent. Perhaps she was contemplating her personal watershed, unable as she was to share it with her husband. Bhaskar brooded in a corner, exchanging sporadic words with Varadan and Father Tobias. Sebastian and Manu were talking in low tones, with Richie listening nervously. Dora and Michelle seemed comfortable with each other's silence. Abbas had returned to his room in the annexe.

Athreya's vivid imagination, which often helped him see beyond the obvious, was hyperactive tonight, showing him glimpses of the phantoms that seemed to be waltzing in others' minds. Several pairs of eyes turned to him frequently, perhaps taking comfort in his presence. All doors, he knew, would be locked tonight, and the sun would be welcomed in the morning with rare fervour.

As the grandfather clock chimed at the stroke of midnight, the gathering stirred uncomfortably. It was getting late. They had to return to their rooms sooner or later. Athreya took the lead despite not feeling sleepy in the least. This festering morbidity, he knew, should not be allowed to get out of hand.

'Time to retire,' he said brightly, smiling with a lightness he did not feel. 'Need to get my forty winks if I have to get up in time for my morning jog.'

'Good night, Mr Athreya,' Bhaskar said, taking the cue. 'I'll retire, too. It's past midnight.'

'Me, too.' Manu broke away from Sebastian and smiled at Athreya, 'Goodnight, sir.' He nodded to his father and continued, 'Sebastian and I will lock up.'

That ended the evening. The four people staying at the annexe went out together, and Sebastian locked the French windows after them. Richie, Dora and Michelle drained their glasses and went upstairs as Manu checked the front door. A few seconds later, Athreya was in his room.

But sleep refused to come. His overactive mind refused to settle down, drawing tenuous links between disparate facts as it strove to stitch them into a patchwork tapestry of sound logic. His practical half, however, reiterated that all the evidence had not yet come in. It would be premature to draw conclusions.

An hour passed as he tossed and turned in bed. Then another. A long while later, he got out of bed and looked at his watch. It was 2:35 a.m. He decided to go to the windows and breathe in the damp night air. The mist had thinned somewhat, but it was still murky outside.

As he stood at the window, it occurred to him that this was the room Phillip had been staying in when the mongrel broke in. The bars on the window had been put in afterwards. All the mongrel had to do was to scale the six- or seven-foot wall below the window, and he would have been inside the room. Easy.

Even as the thought occurred to him, he heard a sharp click. Someone had unlatched a door in haste, shooting the bolt back without regard to the sound it produced. The next moment, he heard slippered feet running down the art gallery. Then came two clicks that he recognized. The person had opened the back door.

Athreya pressed his face against the bars of his window and craned his neck, wondering if he could see the person as he or she emerged from the walkway at the rear. But it was pitch-dark. The night intended to keep its secrets.

Sounds, however, carried well in the still night air. The patter of feet came from the walkway. They hurried away—heading towards the chapel.

As soon as Athreya realized where they were going, the hair on his arms stood on end. His senses sharpened and he involuntarily slowed down his breathing, so it did not interfere with his hearing. He continued to look leftward towards the chapel.

Less than a minute later, a hazy patch of illumination flared. The lights in the chapel were on, and spilling out into the misty night through its door. Judging by the lack of other sounds and the quickness with which the light had appeared, Athreya figured that the door, which he had locked that evening, was already open.

Fifteen seconds later, although it seemed like five long minutes, an inarticulate cry came from the chapel. It was Sebastian's voice, and he was furious. He was shouting as loudly as he could, trying to awaken people in the mansion and alert them to some drastic happening.

Moments later, a gunshot sounded. Then another. Athreya stood riveted to the window, his eyes wide open and his ears primed. He had the rare opportunity to witness the drama as it was happening. It was imperative that he continue to watch—others would respond to Sebastian's call. His eyes focused on the dim blotch of light in the distance.

Even as these thoughts flashed through his mind, he heard sounds from inside the mansion. Manu was opening his door. Feet thudded across the floor of the room above Athreya's.

The hazy light dimmed momentarily as a figure appeared in the chapel's doorway. It kicked at something very close to the threshold, and Athreya saw long legs scissoring as it ran out of the door. It wore darkish trousers and some sort of a jacket.

Just as the figure seemed to have escaped, a hand shot out from inside the chapel and caught it by the jacket. With a jerk, the figure yanked it away and ran, heading down the walkway parallel to the mansion.

Within a few yards of the chapel door, the figure melted away into the night, as the light from the chapel faded. Athreya heard footsteps down the walkway, past his window. But he could see nothing.

Meanwhile, the mansion had erupted in an assortment of sounds. Bhaskar bellowed for Sebastian and Manu. Michelle's and Dora's high-pitched voices were asking questions that drew no answers. Doors thudded somewhere further off, probably in the staff quarters.

When he was sure there was nothing more to see, Athreya turned from the windows, pulled on his jacket and hurried out of his room into the lighted corridor. He ran to Bhaskar's door, knocked perfunctorily and pushed it open.

Bhaskar was sitting up in bed with his automatic in his hand.

'What happened?' he demanded.

'Shots at the chapel,' Athreya snapped back. 'Stay here and keep your automatic handy. Someone has a gun. I'll come back.'

Leaving Bhaskar's door open, he ran out of the back door, towards the chapel. When he got there, he found Manu and Ganesh bending over Sebastian, who was lying in the aisle, close to the door. His nightshirt was drenched in blood from two very visible, gaping wounds. His eyes had glazed over and he didn't seem to be breathing. In his hand was a ripped piece of cloth.

'Get Michelle!' Manu yelled to Athreya.

Athreya spun around and ran to the back door of the mansion, where Murugan and Gopal were standing, having just emerged from the staff quarters. Athreya ran into the gallery, calling for Michelle at the top of his voice.

'Coming!' she yelled back and came down the stairs with her medical bag.

'Sebastian has been shot!' Athreya called to Bhaskar through his open door and ran back to the chapel with Michelle.

Within a minute, he knew that there was little hope. The bullet wounds were near the heart, and Sebastian's eyes had rolled upward. As Athreya stepped around the fallen man, his foot touched something on the floor. It was a soft leather pouch, flat and rectangular. It must have fallen when Sebastian ripped the killer's jacket. At once he knew what the pouch was: a set of lock picks.

Taking a clean cloth from Michelle's medical bag, he picked it up and dropped it into his pocket. Lock-picking, he knew from experience, was notoriously difficult to do with gloved hands. Moreover, the metal handles of the lock picks carried fingerprints very well.

He walked slowly down the aisle and stopped a yard or two from the altar. Someone had opened the two small cabinets built into the wooden stands that supported the ends of the altar stone.

He looked up at the mural of Jesus on the cross. It was looking down at him and the altar. At that moment, things fell into place. He knew what his subconscious mind had been trying to tell him through the last sketch. He knew whose fingerprints he would find on the lock picks.

18

An hour later, Athreya stood where Phillip had been killed, in front of the dais and the altar. So, both murders had something to do with the altar. Blood had been spilled before it, the wooden cabinets below it had been forced open, and the candles on it had been moved around. Something about the altar had instigated two murders. He went up the dais to a cupboard, switched on the lights above the altar and stood behind the altar, studying it.

From his wallet, he pulled out a very thin, flexible strip of plastic. This he inserted between two of the stone slabs—the ones in the middle and on the left side—that formed the top of the altar. The plastic strip slid inside easily. He held it in place and moved it along the hairline crack between the two stones. It went all the way to the far edge of the altar.

He repeated the exercise along the crack between the middle and right-side slabs. The strip slid through the length without resistance. The forensic man had been right. The three slabs that made up the altar stone were not attached to each other.

This meant two things. First, the altar top had been designed as three separate pieces that were structurally independent of each other. And second, since they were structurally separate, they should be able to move independently of each other.

He crouched on the floor and shone his torch into one of the small cabinets—more cubbyholes than cabinets. It was empty. He did the same thing at the cubbyhole at the other end. Same result: it, too, was empty.

Athreya stood up and considered the possibilities. Had the cubbyholes contained something? Had Sebastian's murderer taken away whatever they had contained? Or did they serve an entirely different purpose? If they did, they warranted a closer examination.

He lay down on the floor with his head at the opening of one of the cubbyholes. Resting one cheek on the mat, he peered into the dark recess. The torch that was pressed to his other cheek cast a beam into the space. At first glance, the black-painted interior seemed empty and featureless.

After a few moments, he noticed what seemed to be a small plastic box, also black, attached to the roof of the compartment at the very corner. It seemed to be a small electrical connection box or some sort of device that came along with electronic gadgets. On closer examination, he saw the bulge of a tiny LED bulb peeping out of a hole in the box. It was the kind that served as an indicator whether the box was receiving power or not.

Athreya rose and went to the large cupboard at one end of the dais and opened it. He had seen a row of switches there. Several of them were already on. He flipped down the rest, one by one. A few more lights came to life, but two switches seemed to do nothing.

Leaving those two on, he returned to the cubbyhole and peered into it. The tiny LED was now glowing red. Still lying down with his cheek pressed against the floor, he probed the box with his fingers. He found a small gap between it and the side wall of the compartment. At once, he saw four wires: two black and two red, running from the plastic box into the wood.

He raised himself on his elbows and sat cross-legged on the floor, his mind churning. He was beginning to see why the altar had attracted so much attention. He now viewed the gilded altar with fresh eyes, taking in the solid combination of wood, stone and metal. Two polished wood cabinets and five metal pillars in a row at the centre supported the heavy altar stone, which itself

227

comprised three sections. The two end sections of the stone rested on the wooden cabinets, while the middle section stood on the pillars.

Having studied the cabinets, he transferred his attention to the pillars. They were made of stainless steel, and each was about five inches thick. The bottom ends had been embedded into the stone floor and fastened with metal brackets. But the tops had not.

Rather than being attached to the stone slab they supported, the top ends ran into slightly larger stainless-steel tubes that were about three inches long. The fit was perfect. These tubes, which were attached to the stone slab with brackets, were just large enough for the five pillars to fit snugly into them.

Athreya stood up and looked around. He was alone in the chapel. Sebastian's body lay where it had fallen, waiting for the police and the forensic team to arrive. Athreya went back to the large cupboard at the end of the dais and turned off the switches. The lights over the aisle continued to glow as he made his way to the door.

There, he stood for a moment looking down at the still form of Sebastian. He slowly shook his head and walked out. He now knew the secret of the chapel. He knew what had invited death there.

What he needed was confirmation and corroborative evidence.

Back in his room, Athreya found that he had received a text message. His contact in Delhi had obtained new information from Europe, and had sent it to Athreya in the wee hours of the night. There were seventeen articles related to significant happenings in the art world around Vienna in 1994 and 1995. As Athreya read through them one by one, three pieces stood out:

MARCEL FESSLER KILLED

Marcel Fessler, a reclusive art collector, aged 77, was accidentally killed when a burglar broke into his suburban home with the intent of stealing artworks from his collection. It is believed that the burglar was surprised by Mr Fessler. When the burglar employed force in a bid to escape, Mr Fessler fell and hit his head on the base of a marble statue and died. The burglar escaped without carrying out his intent to steal art. Having been seen by two witnesses while fleeing, the burglar was identified as one Jacob Lopez, and was later apprehended. He was sentenced to twelve years' imprisonment for manslaughter and attempted burglary.

NOTE: Jacob Lopez was released from prison in 2007.

KÜNZI BROTHERS KILLED IN CAR CRASH

The two Künzi Brothers, suspected to be dealers in stolen art, and possibly art thieves themselves, died in a car crash when the vehicle they were travelling in went off a mountainous road in the Danube valley, 40 miles north-west of Vienna. The car is said to have fallen 300 feet into a ravine and exploded, charring its occupants. There were no eyewitnesses to the accident.

BALSANO LANDSCAPES BOUGHT FOR $27 MILLION

Four paintings by renowned artist Fabian Balsano were auctioned for an astonishing price of $26,850,000. The paintings, sold by the estate of the German billionaire Stefan Koch, were purchased by an agent on behalf of an unknown buyer.

Athreya replied, asking his contact to compare Jacob Lopez's fingerprints with the sets that he had sent, and to see if any link between Jacob and Philipose could be established.

He then sent a message to Rajan, asking him to phone once he was awake, and was surprised to receive a call right away. Rajan, it seemed, had risen before the sun.

'Do you know anyone in Coorg?' Athreya asked. 'I need to have some enquiries made urgently, preferably before people start work today.'

'There is a team looking into drug trafficking in the Western Ghats,' Rajan said. 'There is apparently a chain operating from Kodai to Ooty to Coorg. They were here on Saturday. One member of the team has gone to Coorg. I can speak to him. What do you need him to do?'

Athreya told him.

Two hours later, Athreya was riding in the police wagon carrying Sebastian's body to Coonoor for an autopsy. Leaving Greybrooke Manor in Inspector Muthu's charge, with instructions not to let anyone leave, especially Abbas, Athreya had hitched a ride.

His first stop was the police lock-up where the mongrel was being detained. After verifying with the policemen on duty that he had been in the jail all night, Athreya went to speak to the prisoner.

The nickname turned out to be apt. It perfectly described the small-built, bellicose man, who was given to quick movements. He had an angular face with quick, hostile eyes and ears that seemed to stand out a little from his head. A narrow mouth under a drooping moustache and twitching eyebrows completed the picture.

The mongrel watched warily as Athreya entered the cell. He remained silent, made no movement and stared unblinkingly. A constable brought a chair for Athreya, which he took silently.

When the constable left, the mongrel finally spoke.

'Who are you?' he asked, his voice sounding like a soft growl.

'I am investigating Phillip's murder,' Athreya replied. 'I heard about your offer to Mr Fernandez.'

Slowly, the wary look melted, and a smug one took its place. The prisoner relaxed visibly as his eyes ran over Athreya afresh, taking in the lack of uniform or anything else that could be remotely official. Athreya could almost hear his thoughts: *Here is a private representative of Bhaskar, having come to negotiate.*

'I have said what I had to say,' the mongrel declared. 'It is Fernandez's turn to act. There is nothing to talk about till he fulfils his part of the bargain.'

'*Is* there a bargain?' Athreya asked mildly. 'The lawyer carried your offer to Mr Fernandez. What makes you think he accepted it?'

'He has no choice,' the little man snarled, looking more like a mongrel than ever. 'Otherwise, he will never know who took out a contract on him.'

'He already knows,' Athreya countered. 'So do I. So does everyone else at Greybrooke Manor.'

'You lie.'

A moment later, the mongrel grinned as he grew assured. He let out a long chuckle. He seemed to think Athreya was bluffing. He leaned back and laced his fingers.

'I know your type,' he said. 'You have come to negotiate. You will first bluff. Then you will act as if nothing matters to Fernandez. And finally, you will threaten.'

'You seem to be very sure of yourself,' Athreya chuckled. 'For a man who holds no trump cards, you are overly confident and brash. You are playing from a poor hand, my friend. You hold no high cards—no aces or kings. Only small, useless cards.'

'Ah! This is the first scene where you bluff.' The little man smirked. 'Go on, go on. I'll play along.'

'Excellent.' Athreya nodded. 'Since we understand each other, let me tell you a little story. I'm talking about what you did three months ago.

'After dinner, when it was dark and misty, you skulked over to Greybrooke Manor from the Misty Valley Resort. You walked alone with the only companion you trusted—a narrow dagger with a wooden handle bound in leather.

'On reaching the mansion, you waited. You saw Sebastian and the younger Fernandez go about the house, locking the doors and windows. But you were not concerned. You knew that you would have a way in when the time came. You waited for the sign from the window of the middle room on the ground floor, the room I am now staying in. It was then occupied by Phillip.'

The mongrel's smirk faded a little at the mention of the name and the identification of the window.

'At length, the window opened and the sign came. All you had to do was to climb up six or seven feet to the windowsill. You did that, and entered the room. You then opened the door and entered the dark corridor, where you turned right. Old man Fernandez must be asleep by now, you thought. In any case, he was a cripple.

'But you were mistaken. Mr Fernandez was not asleep. Nor was he as helpless as you supposed. You entered and went towards his bed, only to find him rising with a gun in his hand. Did you know that he chose not to kill you?

'You dropped your dagger when the bullet hit your leg. You had a choice to make, as you were already halfway into his room. You could go back the way you came, but Phillip's door might be closed. Alternatively, there was a set of unbarred French windows in front of you. You chose the latter.

'Somehow, you limped your way to the Misty Valley Resort where Ismail hid you. The same night, a vehicle took you to Coimbatore, where a crooked doctor dressed your bullet wound.'

Athreya paused and waited for the mongrel to assimilate what he had said.

'Now,' he continued, 'you have heard me name two people who helped you: Phillip and Ismail. But neither of them was the one who commissioned you. Ismail was an agent, and Phillip was a helper. The boss was someone else.

'I will give you two more names. Then, you tell me if I am bluffing. The names are Abbas and Murthy.'

At the beginning of Athreya's monologue, the mongrel's expression had been of one who had bet everything on a single card, which he believed was a winner. He now looked like someone whose hand had turned out to be a dud. The smirk had been wiped off, and his assurance shattered. He had just realized that he had no more cards to play.

'So you see,' Athreya continued, 'there is no bargain to be made. Mr Fernandez has rejected your offer out of hand. He will have no truck with you. At this point, let me let you in on a secret... Mr Fernandez doesn't know I am here. He doesn't know that I have come to see you.'

'Then why are you here?' the mongrel croaked.

'I will tell you, but before that, I am going to make out another case against you. One that Inspector Muthu is convinced about. What happened three months ago was *attempted* murder. The case against you now is for *murder*: the murder of Phillip.'

'I did not kill Phillip,' the mongrel snarled.

'No?' Athreya mocked. 'Inspector Muthu thinks you did. He can't be convinced otherwise. Permit me to lay out the case against you.'

The mongrel was staring at him with wide, fearful eyes.

'You were at the Misty Valley Resort on Friday night,' Athreya began. 'That too was a foggy, murky night like the one three months ago. Abbas and Phillip were already at Greybrooke Manor. Murthy went there at 11 p.m. You followed him.

'You lurked for a long time as the residents of the mansion wandered about the lawns and gardens. Hidden by the thick fog, you crept about, keeping out of people's way, but overhearing their conversations. You overheard a very interesting discussion between Abbas and Murthy at the rock garden; one that gave you material for blackmail in the future.'

The mongrel's face had turned ashen by now.

'After everyone retired,' Athreya went on, 'you stayed. It was an ideal night for you to complete your unfinished business from three months ago. They had foolishly left the front door open, and the thick mist had always been your ally.

'You went towards the rear of the mansion. Before doing anything else, you bolted the door of the staff quarters from the outside. If you had to leave in a hurry, you didn't want Murugan, Gopal or any of the others cutting off your retreat.'

The little man's eyes almost popped out of his head.

'But just then,' Athreya continued, 'you saw a figure come out in the wheelchair. He had grizzled hair, a greying beard and powerful shoulders. You had no doubt in your mind that it was Bhaskar Fernandez, the man you had been hired to kill.

'He drove the wheelchair along the walkway to the chapel and entered it. Your target was now alone, far away from anyone else; all alone in the chapel. A God-sent opportunity! It couldn't have been easier. All you had to do was creep up behind him, and you were an expert at that.

'You drew the same dagger you had dropped three months ago—Phillip had been kind enough to retrieve it for you. You went in and slit his throat. You ran out, threw the dagger into the stream and went back to the resort.

'There you used the small side gate. You knew that it made a noise that would alert the guard. You lifted the latch slowly and let it down. You lifted the gate an inch or two so that it didn't make any noise, and carefully opened it. Five minutes later, you were in your room, safe and sound.

'But you were in for a shock the next day. The man you had killed was Phillip, not Bhaskar.'

Athreya stopped and watched the mongrel. He was terrified. Conflicting emotions flashed across his face, even as his mouth fell open and his eyes darted about. His breathing had grown shallow, and his face was as white as a sheet.

'This is the case against you,' Athreya said. 'A pretty strong one, don't you think? What I've narrated is what Inspector Muthu believes happened. Of course, I have not given you the evidence; I've only outlined what the police think happened. They are convinced that you killed Phillip, mistaking him for Bhaskar.

'Who saw you, who heard you, what others said about you—all that you will hear in court. Keep in mind, Ismail will sing like a canary. If he doesn't, he will become an accessory to murder.'

'I didn't kill Phillip!' the mongrel wailed. 'You must believe me. I was there at Greybrooke Manor, but I didn't kill him.'

Athreya remained silent, letting the man squirm and agonize.

'I didn't kill Phillip,' he moaned again. 'Yes, I locked the door of the staff quarters. Yes, I was near the chapel. Yes, I overheard Abbas and Murthy plotting. But I *didn't* kill Phillip!'

The mongrel was breathing rapidly now, his breath rasping. The broken man was trembling and wringing his hyperactive hands. His beseeching eyes, bloodshot and haunted, were pleading with Athreya to believe him. When Athreya remained still and silent, a shuddering sob rose from the mongrel's chest.

'I... didn't... kill... Phillip,' he whimpered.

At last, Athreya spoke.

'I know.'

19

The mongrel gaped at Athreya as if he couldn't comprehend the simple two-word sentence. A look of utter bewilderment overtook his face. His eyes bulged and his jaw hung slack.

'You know?' he repeated.

Athreya nodded.

'You *know* that I didn't kill Phillip?' The little man's eyes were searching Athreya's face as the latter nodded again.

'You know who killed Phillip?'

'I do.'

'Then?' he asked. 'Then…' Words failed him.

'You got it backwards, my friend,' Athreya said. 'You thought that I had come here to discuss the offer you made to Mr Fernandez. You see, I have come to make you an offer of my own.'

'Offer?' The stupid look remained on his face. 'What offer?'

'I want you to tell me your story.'

'Why?'

A shrewd look came to the mongrel's face. He was getting back to his old self.

'Because there are multiple crimes here. It's not just the murder of Phillip. I want to expose all of them, and one way to do that is to use your testimony.'

'What's in it for me?'

'For one, if you become the state's witness, your sentence will be much lighter. Second, the murder charge that is hanging over your head will disappear. Third, Mr Fernandez could consider dropping charges against you. I don't know if he will, but it is a possibility.'

'And if I don't?'

'I walk out of here. I will leave you to your fate and at Muthu's mercy.'

'You will let an innocent man rot in jail for the rest of his life?' the mongrel demanded.

'Innocent?' Athreya asked, raising his eyebrows theatrically. 'Show me one innocent man in this room other than me.'

'You said there were multiple crimes here other than Phillip's murder. What crimes?'

'I'm not going to tell you. You confess completely, and answer all my questions truthfully. Only then does my offer stand. If you play games with me, you will end up in the hangman's noose.'

'How do I know you will keep your word? How do I know you will not cheat me after I confess?'

'You don't,' Athreya said evenly. 'But you have no choice but to trust me.'

'Give me five minutes,' the mongrel muttered and turned away.

Athreya rose and went out of the cell. He asked a sub-inspector to prepare to record the mongrel's confession. When he returned to the cell ten minutes later, the little man was ready.

'I'm going to trust you,' he said. 'I will tell you everything. You must keep your end of the bargain.'

'My end of the bargain is this: If you confess and turn state witness, I will make Inspector Muthu drop the murder charges, and ask the prosecutor to recommend a lighter sentence for you. Whether Mr Fernandez chooses to drop his charges of attempted assault is up to him.'

The mongrel nodded slowly and began his story.

'I followed Murthy on Friday night to Greybrooke Manor, just as you said. Ismail had not told me who had commissioned the contract, but it hadn't taken me long to find out. I already knew that it must be Abbas or Murthy. But Murthy had no money, and he was in no position to put out a contract. So it had to be Abbas.

237

'But why was Abbas doing it? What did he stand to gain by having Fernandez killed? All it took was some snooping and eavesdropping. I found out that Abbas had struck a deal with Murthy. The property that would come to Michelle after Fernandez's death would be merged with Abbas's resort.'

'Did Michelle know about the contract?' Athreya asked.

'No. She was kept in the dark. Murthy had beaten and slapped her into submission. He had made her sign an agreement with Abbas, promising to merge her inherited property with Abbas's resort.'

Athreya grimaced at the mention of physical abuse that Michelle had endured.

'As I said,' the mongrel went on, 'I followed Murthy to Greybrooke on Friday night. The fog was so thick that I could easily remain concealed, and my ability to move without making noise allowed me to get close to people. It was just as you said, I walked around and overheard conversations. Dora and Manu, Michelle and Abbas, Michelle pestering the lawyer about the contents of the second will. And the very interesting conversation between Abbas and Murthy, in which they talked openly about Fernandez's imminent death.

'By about 1 a.m., most people had returned to their rooms. Only Abbas and Murthy remained, but they were sitting at the rock garden and smoking. I moved towards the mansion.

'The first thing I did was to lock the door to the staff quarters. I didn't want any of them coming out and getting in my way. I was planning to enter through the back door, as that was the shortest way to Fernandez's room.

'But before I could go in, I heard someone come down the walkway. He must have come out of the front door, and was going towards the chapel. I ran to the trees behind the mansion and hid there, watching. As I watched him enter the chapel, I recognized him. You know who it was?'

Athreya nodded. 'Richie.'

'Yes… Richie. I crept up close to the chapel, wondering what he was doing there in the middle of the night. I had just walked around the building, when I saw someone in a gown come down the path from Sunset Deck.

'I stood flat against the chapel wall and watched. To my surprise, it was a woman in a nightgown—the major's wife. She passed within ten feet of me, and entered the chapel through a window. I needed no imagination to know what was going on.

'With two people inside the chapel, it would be risky for me to attempt my work. I decided to wait. Just then, I saw someone else, again dressed in a gown. I was too far away to make out who it was, and even to make out for sure whether it was a man or a woman.

'This newcomer was about to enter through the chapel door when muted sounds came from inside. The woman's giggling carried far in the night air. The intruder stopped and went to the trees behind the mansion and stood there, waiting for Richie and the woman to finish and leave. I could no longer see the new arrival.

'We must have waited for half an hour or forty-five minutes. At last, the woman left the way she had come, and Richie slipped out through the door and returned to the mansion. The stranger then waited a little more before entering the chapel.

'A minute later, I heard a loud gasp from there, as if the intruder had seen something surprising and terrible. The next moment, I saw the figure run out and down the walkway past the mansion.

'By this time, I was getting jittery. I had encountered too many unexpected hurdles. It was not my lucky night. Experience had taught me not to carry out my work when luck was not with me. I aborted my mission and returned to the Misty Valley Resort.

'The next day, I heard about Phillip's death and thanked my

stars for having aborted my mission. That, sir, is my whole story. I have left out nothing.'

'OK,' Athreya nodded. 'But you know more about Abbas than you have told me.'

'About the murder?' the mongrel asked. 'No, there is nothing more.'

'Not about the murder… but about something else. About Abbas's business.'

'I know nothing about his resort.'

'Not the resort, my friend. His other business. The one that brings him money by the truckload. The one he runs across the Western Ghats.'

The little man blanched. He looked away, muttering, 'I don't know what you mean.'

'Oh, you do,' Athreya disputed. 'You have been around here long enough to know what I am talking about.'

'I… I have nothing to do with it. It is not something I touch even with a pole. It's a dirty business… I've seen what it does to young men and women. It converts boys into thieves and makes girls sell their bodies. I've seen how addicts die… My father was one. I don't touch it.'

'I am not saying you touch it. I'm saying that you know something about Abbas's drug business. You are a man who watches, a man who listens. The resort has been raided several times, but nothing has ever been found. And the stock is being stored somewhere not far from here.'

The mongrel licked his lips and remained silent.

'An anti-drug team is in town now,' Athreya persisted, trying to persuade him. 'If you help them crack the case, the police and the judge will count it in your favour.'

The little man hesitated. He was in two minds. Athreya knew what he was thinking.

This was an opportunity for him to play his card for his own benefit. Abbas was already neck-deep in trouble by having put out a contract on Bhaskar. Milking him now would be difficult. On the other hand, what Athreya had said was true—the police and the courts tended to look favourably upon those who helped fight drugs.

The mongrel looked up.

'Abbas has a hidden cellar at the Misty Valley Resort,' he said. 'And there is this shack in Coonoor…'

The shack turned out to be one among a dozen that stood scattered on a slope beside a potholed lane on the outskirts of Coonoor. A hundred feet below was a black-topped road that ran north from the town towards the valley that housed Greybrooke Manor and the Misty Valley Resort.

Near the shacks was a tea shop that doubled as a small restaurant, and a cigarette stall. A clutch of idle men loitered around, smoking and sipping tea.

Half an hour after Athreya spoke to the mongrel, a man who appeared to be a daily-wage worker sauntered in and struck up conversation with the cigarette-stall owner. Another man wandered into the crowd near the tea shop.

A little later, these two men had learnt that three men visited the shack after dark a few days a week, but always separately. One was Ismail from the Misty Valley Resort, and another was a man who worked at a restaurant near the bus stand at Coonoor. The third name came as a surprise to the anti-drug team.

When a lorry blocked the view from the tea shop and the cigarette stall, a man materialized in front of the shack. Within thirty seconds, the lock was open. He stepped in and closed the door behind him. Inside, he found unquestionable evidence of drug trafficking.

The shack was put under round-the-clock surveillance. Before the next day dawned, the three men who frequented the shack would be apprehended.

Once the shack had been searched, the team prepared to raid the Misty Valley Resort. Their primary target was the hidden cellar under Abbas's office that was accessible only through a trapdoor concealed under a thick rug behind his desk.

Meanwhile, at the Coonoor town police station, an officer had been busy on the phone, calling nearby hotels and resorts in the hope of finding a man whose name he had been given by Athreya. He started with hotels in the heart of town, and then moved outwards.

The first hours had been fruitless as none of the hotels reported having hosted anyone by that name. After all, it was an uncommon name in this part of the world. Each call took several minutes. First, the officer had to get to the manager or his representative. Then, he had to convince the person that he was indeed a policeman calling from the station. And finally, he had to wait for the person to go through the guest register and report back.

By the end of the second hour, he was growing frustrated. He had called twenty-odd hotels without success. An hour later, his hopes were fading. All the hotels in and around the town, including the few that were close to Wellington, had not hosted the man. Athreya's hopes were also fading, but he insisted that they go through the entire list, and call all hotels and resorts.

Suddenly, the officer hit pay dirt. When he called a high-end resort to the south-east of Coonoor, he had a pleasant surprise waiting for him.

'Yes,' the hotel manager said. 'We have a Mr Enrico staying with us. He checked in on Saturday, and is expected to be here for two more days.'

Enrico, the art valuer, had come to Coonoor after all. Disregarding his growling stomach, Athreya jumped into a police vehicle and hastened to the resort, which was half an hour away.

'Mr Enrico?' he asked when he met the surprised foreigner. 'I have come from Greybrooke Manor. I want to speak to you about some paintings.'

'What paintings?' Enrico asked.

'The Balsano landscapes.'

Back in Coonoor, a ravenous Athreya sat down to eat lunch with Rajan. News of the anti-drug team's discovery at the shack had come in, delighting Rajan and the local police. If Rajan had been expecting Athreya to be surprised at any of the three names that had emerged in relation to the shack, he was disappointed. In fact, the third name, which had surprised everyone else, was the very one Athreya had asked Rajan to enquire about in Coorg.

Rajan's contact in Coorg called when they were in the midst of lunch. He had completed the enquiries, and found out something that left Rajan astonished.

'The person you asked me to find out about is dead,' the man said. 'Died ten years ago.'

'You were right,' Rajan said, once he had hung up.

'Things are falling into place,' he continued. 'We now have enough evidence for a conviction. In addition, Abbas, Murthy, Ismail and a few others will also see jail terms.

'The local police are thrilled that they have finally been able to nail Abbas. They have been after him for a few years now, and suspected that he was somehow involved in the drug trade. But they had nothing definite. Now, they have him.'

'Bhaskar Fernandez, too, suspected that Abbas was in the drug trade,' Athreya said. 'In fact, he was very sure of it. It was his conviction that set me on to Abbas. A very sharp man, Bhaskar. He will be delighted to hear this news.'

'That's all fine,' Rajan said with a frown. 'But how does all this fit in with the murders at Greybrooke Manor? Why was Phillip killed? We know that he was involved in the attempts on Bhaskar's life. But who killed him? And Sebastian? I suppose he surprised someone at the chapel last night and paid the price for it.'

'That is what I am waiting for,' Athreya replied. 'The last piece of the puzzle. The final piece of evidence that links the residents of the valley to art-related crimes in Europe.'

'What kind of evidence?' Rajan asked.

'Fingerprints. I expect one set of prints from here to find a match in the Viennese police records.'

As if on cue, Athreya's phone rang. It was the man from Delhi. He sounded excited.

'We have a match!' he exclaimed. 'We finally have a match.'

20

Back at Greybrooke Manor, Athreya was standing over Bhaskar in his wheelchair in the study. Sebastian's murder had broken him. He sat slumped now, pale and drawn, his eyes deep-set and empty. Without Sebastian standing behind him, Bhaskar somehow looked lonely. It was no secret that Sebastian had been like a second son to him.

Sebastian had been with Bhaskar from the time the younger man had been an uneducated, wayward seventeen-year-old. As a Spanish immigrant and a recent orphan, Sebastian had been unemployed and penniless in Austria. Bhaskar had pulled him out of the mire that many boys of Sebastian's economic standing were prone to sink into. He had offered the lad a job at his antique shop and had given him a roof over his head.

Most importantly, he had given the young orphan hope, and something to look forward to in life. Alongside this, he had educated Sebastian and taught him many things, small and big, that enabled him to move in the circles of law-abiding, self-respecting citizens. Sebastian had, in turn, demonstrated an eye for antiques and the ability to distinguish between genuine artefacts and fakes. He had picked up the trade quickly and become indispensable to Bhaskar.

For over thirty years, he had been Bhaskar's right hand, from before Bhaskar became confined to his wheelchair, from when he ran a flourishing antique business—first in Europe, then in India. In Bangalore and Chennai, and later, after Thomas Fernandez's death, at Greybrooke Manor, as his caregiver, secretary and major-domo.

Now with him gone, Bhaskar was at a complete loss. He seemed paralysed physically and mentally, unable—or unwilling—to be the dominant force he had always been. Since morning, Manu had stepped into the vacuum left by Sebastian's death, taking charge of the mansion and administering tender care to his father. Dora, too, had stepped up to the occasion, quietly working with Manu to run the household.

Looking down at Bhaskar, Athreya felt sorry for him. He had faced the prospect of his own unnatural death with equanimity, even élan. He had devised a scheme to thwart his would-be killers, and had written two conflicting wills. But the murder of Sebastian seemed to have blindsided him.

Be that as it may, Athreya still had a job to do. Bhaskar had commissioned him to solve the murders, and he was on the verge of doing so. But first, he had to confront the older man and get him to speak of the secrets he had so far withheld.

'It is time,' he said softly to Bhaskar, 'for us to have a little chat. The time has come for you to take the cover off what has been hidden for almost twenty-five years. Only then will there be a resolution to this affair. Only then can you rest in peace.'

Bhaskar looked up at Athreya with hollow eyes and said nothing.

'I know about Marcel Fessler's death,' Athreya continued. 'About the Künzi Brothers and the Balsano landscapes. And about Jacob Lopez. I have all the information that is publicly available in Vienna, and some that is not. I have also spoken to Enrico. But there are gaps that only you can fill. What you choose to tell the world is entirely up to you. But having commissioned me, you must let me into your confidence.'

Bhaskar let out a long sigh and nodded his head.

'I owe it to you,' he concurred. 'If you indeed know about what you have just mentioned, I am amazed. Today is only the third day after Phillip's murder. How you managed it is beyond me. But you have more than justified the faith I put in you.'

246

He looked out of the window and went on.

'Shall we go outside?' he asked. 'The vale is bright and sunny today. The fog has lifted. Do you really know who killed Sebastian?'

'I do.'

'Then the fog has lifted in your mind as well. It's appropriate that we go outside. I hope you don't mind a stroll.'

Five minutes later, they were moving slowly along the walkways.

'I believe you have called a gathering at 7 p.m.?' Bhaskar asked. 'What do you have in mind?'

'I hope to introduce you to Sebastian's murderer.'

'Really? I look forward to it. But now, let me tell you what I haven't told anyone since I let my father into the secret. He carried it to his grave, as did my dear wife, Sujata.

'As you know, I used to deal in antiques and other forms of art. I ran a tidy business for many years in Vienna, a crossroads for art of all forms. Sitting between eastern and western Europe, cheek by jowl with Italy and other cradles of art, a stone's throw from France and the erstwhile Soviet Union, Vienna saw a lot of art pass through it. Even decades after the Second World War, it was not uncommon for a forgotten Nazi treasure to surface every once in a while. The collapse of the Soviet Union unleashed another wave of discoveries. In other words, Vienna was just the place to be for someone like me.

'Sujata and I had decided to return to India soon. Manu was approaching ten, and we wanted him to grow up in this country. We had already delayed our return by three or four years more than we had intended, and so Sujata and Manu moved to India. That was 1993. I was to follow in two or three years. I was not crippled then.

'But one day—a single day—in 1995 changed our lives. Forever.'

Bhaskar pulled out his pipe, filled it slowly with tobacco from a leather pouch and lit it. He fell silent as he puffed on it, gradually building the fire in the bowl, his eyes gazing unseeing past Sunset Deck at the hills beyond. Athreya waited, leaning against a stone bench.

'It was a fine day that dawned with no indication that it would wreck my life in so irreversible a manner. Sebastian had gone out to show some pieces to a customer, and I was alone in my shop. What I did not know was that something had happened the night before that would plunge me into hell.

'The Künzi Brothers, along with their break-in man, Jacob Lopez, had entered the house of Marcel Fessler, a reclusive art collector. Two days earlier, Fessler had anonymously purchased four paintings by the famous Fabian Balsano through his agent for an astonishing twenty-seven million dollars.

'The four canvases were still in their packaging—a long metal tube—when Jacob and the Künzi Brothers broke into Fessler's house. They were yet to be catalogued or added to Fessler's list of paintings. The world was not aware that he had bought them, and did not expect to see the four paintings for many years.

'Reclusive collectors, who purchase art anonymously, often keep them in their private collections, away from the eyes of the world. An item bought by such a collector could disappear, for all intents and purposes, for years, sometimes for the rest of the collector's lifetime. It was only when such a collector died that the world would come to know about the purchase, and say, "So *he* was the one who bought *that* painting."

'As luck would have it, the only thing Jacob stole before being surprised by Fessler was the tube with the four Balsano landscapes. He had passed it to the brothers, who were outside the Fessler house.

'When the alarm was raised, all three thieves fled. Jacob, being of darker skin by virtue of his Indian origin, was recognized, but the Künzi Brothers, who were outside and had a head start, escaped unseen. They had made away with the landscapes, and nobody knew that they had taken them. In fact, nobody knew that the Balsano paintings had even been stolen.

'So the Künzi Brothers found themselves in possession of some seriously hot property at a time when the police were buzzing around, as they had responded very quickly to the alarm. The brothers had to find a hiding place, and, as luck would have it, they chose my antiques shop. They apparently threw the tube in through a window, with the intention of retrieving it early the next morning. I was, of course, totally unaware of this.

'But in the morning, Sebastian, who always rose early, found the tube, and stuck it among the rafters. There was some space between the thick horizontal beams and the slanting thinner ones, and Sebastian kept it there. He later told me that he hadn't known what the tube had contained, but that it had knocked down several antiques, and he had just put it away. With my shop crammed from floor to ceiling, there was no place to store a long tube, so he had therefore decided to put it in the rafters.

'But before I came to the shop that morning, he had left to meet a customer and didn't have an opportunity to tell me about the tube. So, I came to the shop unaware of what had transpired. Hardly had I stepped in when two men entered after me. They were the Künzi Brothers.'

Bhaskar paused, and they resumed their slow journey down the walkways. Athreya remained silent, letting him tell his story the way he wanted to.

'What happened in the next one hour was sheer hell. The brothers shut the door from inside and assaulted me. When I professed ignorance of their metal tube, they thought I was lying. They tied me up and ransacked my shop. But they didn't find their precious paintings.

'In anger, they turned on me. Not believing that I had no clue to where the paintings were, they brought two lead pipes from their car and began thrashing me. Lead pipes wrapped in cloth tend to cause serious injuries that may not be visible from the outside. They may not break the skin, but they will shatter the bones.

'They pounded me mercilessly and broke my legs in multiple places. Several times, I lost consciousness, but they splashed water on me and woke me up. Each time they would ask, "Where are the paintings?" How I endured that hour, I don't know. But I will never forget the agony of it.

'Just as I passed out for the last time, I saw a familiar figure materializing behind the Künzi Brothers: Sebastian. He hit one of the villains on the head and knocked him down. After that, I don't know what happened...

'The next thing I remember is waking up in a hospital three weeks later. It was the middle of the night, and Sebastian was beside me. He told me what had happened, and said that he hadn't told anyone about the Künzi Brothers assaulting me. The story he had told everyone was that I had been badly injured in a car crash. I didn't know why he asked me to do this, but I played along. After all, he had saved my life.

'Over the next few weeks, the rest of the story slowly emerged. That's when I learnt of Fessler's death and Jacob's arrest. I also learnt that the Künzi Brothers had died in a car crash in the Danube valley.

'At first, Sebastian feigned ignorance. But I knew better. I knew that he had somehow engineered a car crash forty miles from where we had lived. He never told me the details, but I had no doubt that he had wreaked revenge on those brothers for what they had done to me. I saw it in his eyes, in his young face that I knew so well. Each time he saw my mangled legs, he would shed tears and a look of grim satisfaction would shine through.

'I still had no idea what had become of the Balsano landscapes. In fact, I was under the firm impression that the brothers had been mistaken in the first place. When I came out of the hospital two months later, I was confined to a wheelchair. I couldn't go around my shop very much, and it was Sebastian who managed everything.

'It was only four years after I had returned to India that I discovered the paintings. When I confronted Sebastian, he was unapologetic. In fact, he was surprised and offended. The paintings were mine, he said. They were small compensation for what those brothers had done to me. They were mine to do what I chose with them.

'Fessler had died heirless, and had drawn up an elaborate will, dividing his collection among a dozen museums. The Balsano landscapes, never having been added to his collection, were not missed. His will had long since been executed and his assets distributed as per his instructions. That was essentially a closed chapter.

'As far as the art world knew, the Balsano landscapes were owned by someone somewhere, and there wasn't even the faintest suspicion that they had been stolen. Which meant I could sell them openly if I chose to do so, and they would fetch a handsome price. Whether to keep them or to sell them, Sebastian said, was my decision.

'I consulted my Sujata. She agreed with Sebastian. She too said that they were small compensation for what I had suffered. Providence had gifted me the paintings. After all, I had spent a fortune on medical bills.

'I then went to my father. He too was of the same view as Sujata and Sebastian. Besides, he told me, if I were to rake up the old story and tell the world that the paintings had been stolen, I would leave myself open to criminal proceedings. The fact remained that they had been in my possession all these years, and I had kept quiet.

'In addition, I would bring down serious indictments on Sebastian—the very man who had saved my life and had stuck with me through all this. He could have chosen to sell the paintings himself and pocket the money. He would have been a rich man.

'I thought about it, and decided to remain silent. There was no risk in it except one: Jacob Lopez. He would soon be released, and we did not know how much he knew. Did he know what the Künzi Brothers had done with the tube with the Balsano landscapes? We had no idea. It was best that we stayed low.

'That's what I did, Mr Athreya. I stayed low. I spoke nothing of the four paintings. Wherever I happened to be—Bangalore, Chennai or here—I always found a safe hiding place for them. That is the story of my legs and of the Balsano landscapes.'

They continued silently along the walkways. Athreya considered all that he had heard, and decided that Bhaskar had spoken the truth. That is what had happened in the past.

Now, they had to deal with the present; the present in which Jacob Lopez had probably come to India. If the paintings had been worth twenty-seven million dollars then, they would be worth much more now. That was enough to kill for.

By this time, they were near the chapel. Athreya stepped towards it. After a moment's hesitation, Bhaskar followed. Athreya unlocked the padlock and they entered the building together and went up to the altar.

'You always found a good hiding place for the paintings,' Athreya said quietly. 'That's what you said. When you renovated Greybrooke Manor, you actually built a hiding place for them, didn't you?'

Bhaskar stared silently at Athreya, his facial expression giving nothing away.

'That is what led to the murders,' Athreya went on. 'Somehow, Jacob Lopez discovered the hiding place.' He turned and faced the dais. 'The altar. Four of the five metal tubes that support the middle slab are hollow. Four tubes for four paintings. The central one houses the mechanism to open and close the hiding place.'

He went up the dais and opened the large cupboard at one end of it. There, he turned on the two switches and returned to Bhaskar. Both of them stared at the altar.

'The mechanism to open the altar is operated wirelessly,' Athreya continued. 'It is operated from the console of the wheelchair. It is indeed a good piece of work, well designed and well executed. I did not have the heart to force it open.'

Athreya turned to Bhaskar and spoke softly.

'The chapel door is locked,' he said. 'Please open the altar.'

Bhaskar stared at the mural of Jesus for a full minute, his face etched in tragic lines. At length, he moved his hands and touched the console. Seconds later, a soft click sounded from the altar and the middle portion of the altar slab rose by about four inches.

'Rotate the stone clockwise by ninety degrees,' Bhaskar whispered. 'That will expose the tubes.'

Athreya pulled out a pair of gloves from his jacket and put them on. He rotated the altar slab clockwise. As the stone turned, the openings of the four tubes became visible, and Athreya shone a torch into them.

'There is something here,' he said.

'Can't be,' Bhaskar said in alarm. 'The paintings were removed after Phillip died.'

'These are not paintings,' Athreya replied quietly, as he dipped his gloved fingers into one of the tubes. 'They contain something I have been looking for… blood-soaked floor mats. The ones that were under Phillip when he was killed.'

One by one, he pulled out the contents of the tubes. The two missing mats, each cut into two pieces so that they could fit into the tubes, came out. Four pieces in all. And in one of the tubes was a pair of gloves.

'These are Phillip's gloves,' Athreya continued. 'The ones he used so that he left no fingerprints. He had somehow figured out how to operate the console and open the altar. That's why he had to bring the wheelchair to the altar that night. Without it, the altar could not be opened.' Athreya rotated the altar slab anticlockwise, and when it was aligned with the tubes below, he pressed it down. It didn't move.

'I'll have to do it from the console,' Bhaskar said and touched the screen a few times.

The slab sank smoothly and clicked into place. The altar now looked as it always had, smooth and even. On the floor lay the bloodied mats and a pair of gloves.

'So, Phillip opened the altar that night,' Athreya concluded. 'But, unfortunately for him, the rest didn't work out as he had intended, and he ended up paying the ultimate price.

'Now, Mr Fernandez, tell me the rest of the story. The story that Sebastian told you early Saturday morning.'

'OK… I will tell you. As I said, I probably owe you this. Besides, there may be no getting away from it as far as you are concerned. I will narrate what Sebastian told me, but I reserve the right to say nothing to the police. If you repeat what I will now say, I might deny it altogether.'

'I understand. The choice will be yours.'

'At about 3 a.m. on Saturday, Sebastian shook me awake. This is what happened…'

'What is it?' Bhaskar asked Sebastian, waking up with a start. 'Some problem?'

'Jacob Lopez is here,' Sebastian said. His face was suffused with alarm and anger. 'The swine has found the Balsano landscapes.'

Sebastian held up the four rolled canvases to support his claim.

'Jacob?' Bhaskar sat up in shock. 'How do you know? Neither of us know how he looks. We've never seen him.'

'We do now,' Sebastian snarled. 'We know him by a different name.'

'What name?'

'Phillip.'

'Can't be, there must be some mistake, Sebastian. Phillip is a good man.'

'Remember how much interest he has been showing in your wheelchair lately? Especially the console. Your wheelchair is missing. It's been taken from the charging point to the chapel.'

'Good Lord!' Bhaskar struggled out of his bed and stood up unsteadily. He tottered to a nearby chair and lowered himself into it. 'Tell me from the beginning. What happened?'

'After settling you in, I was in my room, reading. I heard a click that sounded like the back door, but I didn't give it much thought. There were so many people about; any one of them could be going out. Or Murugan could be coming in. I dismissed it from my mind and continued reading.

'A short while later, I heard the whir of the wheelchair. That is a distinct sound, one which I can't mistake for anything else. The funny thing was that it seemed to be coming from the window, and not the corridor. It was as if you were on the walkway outside.

'I went to my window and peered out. It was murky and dark, and I could see nothing. But the whirring continued, although softly. It seemed to be fading away towards the chapel.

'I came out of my room and went to the charging point. The wheelchair was missing and the back door was open a crack. I opened the door to your room and peered in. I was shocked to see that you were in bed, sleeping. I came in and looked at you closely. You were snoring.

'So, someone else was using the wheelchair. I stood there undecided for a long while. Could it have been Manu or Dora who had borrowed it? Perhaps they were pulling a prank on someone. If that was so, I didn't want to spoil their fun.

'Gradually, another thought dawned on me. Whoever had taken the wheelchair had taken it to the chapel. If it was not Manu or Dora, and if the intent was more serious than playing a prank, the consequences could be profound. As I thought about it, the combination of the wheelchair and the chapel set off alarm bells in my mind. I hurried back to my room and pulled on a pair of shorts and a T-shirt; I went to the back door and made my way to the chapel.

'When I reached the chapel, I saw a faint glow inside. I pushed open the door and stepped in. Near the altar was a light from some kind of a torch. What I saw made my blood run cold. There was Phillip, at the altar with the slab raised and rotated. On the first row of pews were two canvases. He was pulling out the third from its tube in the altar.

'I crept up, making no noise. He was so engrossed in what he was doing that he didn't hear me. He put the third canvas beside the first two and began pulling out the fourth. By now, I was within a couple of yards from him. I crouched, trying to decide my course of action.

'The only person who could have known that the Balsano landscapes were with you was Jacob Lopez. The agent who had bought the paintings on Fessler's behalf wouldn't have known that you had them.

'As I thought about it, I realized that Phillip had just turned up in the valley seven years ago. Where he had come from, nobody knew. He had shown tremendous interest in your painting collection and subsequently in your wheelchair. Suddenly, everything clicked into place.

'Phillip was Jacob Lopez. That was the only possible answer. He had tracked you down to Greybrooke Manor, and had bided his time. Eventually, he had figured out where the paintings were and how to reach them.'

'How?' Bhaskar asked, his face set in grim lines. 'How did he figure it out?'

'Remember the deluge we had two months ago?' Sebastian asked, his gaze fiery. 'When the chapel was in danger of getting flooded from the water flowing down into the vale from the hills?'

'Yes,' said Bhaskar, nodding. 'The water was rising, and we had to bring the paintings into the mansion for a few days.'

'Phillip was staying here then,' Sebastian hissed. 'He must have seen us go to the chapel in the pouring rain. He must have wondered why. And he must have seen me transporting the tubes containing the paintings to the mansion.'

'Yes… yes. I fell ill after that drenching and was confined to bed. After the water receded a few days later, you put the paintings back in the chapel. Phillip must have wondered also why you were wheeling the empty wheelchair to the chapel and back. Especially both times in such bad weather.'

'Not just an empty wheelchair,' Sebastian corrected him. 'Four aluminium tubes too. He must have scrutinized the chapel and the altar thereafter. He must have figured out that the paintings were hidden in the altar, and that the wheelchair unlocked it.

'He then inveigled himself into your confidence, and found out how to operate the wheelchair and its console. He must have obtained your access code by pinching the pocket notebook in which you had written it. He then pretended to find it and returned it—all within ten minutes of your missing it.'

'The snake!' Bhaskar exclaimed. 'Continue with what happened tonight, Sebastian. You were telling me about how you had crept up to Phillip at the altar. What happened then?'

'As I watched him, I realized that if I let him go, we would never see the paintings again.

'My mind went back to 1995, to when the thugs had mangled your legs forever. It went back to how you lay broken, within an inch from death that morning. The Künzi Brothers had done it to you for their own selfish ends. They had done it to a good man, an innocent man. They had done it to the only father I had known.

'After a long struggle, your father and your wife had helped me finally convince you to keep the paintings. Now, Jacob Lopez, the snake in human form, posing as your friend Phillip, was stealing them from you. I had to stop him.

'By now, he had pulled out the fourth painting and they all lay together on the pew. Beside them was something long and slender, glinting in the soft glow from Jacob's torch. It was the dagger the mongrel had dropped. Phillip had taken it from the drawer in the hall. His intent could not have been honourable.

'As Jacob returned to sit in the wheelchair to close the altar, I reached for the dagger. My blood was boiling. I knew what I had to do.'

'Sebastian!' Bhaskar cried in horror, half rising from his chair. Blood had drained from his face, and his eyes were open wide in alarm. 'What did you do?'

'I slit his throat.'

21

Twelve people sat in the drawing room once more. This time in uneasy silence, not knowing what to expect from the gathering Athreya had called. The five members of the Fernandez family sat together. The four neighbours were there: Abbas, Ganesh, Jilsy and Father Tobias. Two outsiders—Varadan and Athreya—made the count eleven, and the twelfth was a surprise. Murthy had been prevailed upon to join the group.

Athreya waited for a few moments, and when it was precisely 7 p.m., he rose.

'We were here less than seventy-two hours ago,' he began. 'The people were much the same then, with a few exceptions, but the mood was very different. A lot has happened since then, and many illusions have been shattered. I've called you all together now to conclude this sordid chapter in your lives.

'Some of you, especially those from the Fernandez family, have a shadow hanging over you. When you walk out of here later this evening, the shadow will be gone. That was the assignment Mr Fernandez gave me: to lift the shadow of suspicion from the innocent. I intend to do exactly that over the next fifteen minutes.

'Let me begin with Mr Fernandez's first will, which he wrote a year ago. It bequeathed certain assets to some of you unconditionally. By unconditionally, I mean that the assets would come to you irrespective of how Mr Fernandez died.

'But once he wrote that will, strange things began happening. His car's brakes failed; a venomous snake materialized in his bed; he was almost run over in Coonoor. And, to top it all, an intruder broke in and tried to kill him. Someone was trying to hasten Mr Fernandez's death.

'Let's look at it from a motive perspective. It was at once apparent that multiple people potentially had motives. It was not only Mr Fernandez's relatives who might want him dead, but others too, including his neighbours: Phillip, Father Tobias and Abbas stood to gain from his death.

'It didn't take much for Mr Fernandez to realize that someone had hired an outsider to kill him. And so he decided to scrap his earlier will and write two new ones. The first would take effect if he died naturally, and the second, if he was killed. The attacks stopped after that, but it was not clear if they had stopped because of the new wills, or because the wounded intruder was lying low.

'It so turned out that he was lying low and was planning to return. And return he did, on the night Phillip was killed. For those of you who aren't sure of his identity, the intruder's nickname is "the mongrel". We know now that it was Phillip who had let him into the mansion that night three months ago. It was amply clear that someone here had hired the mongrel to kill Mr Fernandez.

'So Phillip's death begged the obvious question: Did the mongrel kill Phillip by mistake? Did he think Phillip was Mr Fernandez?

'That was certainly a possibility, as some of you have suggested, except that it didn't answer one all-important question: What was Phillip doing in the chapel in the wheelchair?

'That meant that there was more than one crime playing out at Greybrooke Manor. The first was the attempted murder of Mr Fernandez, but there was at least one other plot that needed to be unearthed. To do that, I went into the past, and to Vienna.

'Soon, I discovered two things. First, it was very likely that Mr Fernandez possessed four very valuable paintings: the Balsano landscapes. Enrico confirmed that Mr Fernandez had spoken to him about them. Second, there was an art thief called Jacob

Lopez, who might have come to India under an assumed name. Not just to India, but to this valley. Lopez was the son of Indian parents who had emigrated to Europe when he was a boy.

'When I looked at the chronology of events that unfolded in Vienna, I discovered that Jacob Lopez had been released from jail late in 2007. And Phillip, who was a newcomer to Vienna, appeared in early 2008. Then, had Jacob reappeared as Phillip?

'Simultaneously, I was investigating the chapel here, and it became apparent that the altar was the most important piece of the puzzle—all roads seemed to lead to it. On closer examination, I found that the altar was a hiding place. Something of great value had been hidden there. The obvious candidates were the Balsano landscapes.

'It didn't take much to put two and two together. Phillip had somehow found out that the paintings had been hidden inside the altar, and that the mechanism to open it was operated by the console of the wheelchair. That is why he had gone to the chapel that night in the wheelchair—to steal the paintings.

'But someone surprised him that night and slit his throat.

'Meanwhile, a third development had taken place: the mongrel was caught. It didn't take long to break him. Within half an hour of making him a proposal, I had his story.

'He had been skulking around the chapel the night Phillip was killed, and had seen enough to confirm my suspicions. Some of you had been in the garden when you claimed to be in your rooms. Some of you had stayed out longer, and some had gone out after retiring.

'The mongrel has given a complete confession in writing. He was hired by Ismail—one of the staff members of the Misty Valley Resort—to kill Mr Fernandez. But Ismail was only an agent. He was working on someone's behalf. We have the name of the person Ismail was representing. Ismail is already in custody.'

Murthy, who had been growing paler by the minute, threw a terrified glance at Abbas. Abbas himself might have turned to stone. Dora was glaring at him, while Bhaskar kept his eyes on Athreya.

'The mongrel overheard several conversations that murky night,' Athreya continued. 'Hiding in the mist, he snuck up close to people as they talked. He narrated a particularly interesting discussion that took place between 1 and 1:45 a.m. that night at the rock garden. There is no doubt now as to who had commissioned the mongrel to kill Mr Fernandez.'

By now, Murthy was visibly trembling. He stole glances at his wife, who sat staring at the carpet with her lips compressed into a hard, straight line. Dora, sitting beside her, slipped a hand through Michelle's, trying to comfort her.

'That was not all,' Athreya went on. 'We also found out enough to crack a case that the anti-drug team had been working on for some time. There was a drug-trafficking network operating across here, Kodai and Coorg.'

Athreya paused and looked at his watch. It was 7:10 p.m. He glanced out of one of the French windows. Muthu was standing just outside. The inspector nodded.

'This is the reason I waited till 7 p.m. to begin,' Athreya said. 'As we speak, the anti-drug team is raiding several places, including the Misty Valley Resort. They have jammed mobiles, so no calls can go out or come in. Of particular interest is a hidden cellar at the resort.'

Abbas looked as if he was in a trance. He sat still and silent, hardly breathing. Bhaskar threw a quick glance at Michelle.

'So,' Athreya said, 'there were three crimes playing out at Greybrooke Manor: the attempted murder of Mr Fernandez, Phillip's murder and drug trafficking. Abbas is the mastermind behind the first and the third. Murthy is involved in the first.

While he didn't have the resources to hire anyone, he certainly was a part of the plan to kill Mr Fernandez. I believe he also actively abetted the mongrel, just as Phillip had. Whether that is indeed so is for the courts to decide.'

Michelle was now shuddering as she took deep breaths. Her world had just collapsed around her, but she was dry-eyed. Dora clutched one hand as Manu now held the other. At least her cousins were with her.

'When it came to drug trafficking,' Athreya went on, 'the police were in for a surprise. One of the main distributors was a man they had never suspected. He was the one who handled the distribution of drugs to the Coorg area, including Madikeri. He was none other than Jacob Lopez, operating under a different name.

'Jacob had come to the valley in 2009 and had taken on the identity of a man who had died two years earlier. He took the name of the dead man, and claimed the dead man's relatives to be his. Unfortunately, Jacob's adopted vocation was such that nobody questioned him.

'It was he, Jacob Lopez, who killed Sebastian last night.'

'What!' Bhaskar exclaimed. 'That can't be. Phillip was already dead; Jacob Lopez was already dead.'

'No, Mr Fernandez… that is the mistake you made. You assumed that Phillip was Jacob Lopez. He wasn't. Jacob has been in front of you all this time under a different name, hidden in plain sight. In a garb that defies suspicion. He is in this room now.'

'Who?' Bhaskar thundered.

Athreya paused and turned to the robed figure near the French windows.

'Father Tobias.'

A stunned silence enveloped the room. All heads snapped to the priest, who sat motionless, staring into the distance.

'The proof?' Athreya continued. 'His fingerprints. Under the pretext of getting him to identify some items, I got him to handle a silver cigar case and a glass paperweight. I had his prints taken from them and sent them to Vienna, where they matched with the police records. There is no doubt about his real identity.'

Inspector Muthu walked in through the French windows, carrying a black bag.

'This is from Father Tobias's room in the annexe,' the inspector said. 'It has a false bottom. Inside, we found an Italian handgun.'

'And I found this,' Athreya added, pulling out the flat leather pouch that he had picked up in the chapel beside Sebastian's body. 'It is a set of lock picks that his murderer dropped when Sebastian ripped his jacket. I haven't opened the pouch yet, but there's no doubt in my mind that the picks will have Father Tobias's fingerprints. Lock picks are notoriously difficult to use with gloved hands.

'Phillip and Jacob Lopez knew each other from Vienna, where Phillip used to copy paintings for Jacob, which the latter then sold at a huge profit. They renewed their relationship here, after which Jacob must have told Phillip about the Balsano landscapes.

'On Friday night, Phillip and Father Tobias were working together. Their original plan was that Phillip would steal the paintings and Father Tobias would take them away early in the morning, probably in cardboard tubes. The mongrel saw a person "dressed in a gown" lurking around the chapel, but didn't realize that it was Father Tobias in his cassock.

'Unfortunately for them, Sebastian intervened and killed the thief.'

Several sharp intakes of breath sounded and shock sprang to all the faces gathered around, except Bhaskar's and Father Tobias's.

'Sebastian!' Manu exclaimed. 'How did that happen?'

'Alas, we'll never know,' Athreya lied. 'Both of them are dead now. But let me continue with what I was saying.

'As a result, Father Tobias had to go to Phillip's house to return the cardboard tubes he was carrying. Not only did I see the tubes there, I also saw damp footprints Father Tobias left. With Phillip dead, he had no idea what had happened to the paintings. Even at the risk of being found out, he had to return to the chapel last night to check the altar, but the vigilant Sebastian intervened again.'

Suddenly, the man who had been unmasked as Jacob Lopez leapt up. From inside his cassock, he drew another pistol. Athreya and Muthu were taken completely by surprise. They had not expected him to have a second gun. Having confiscated the weapon in his bag, they had become complacent.

Jacob lined up the pistol to fire at Athreya. Jilsy screamed, her high-pitched shriek piercing the air. For a moment, Jacob's aim wavered between Athreya and Bhaskar. Before he could decide, a gun boomed twice. Jacob was thrown off his feet. His pistol clattered to the floor.

Athreya turned in astonishment towards where the gunshot had come from. There sat Bhaskar in his wheelchair, his face set in humourless lines. A thin strand of grey smoke curled up from the barrel of his gun.

'I told you,' he said grimly. 'I *am* a pretty good shot.'

EPILOGUE

The next morning, Jilsy and Ganesh came to Athreya and said that they had decided to move out of the valley and, most likely, back to Pune. They didn't want to stay opposite a drug-tainted resort, and next to Phillip's house. Further, they were concerned about ramifications when the mongrel was released from jail. After all, they were the ones who had tipped off Athreya about his involvement. All things considered, they had decided to move to Pune.

Immediately afterward, Athreya took Richie aside and warned him. If Richie were to do anything to tarnish Jilsy's reputation, he said, Bhaskar would come to know of how he had defiled the altar at the chapel. Considering that Bhaskar had already warned him about spoiling the family name, that would be enough for him to cut Richie out of his inheritance.

In private, Bhaskar let Athreya into a secret. Sebastian, he said, had disposed of his bloodstained shorts and T-shirt among the landslide's vast debris. He had done that when he had ridden his mountain bike to bring the police inspector to Greybrooke Manor. They would be so muddied and stained now that they would be unrecognizable, even if they were found.

Michelle began drawing up the relevant papers with Varadan's help, and before the week was out, she would file for divorce.

With Manu's support, Dora convinced Bhaskar to give her money instead of becoming a co-founder in her fledgling fashion business. But first, Bhaskar extracted a promise from Dora and Richie in front of Manu that the money would not, under any circumstances, go to Richie.

Abbas and Murthy, who had been taken away by Inspector Muthu after Athreya's little show, were remanded in custody along with Ismail and some others.

A search of the church revealed a set of old British Army uniforms. These were what Jacob Lopez had used to masquerade as Parker's ghost. Much of the drug movement from the Misty Valley Resort happened under the cover of darkness, and it was desirable to empty the vale of casual walkers. The story of Parker's ghost wandering about was enough to discourage people from strolling around the vale after dark.

Jacob Lopez never regained consciousness and died two days later. Bhaskar had indeed been an excellent shot, and Jacob pulling a gun on him and Athreya had given him the freedom to take revenge for the death of the man he had considered a second son.

AVAILABLE AND COMING SOON
FROM PUSHKIN VERTIGO

Jonathan Ames

You Were Never Really Here

A Man Named Doll

Olivier Barde-Cabuçon

*The Inspector of Strange and
Unexplained Deaths*

Sarah Blau

The Others

Maxine Mei-Fung Chung

The Eighth Girl

Amy Suiter Clarke

Girl, 11

Candas Jane Dorsey

The Adventures of Isabel

Martin Holmén

Clinch

Down for the Count

Slugger

Elizabeth Little

Pretty as a Picture

Louise Mey

The Second Woman

Joyce Carol Oates (ed.)

Cutting Edge

John Kåre Raake

The Ice

RV Raman

A Will to Kill

Tiffany Tsao

The Majesties

John Vercher

Three-Fifths

Emma Viskic

Resurrection Bay

And Fire Came Down

Darkness for Light

Those Who Perish

Yulia Yakovleva

Punishment of a Hunter